HIGH MOUNTAIN WINTER

Borgo Press Books by Ardath Mayhar

The Absolutely Perfect Horse: A Novel of East Texas (with Marylois Dunn)
The Body in the Swamp: A Washington Shipp Mystery [Wash Shipp #2]
Carrots and Miggle: A Novel of East Texas
The Clarrington Heritage: A Gothic Tale of Terror
Closely Knit in Scarlatt: A Novel of Suspense
Crazy Quilt: The Best Short Stories of Ardath Mayhar
Deadly Memoir: A Novel of Suspense
Death in the Square: A Washington Shipp Mystery [Wash Shipp #1]
The Door in the Hill: A Tale of the Turnipins
The Dropouts: A Tale of Growing Up in East Texas
The Exiles of Damaria: A Novel of Fantasy
Feud at Sweetwater Creek: A Novel of the Old West
The Fugitives: A Tale of Prehistoric Times
The Heirs of Three Oaks: A Novel of the Old West
High Mountain Winter: A Novel of the Old West
How the Gods Wove in Kyrannon: Tales of the Triple Moons
Hunters of the Plains: A Novel of Prehistoric America
Island in the Lake: A Novel of Native America
Khi to Freedom: A Science Fiction Novel
The Lintons of Skillet Bend: A Novel of East Texas
Lone Runner: A Novel of the Old West
Lords of the Triple Moons: A Science Fantasy Novel: Tales of the Triple Moons
Makra Choria: A Novel of High Fantasy
Medicine Dream: Being the Further Adventures of Burr Henderson
Messengers in White: A Science Fantasy Novel
Monkey Station: A Novel of the Future (Macaque Cycle #1; with Ron Fortier)
People of the Mesa: A Novel of Native America
A Planet Called Heaven: A Science Fiction Novel
Prescription for Danger: A Novel of the Old West
Reflections; & Journey to an Ending: Collected Poems
A Road of Stars: A Fantasy of Life, Death, Love, and Art
Runes of the Lyre: A Science Fantasy Novel
The Saga of Grittel Sundotha: A Science Fantasy Novel
The Seekers of Shar-Nuhn: Tales of the Triple Moons
Shock Treatment: An Account of Granary's War: A Science Fiction Novel
Slewfoot Sally and the Flying Mule: Tall Tales from Cotton County, Texas
Soul-Singer of Tyrnos: A Fantasy Novel
Strange Doin's in the Pine Hills: Stories of Fantasy and Mystery in East Texas
Strange View from a Skewed Orbit: An Oddball Memoir
Through a Stone Wall: Lessons from Thirty Years of Writing
Timber Pirates: A Novel of East Texas (with Marylois Dunn)
Towers of the Earth: A Novel of Native America
Trail of the Seahawks: A Novel of the Future (Macaque Cycle #2; with R. Fortier)
The Tulpa: A Novel of Fantasy
Two-Moons and the Black Tower: A Novel of Fantasy
Vendetta: A Novel of the Old West
Warlock's Gift: Tales of the Triple Moons
The World Ends in Hickory Hollow: A Novel of the Future
A World of Weirdities: Tales to Shiver By

HIGH MOUNTAIN WINTER

A NOVEL OF THE OLD WEST

by

Ardath Mayhar

Writing as "Frances Hurst"

THE BORGO PRESS

An Imprint of Wildside Press LLC

MMIX

CONTENTS

FOREWORD

With the westward journey of Marcus and Narcissa Whitman, in 1836, expansion of the United States to the Pacific began in earnest. That first trek proved both women and wagons could make the almost two-thousand-mile migration, and by 1850 the ruts were already worn deep.

Starting at either Westport Landing, Missouri, which was later to be named Kansas City, nearby Independence, or at Kanesville, Iowa, now Council Bluffs, the emigrants set off across the plains toward their goals. Some headed for the rich valleys of Oregon, while others, lured by the promise of the 1849 Gold Rush in California, turned west, past the Rockies, toward the Sierras.

Both routes involved crossing long miles of plain, seemingly endless stretches of desert and mountain terrain. At the rate of ten to twelve miles a day (on good days), that journey required just under six months to cover, and families walked, most of them, the entire distance in order to save wagon-weight that might overwork their precious oxen. Although mules were tougher and stronger than horses and were sometimes used, the patient ox could live off sagebrush, and because of that was most often the chosen animal for the teams that pulled the wagons west.

Many kinds of people ventured along those trails. Easterners, Southerners, Europeans from many nations turned their faces westward and set out to make their fortunes, to find good free land, or simply to see country that none of their kind had known before. In addition, the United States government was encouraging its citizens to colonize that distant country, in order to secure it for their nation.

But there were other kinds of people, too. In 1848, revolutions took place in several areas of Europe. Austria was the site of one such upheaval, and it is quite possible that displaced Austrians fled the turmoil of their own country and went west to America. Perhaps some of those even journeyed along the Oregon Trail as a result of being uprooted from their normal lives.

It must have been a rich brew of cultures that trudged along behind the overloaded wagons, eating dust and stepping into cattle dung and wondering, probably, why on earth they had risked everything on this drastic venture. Yet few turned back, though many died along the way and never saw the Promised Land toward which they moved.

They were stronger than modern people tend to be, tougher, and less spoiled to the easy life. Heat and cold, dust and floods, and catastrophes didn't stop their progress across the wide land. Those spared by cholera and accidents and occasional Indian raids became the ancestors of at least some of those now living in the West.

Maryla Stoner's winter sojourn is based upon an actual occurrence. Years ago, while researching some articles for a colleague who was compiling an anthology of nonfiction about the early west, I ran across an account of just such an adventure.

Sadly, I cannot recall her real name, but there was, indeed, a young woman who survived a high mountain winter all alone in a covered wagon, after her father and brothers went away to hunt and never returned. She walked out the next spring.

Now go with me and follow the Oregon Trail in 1850, with the last wagon train to leave Westport Landing before the season was too far along to allow safe passage. Meet the assortment of people who set their faces toward the setting sun, in pursuit of a dream that our kind has never quite lost.

—Ardath Mayhar
Chireno, Texas
April 2009

CHAPTER ONE

Albert Stoner straightened his back and stared across the rocky field. In the harsh light of late spring, yellowish shoots of corn were prying their way painfully out of the ground, a poor stand of what promised to be an even poorer crop, he thought.

He and his father had claimed this mountainside when he was a young man. Then the undepleted soil seemed to rush seeds into sprouting and stalks into reaching for the sky, bearing six ears each. He thought of the dark leaves rustling in the breeze off the mountain, the rich promise of the fat ears.

Now if he got two scraggly ears of corn to the stalk it was considered a good year, and the rest of his hillside farm suffered from the same problem. As the soil washed away down the plowed slope in the heavy winter rains, every year it became harder to feed his brood of children. And there was no fresh land, this side of the Rockies, where he might do better.

His oldest three children worked with him, trying their best to grow enough corn to ferment into whiskey and grind into meal for the winter. The whiskey he distilled, his method based on his great-grandfather's Old World recipe, sold for the only cash they saw from year's end to year's end.

Albert Stoner's method still produced prime corn-juice, and he blessed his sailor father for preserving the formula that had been passed down in his family through the generations. Many a hard-earned coin came into Albert's hands only through its sale, though he sometimes wondered how one of his own scholarly bent had ended up as a farmer and distiller instead of a schoolteacher.

Cornmeal, pork from their hogs, beef from slaughtered steers, as well as fruit, peas, beans, and squash that Elizabeth dried in the sun on their shed roofs, kept them going through the winter. Life seemed to get harder all the time. Without rich soil, even the best of farmers could not grow good crops, and he was never quite as dedicated to the task as his father had been.

All the talk, when the circuit rider came through to hold services at the church, had been about the rich land people were taking up in Oregon. He'd looked that country up in his big leather book of maps, although the names and ownership of whole areas of the world had changed since it was printed.

Much of the western continent except for the coast was marked UNKNOWN; still, he could trace the seacoast and the mountain range running parallel to it. The Rocky Mountains were sketched in inaccurately, he knew from talking with occasional mountain men who drifted through the area.

The long expanse of desert country that ran down the length of that territory was a blank space. Now, even people he knew were heading in that direction, crossing the flat, dry country, seeking for new land. Free land. The landless generations of his ancestors in Europe had waked in his blood at last, matching the soil-hunger of his sailor father.

That hunger filled his heart and his long, square-shouldered body. Land that was flatter than this and would grow just about anything you planted—that was the dream that had brought his father to Missouri. It had been impossible for Albert to let his parents come alone, so he had brought his own growing family along.

People surely needed someone to teach their children, he had hoped, but that had never been needed here. Those already here had a teacher, he found when he arrived.

They'd stopped in the edge of these mountains because his father fell ill and could travel no farther into the rich country he coveted. This land was open for homesteading. It was not bad soil, at that time; the underlying rock had not been obvious at first. Once the forest was cut away, allowing the heavy rains to erode the topsoil, life became harder than they had planned or wanted.

Now the farm was worn out, the soil washed away down the stony slopes, all but useless. Elizabeth might look martyred, but one day he would pick up stakes and follow those of his neighbors who had already made plans to emigrate. His sons would have good land to farm, when he was gone, and surely in that new country there would be need for a teacher.

His daughter never entered his thoughts. She was a woman. Some man would marry her and take her off his hands; until that happened she'd be working beside him, matching his abilities more than either of the older boys. Albert seldom allowed that thought to enter his mind.

She was useful, there was no doubt of that, but only a woman, when all was said and done. All the books, all the preachers, all the ancient writings said she was of no worth.

Maryla came up behind him and paused. "You tired, Papa?" she asked. "If you want to go sit in the shade, I'll finish weeding your row."

She was a good girl, and he was fond of her. Still, she lacked a lot. She had no feminine graces, though she was pretty enough, entirely too tall and strong ever to be considered feminine. Her large, bony frame, in addition to her mane of coppery hair, was enough to put off almost any suitor.

Working in the fields, she insisted on wearing his old clothes, for skirts were impractical for hoeing or cutting and raking hay. It wasn't proper, but she got her hard head directly from him and his mother, he knew. There wasn't much he could do about that.

In a girl, it was inconvenient. He sometimes wondered that his father had never objected to that trait in his own wife. Mama had been different from any other woman he ever knew; most men had disapproved of her, as well as just about all women. Maryla was too much like her for comfort.

Maryla looked like a gawky boy, in her loose linsey-woolsey shirt and baggy pants held up with a length of rope. She even wore her hair pulled back into a single pigtail, as he and the boys wore theirs. From a distance, nobody could tell the difference between the male Stoners and the female.

It would be nice to have a sweet, gentle daughter like the Fosters' girl. Josephine was soft-spoken, her skin pale, her eyes properly downcast. He knew Elizabeth envied Mrs. Foster her daughter, and so, at times, did he.

Yet as he turned back to work, he admitted to himself that Josie'd be no earthly use weeding a cornfield. Better the bird in hand, the one God put in your nest, he supposed, than the bright-feathered one perched in someone else's bush.

He smiled at his daughter. "No, I'm not tired. Just worried, perhaps. If your mother could bear it, I'd buy that big wagon John Wilden has for sale and set out westward. I saved enough of last year's whiskey money to manage that.

"Good land...new schools...." He stopped, unwilling to sound disloyal to Elizabeth.

Maryla was busy again, moving steadily up her own row, her hoe scraping out weeds without touching one of the young sprouts. She was a good hand. Better, if he was honest, than either of her brothers, who tended to daydream and cut corn along with weeds.

He thought again of the words of Brother Sam, the circuit rider. "Folks are thinking about moving out," he'd said. "A good half dozen families have already headed for Westport Landing to join up with trains that are organizing.

"This is the time of year to head west, to get over the mountains before the snows stop up the passes. If I hadn't my circuit to ride, I'd consider heading that way myself. Folks are going to need preachers and teachers, as well as farmers." There had been the ghost of a dream even in the preacher's eyes.

His words haunted Albert, even while he finished his work and led his weary children homeward for supper. This was no land, no work for a scholar. He could teach the children of those who went west, leaving behind the years of bone-wearing toil he had known here in Missouri.

There had been a schoolmaster here before he arrived, and the old fellow seemed bent on living forever. There had never been any opportunity for Stoner to show his abilities, except in teaching his own young ones. He had to admit he'd done pretty well with them.

The boys had been apt scholars, loving the classics and poetry and history. Maryla—he sighed. She should have been his son, he realized. She certainly wasn't studious. Though quick to learn, she had never shown any hint of his own love for reading and mathematics.

Rags, the ancient dog, wagged up to greet him as he stepped onto the back porch of the log house and poured the wash-pan full of water from the bucket standing full, still cold from the well. He scrubbed his arms and hands, face and neck, and finally submerged his head and let the soapy water rinse the sweat from his scalp. Rubbing heartily, he gave place to Jon and went into the house, toweling his wet hair, while his sodden red pigtail dripped down his back.

Elizabeth stood beside the fireplace, stirring the contents of the iron pot hanging from a hook that swiveled from an iron arm. As she looked up to see him, she pulled the Dutch oven out of the coals and lifted its lid. The smell of hot cornbread filled the kitchen.

Albert sat in the hickory splint chair at the head of the table, resting while he waited for the others to come. He felt his wife's eyes on him, pleading silently, he knew, that he forget his notion to move away from this familiar place. She could read his mind, after so many years of marriage, and she understood as well as he that one day he would make that decision.

A wave of irritation swept over him. Since his wife began to ail, she had not been the brisk, determined woman he knew. That bright-eyed wife had come willingly, infant in arms and pregnant again, as he helped Papa search for good land on which to rear his brood.

Now she was pale, thin, sometimes querulous. Her unspoken resistance to any change had worn him down to the bare nerve. She was obedient, it was true, and said almost nothing when she disagreed with him. Yet her gaze could carry more messages than any words were capable of, and he knew her thoughts, no matter how he tried to ignore them.

As his sons and daughter entered the kitchen, he made a sudden, angry decision. "We'll finish the crop, what there is of it," he said. "Then we'll pack up and go. I'll see John Wilden tomorrow to trade for his wagon. He might just take whiskey in lieu of part of the money. We can put everything we need and more into that thing; it was built to carry a couple of tons."

Lizzie sank into her chair, her hands pressed hard over her heart. Tears filled her eyes, but they didn't fall. She still had a lot of control, he admitted grudgingly.

Maryla's eyes were wide, bright with excitement. "We don't have enough oxen to pull it. Takes a half-dozen, from what I heard Preacher say. Is there enough money to buy that many?"

"We've got four. I'll trade those for three younger ones. We can sell all the livestock but a cow and a riding horse—it'll be Petronius, of course—for enough to buy everything we need.

"We'll make it without spending any of the whiskey savings. The wagon will take all the coin I can spare at this point." He was already doing mental arithmetic, calculating weights and distances.

They'd need some cash in hand when they got to Oregon, whatever happened, and he didn't intend to arrive in that new country without a penny in his pocket. For the thousandth time he blessed that recipe for corn whiskey his father had evolved from his own father's Old World method. That was the most reliable money crop possible.

His sons plopped onto the bench where the youngsters had always sat, two on either side of the table. Though they were too shocked to speak, yet, he could see by their expressions they were fully behind this move.

Lizzie couldn't know the discouragement of working yourself into the ground in the blazing sun, only to see the crop dwindle every year. Since she felt too poorly to do field work any longer, she had lost touch with the farm. Their sons and Maryla, who worked beside him, realized as she could not the change this would make, the hope it would give them all.

Albert felt suddenly guilty. "It won't be so bad, Lizzie," he said. "We'll do all the hard work, packing up and such. And maybe you can ride in the wagon most of the way to Oregon. The five of us will take care of you and the baby. You'll see."

But early summer still stretched before them, filled with farm work and the added burden of deciding what to take and what to sell or give to neighbors and friends. Although the decision was made, it would be next season before they could take the trail, for by harvest time it would be too late to catch a train heading west.

It seemed, sometimes, that the time to go would never arrive, as groups of wagons or single families passed along the road, heading for Westport Landing and the trailhead. Those who lived farther to the east and north would take off from Kanesville, Iowa, where there was a ferry to take the wagons across the Missouri River. Albert seemed to feel in his very bones the movement of endless strings of wagons across the land.

Every time another group paused to water their stock at his creek or to share a meal, Albert envied those already on their way. But the time would come, he knew. The time would come, and he would take his family west into that Promised Land that would change their lives forever.

Just knowing he had decided, that a fresh start lay before him, made Albert feel younger, less dragged down by the work and worry of the farm. It was good to feel free, even though at this point that freedom was only a dream.

CHAPTER TWO

Philip Stoner bounced around the yard, arms spread wide, screaming like a chicken hawk. Rags flopped along at his heels, his scruffy tail wagging in circles, his gruff bark adding to the noise. All Elizabeth's shushing couldn't quell Phil's high spirits, for he knew that though their neighbors were saying goodbye, it wouldn't be long before the Stoners would follow.

Charles Foster was keeping pace with him, though the younger boy wasn't making much noise. Phil thought he might be a little sad about leaving home and everyone he had known all his life.

Feeling some sympathy for Chuck, Phil paused in the shade of the chinaberry tree and plopped onto the dusty ground. "Sit down, Chuck," he said. "It'll be a long time before we see each other again."

That was the wrong thing to say. Tears welled up in the child's eyes and made muddy furrows down his fat cheeks. "I don't want to go, Phil," he said. "I want to stay and play with you and Danny Letterman."

Phil thought hard. He'd brought up the subject, and now it was up to him to fix what he'd busted. "Why, Chuck, Danny and his folks are going before we do. None of us are going to be here for all that long. And maybe we'll see you in Oregon! Wouldn't that be fine?"

Seeing the round face brighten, he rose hurriedly and pulled the younger boy to his feet. "You come say goodbye to Jon and Mark. Your folks are gettin' ready to pull out.

"The oxen have drunk all the water they can hold. I expect they'll piss a trail we can follow all the way to Oregon." He grinned wickedly, knowing his mother objected to rude words.

Chuck smiled back, suddenly ready for this adventure. "Where's your sister?" he asked. "Josie was lookin' for her, but we couldn't find her."

Phil snorted. "Girls! She went off to hunt. Didn't want to have to say goodbye to her best friend, I 'spect. Girls are sissies, you know."

Though Chuck understood all too well that his own sister might be a sissy, Phil knew that Maryla was tougher than he let on. Still, Chuck nodded. Obviously, there was no use getting into a fuss on their last day together.

* * * * * * *

The hunter lay flat, still and silent, waiting for the buck to raise his head. The barrel of the flintlock was as motionless as the stone on which her elbow rested; when the animal finished drinking at the small stream and turned to go, her shot took him in the angle of the neck, slanting toward the heart. He ran a few steps, coughed deeply, and fell forward, fragile legs crumpling beneath his body.

Even now, with the local Indians pushed out into the plains, it was unsafe to be on the mountain with an unloaded weapon. Maryla sat and re-charged the old gun, ramming home powder, then setting patch and ball on the end of the barrel and pushing them in with the tool she kept for the purpose. Her ramrod sent them down against the charge of powder, and she checked the flint. All was well again.

She knew her shot would have been heard below, where her family was saying goodbye to the Fosters. She didn't care. The Fosters were all right, but they were no special friends of hers.

Mrs. Foster had made it quite plain that she felt Maryla was a bad influence on her blond, dimpled Josephine. The young woman looked down her gawky length, smiling at her long legs in her father's outworn trousers. She had nothing but contempt for the frilly nonsense her neighbors' daughters seemed to like so much.

Mama hated for her to wear pants, but when you went into the woods to hunt, skirts were ridiculous. She might be seventeen and a bit, but she didn't intend to be hurried into becoming a lady. Those she knew on her rare visits to the neighbors or to church were a bunch of ninnies.

She moved to kneel beside the buck, gutting him so she could lift him onto her sturdy back. He'd be welcome—with seven mouths to feed, Pa was hard put to supply enough food. The farm was producing less every year, and she knew it as well as the menfolk did.

Their neighbors knew that, too; it was the reason they were leaving these familiar rocky hills and fields for the rich, free land in Oregon. Maryla's main reason for avoiding goodbyes was her violent envy; she would have gone with them right now, if she could.

Pa had obviously wanted to join them for a long time. She recognized her own hidden feelings in his steel gray eyes, though until that fateful evening he had said little.

Still, he'd promised to finish out the crop, and both of them knew how Mama hated the notion of leaving her home and the few friends still left. Papa was giving her some time, but he wasn't red-headed for nothing. He always got his way, in the end.

Not that Mama said anything—she'd been raised to accept whatever her man decided. But there were more ways than one of making one's feelings known, and nobody in the Stoner family had any doubt of her thoughts on the subject.

It was hard to see those others trundle away in their wagons, leaving behind only rooster tails of dust and the memories of grow-ing up with their young ones. That was why Maryla had taken to the hills with the ancient Hawken her grandmother left her.

Jon and Mark had tried for years to wheedle it away from her, but she was firm. This was her key to the freedom of the woods, and as long as she brought back meat, nobody in the family could really fuss too much.

By now the last of the dust trail should have settled, she thought, rising to bind the deer's delicate hooves together. She heaved the carcass onto her shoulders and started down the moun-tain, hardly feeling the weight.

Her brothers might be almighty males, she thought, but she was the only child to inherit her father's height and red hair and strong-boned build. It drove her mother wild, but she was glad of her size. She never had to call on one of the men to lift or hoist or lever heavy items.

Her father worked alongside her in the fields, as well as tending the cattle and making hay, and while they worked, he treated her as a son. It was only when they returned to the house that things changed.

Then, though she had worked step for step with him and ahead of his sons, she was expected to help her mother set food on the ta-ble, draw water, wash up the pots afterward and such, for that was woman's work. A man tired from the fields could not be expected to take a hand in such things.

A woman tired from the fields was still a woman. Until the baby came and left her so weak and ill, Mama worked along with the men and still did all her other work as well.

The injustice of it galled Maryla, who had even tried arguing her case with Albert. But he was a deep thinker, a scholar who had read and thought about all the books in the great trunk he kept in his and Mama's bedroom. Out-arguing him was like trying to talk a tree off its stump or a rock out of the mountainside.

When he ran out of Greek philosophers and Calvinist preachers to quote, he started on the Bible, and who could argue with that? Though she wondered, thinking of Pa's saying how many times the Bible had been translated, if some of those far-off males who did the work hadn't made some mistakes in deciphering dead languages. Which was blasphemy, but who gave a damn?

She grunted, shifting the buck's weight to the other shoulder. Mark couldn't carry a big carcass like this, nor could Jonathan. Philip, at eleven, showed signs of inheriting his mother's slight frame as well.

Would she work her back into a permanent crick and her hands to gnarled roots without ever getting credit for what she did? She thought of old Mrs. Deeson, who had shriveled away to knotted muscle on tough bone as she labored beside her husband.

Her face was brown as a boot, her skin wrinkled and liver-spotted. And Zwing Deeson often complained because she'd got old and homely, when he much preferred a likely young gal like Maryla.

She chuckled, remembering his only approach to her, after church one Sunday while families picnicked together beneath the big elms and maples of the churchyard. Not for nothing had she listened to her father's sometimes profane comments to the oxen who pulled his heavy plow.

"Take your bloody hands off me, you jackass!" she'd grated. "I'll kick your tail up around your ears, if you ever say another word to me."

His shocked expression was wonderfully funny. Zwing had stepped backward, stunned by her ferocity, caught his heel on a stub of root, and fallen on his backside.

Maryla hadn't waited for him to gather his wits. She'd hitched up her hated skirt and headed for Mrs. Deeson's table, where the woman's custard pie and roast venison had gathered a crowd to sample her cooking.

Maryla stepped up beside the weathered woman and helped her serve, not resenting this voluntary contribution to someone who was obviously not appreciated by the very one she had all but killed herself helping. The poor woman had lost seven babies, they said, one after the other. As if that wasn't enough trouble for one lifetime! It was enough to make you decide against marrying at all, no matter what anybody said.

Maryla came over the ridge that sloped down to the sheltered cup where Pa and Grandpa had built the house, when Jon was just a baby. The lower ridge around which their road curved was still below her, and she could see a line of specks, antlike, moving in a cloud of dust.

The wagons, some huge, some smaller, some merely gussied up farm wagons, were going away from Missouri, away from the stony soil and the troublesome night-riders, into the clean land beyond the prairies. What awaited them there?

She sighed and started down, stepping carefully. Two years ago Jonathan had broken his leg coming down this ridge carrying a new calf. He still walked with a limp, though Maryla suspected he exaggerated that to get sympathy. Jon loved to be coddled, and that was all there was to it.

Now there was going to be an end to this life, a beginning of another she couldn't even guess at. There was the long trail west, the company of people she had never met, the possibility of bad weather and Indian raids.

Though she knew she should shudder at the thought, Maryla found her heart beating faster, hoping she would have some chance of adventure before she had to grow up and become a dratted lady. Surely there would be some chance of that on a journey of two thousand miles!

Whistling (another habit her mother deplored), she stepped down the steep slope, balancing the deer and her rifle effortlessly. Whatever came, she was a Stoner, hard of head and strong of back. She could handle it, she reckoned, if anyone could.

CHAPTER THREE

It was dry in late spring and early June, and the painfully culti-
vated corn shriveled in the fields. The small crop Albert had expected was going to be even smaller, he thought, staring down the
slope at the curling leaves and stunted, yellowing stalks of the young
corn. The crop was hardly worth staying to harvest.

He longed to go down the hill and tell Lizzie to start packing up
their goods. He turned toward the woods path, grateful for the shade;
the heat, this year, was terrible. It would be hot on the Plains as well,
but beyond—he let his imagination soar. Beyond were forested
mountains and long valleys deep in grass.

As he moved down the crooked way, his quick ear identified the
calls of catbirds and jays and crows, the distant cry of a hawk. Amid
the familiar sounds he heard something else, alien and disturbing.
What sort of bird whistled like that?

He stopped, listening intently. Ahead of him Rags paused, too,
his ragged tail stiff, his ears pricking up. A grumble sounded in the
old dog's chest as he gazed off into the woods.

Again Albert heard the call, not from a bird. Not from an Indian, for he knew he would not have been able to distinguish one of
their calls from the real bird itself. No, this was a signal. A white
man's signal.

He forgot the heat, the baking crop, and sped down the hillside
toward his home. There had been isolated raids in southern Missouri
over the past year, the circuit rider said. All had been night attacks
against farms and homes known to hold cash money or stores of
portable foodstuffs. This bad summer had made such raids more frequent, as crops failed all over the area.

It was broad daylight now. Did that mean this was someone
else, or were the nightriders scouting out his farm to raid after nightfall?

However it might be, he intended to get home and make sure all
the weapons were loaded. Anyone trying to take the little he and his

family had saved or intending to burn his house was going to get a bad shock.

Rags dashed ahead of him as he strode hastily down the mountain. He found Jon standing in front of the cow shed, his head cocked, his eyes scanning the forested slopes to the north of the house. "You heard it, Papa?" he asked.

Albert saw with approval that he had his rifle at hand, primed and ready for action. He might be small and fragile-boned, but Jon was no fool. He had the Stoner hard head, if not the sturdy build.

"Let's go in the house," Albert said. "I don't know what that is, but I don't think it means us any good. The raiders haven't come this far north before, but I heard the folks down a way have been making it hot for them. Maybe they've moved themselves someplace where they won't be expected."

The two slipped around the cow shed, approaching the back door of the house by way of Lizzie's long row of crape myrtles, which gave good cover from anyone watching on the mountain. Inside, Albert found his wife and daughter busy folding winter clothing, colorful quilts, and hand-woven blankets into one of the trunks he had built for the trip.

Another trunk held his books, and still another material for making clothing for every member of the family. The trunks were built flat on top, so family members could sleep on them if the weather made sleeping on the ground beneath the wagon unhealthy.

Mark and Philip were in the attic; he could tell that from thumps overhead and the drifts of dust that curled downward between the beams. So much bustle was good—when Lizzie was busy, she forgot to worry.

Albert hated to spoil her present mood with his warning, but everyone had to be on guard, if prowlers were watching the house. He wiped his feet carefully, trying to put off the moment as long as possible.

Lizzie looked up instantly. "Albert, what's wrong? You never wipe your feet unless you have bad news. I've seen it for twenty-three years. Go on, tell me. It won't get any better for holding it in."

He sighed. Being married for so long meant you couldn't keep a secret, no matter how you tried.

"All right, Lizzie," he said. "And I'm not dead certain I'm right, remember that. I heard a signal whistle that didn't come from any Indian. I'm afraid it may be some of those bandits they've been having trouble with down to the south of us."

She dropped the quilt she held and sat suddenly on the side of the trunk, her hands clasped tightly to her chest. He knew she had been worried about a lot of things, but this hadn't been something anyone could foresee.

Still, she was a strong woman, in spirit if not in body, and she had survived skirmishes with various groups of Indians, unhappy at being driven away from their hunting lands. She'd had five children, alone except for him and his parents, and Albert felt with some shame that if it had been him, he'd have stopped with the first and moved out of the house to prevent ever having any more.

Now he grinned at her. "We may not have any trouble at all. And if we do, we're forewarned and armed with plenty of good weapons, powder, and lead. Get out your father's blunderbuss, my love. I've seen you use that to good advantage, more than once."

She smiled back, and he knew she was remembering the days when they were young, working together to feed their small brood and to keep the world from trampling them all flat. Her hands might be thin now, her arms more frail than they used to be, but she understood what had to be done in an emergency.

His daughter looked far more eager than afraid. It made him fear for her future—what use had the world for a girl who went out looking for a fight? He recalled one of her bouts with the Fosters' oldest son Gerald, when she was about ten. If Lizzie hadn't been at hand and broken up the brawl, Maryla would have beaten the boy senseless, even though he was quite a bit larger than she at the time.

When asked, she had refused to explain the cause of that fight. But Mark, who had been present, said, "Gerry called her 'nothing but a weak little old girl.' And she told him she'd make him think 'weak little old girl.' She whipped him good and proper."

That was Maryla, not in any way a lady. He sighed as he went to check the stock of lead.

"Might as well build up the fire in the stove," he said. "We have time to mold some rifle balls, while we wait to see what happens. There's plenty of powder, because I bought all I could afford for the journey; if we have enough ammunition ready, we can stand off an army. These log walls will turn anything but a cannonball."

Maryla volunteered to melt the lead and pour it into the molds, a hot job that none of her brothers envied. She had rows of bright-shiny rounds ready, long before there was any need for them.

Before nightfall, Albert closed and barred the heavy shutters over the two windows. He hitched the two remaining horses in the shed room off the kitchen porch, thankful that his new oxen, for which he had traded the older animals, were still with their original owner. Then, as crickets and locusts and katydids began to zoom and chirr, he set himself to wait for what might happen.

Now it was plain that strangers were on the mountain above the house. Whistles and even low calls sounded when any of the family risked opening the door a crack. Whoever was out there was coming closer, as night drew in. The whistles grew louder as twilight descended.

"Let me go out, Pa, and catch 'em in the rear," Maryla pleaded.

Albert shook his head. "No use risking getting blown to Kingdom Come, girl! They'll come when they come, and we'll watch through the loopholes and get them as they step into range."

Mark and Jon were already standing beside the north and east loopholes. Maryla, frowning, took her place on the south side of the house. Albert bent to kiss his wife and moved to the west wall, while Philip readied himself to help his mother reload the weapons as they were fired.

Having two flintlocks each meant there was no long period of vulnerability while the shooter reloaded. It had been expensive to provide them, but he and his father had traded whiskey for what they could and painfully saved for the rest. When Albert's family came west to Missouri, they all understood there was still frequent Indian trouble, and they had taken pains to provide enough weapons.

Now that his parents were gone, there were enough weapons, even without much time to reload. Lizzie's huge blunderbuss, which she loaded with gravel or nails or whatever else she could find, wasn't much for accuracy, but anything coming within its range would be chopped to mincemeat. If any raider managed to get into the house, Lizzie would get him.

Phil knew to stay low, retrieve spent weapons, and reload them with lightning speed. That meant that no area of the house would remain unguarded while someone fumbled with reloading.

Albert and his parents had put a lot of thought into designing the cabin. Knowing there would be times when it must double as a fort, they had drilled loopholes through the stout log walls in sets of three: one aimed straight ahead, one angled to the right, the other to the left. Because of that, the person on guard at each point of the compass was not limited to shooting only those who stepped in front of the forward loophole.

This was so unusual that more than one Indian raider or would-be scavenger had died when he thought he was perfectly safe. Now Albert knew anyone trying to get close enough to pitch a torch on the slab and shingle roof stood a good chance of dying in the attempt.

Even as he thought that, a shadow darted across the yard toward the shelter of the cowshed, and he fired before it could reach its goal.

The man dropped and yelled. Then he began crawling painfully toward the shed.

Jon shot, then Mark. Albert concentrated on watching his own field of fire. Smoke started filling the big square room and drawing lazily up the chimney.

The baby began crying. Lizzie finished reloading for Jon and took the infant up to nurse it. His small daughter's contented gurgles made a strange counterpoint to the deadly mood of the evening.

Mark fired again and exclaimed, "Got him! He fell and is twitchin' around like a chicken with its neck wrung."

Phil crawled over and reloaded that weapon, while Mark kept his eye on the dark space that was the kitchen garden. From the corner of his eye, Albert saw Maryla aim through the left-slanted bore. The roar of her old weapon deafened him for a moment, and a scream of agony outside told him the raider had taken a painful wound.

It grew even darker. Then a light sprang up—a torch. "They're going to try to fire the roof," Albert said, just loudly enough to be heard inside the room.

"Jon, you go up to the bedroom loft. Get anyone who sets himself to pitch a torch or to climb onto the roof."

Jon caught up two loaded rifles and moved silently to the rude stairway and out of sight. Maryla went to cover his loophole, and Phil took his place at hers with the extra weapons. Lizzie put the now drowsy infant in her cradle and took up her post for reloading.

A shot from upstairs was followed by an angry yell. Albert moved to peer through a chink toward the spot where the torch had been seen last. Phil and Maryla blasted, almost at the same time, and Jon, having had time to reload, fired once more from the loft.

There was a string of curses fit to blister anyone's ears. "Don't listen, Maryla!" Albert snapped, without thinking. He was concentrating on the sounds of feet moving through the dry vines and stalks of the garden...moving away now, and up the hill.

Phil's gun boomed. Turning to his youngest son, Albert saw that the boy's eyes were wide and beginning to fill with tears.

"I kilt him, Pa. He was sneakin' up toward the house, while the others stomped off to make us think they were all goin'. He dropped right down, and now he's lyin' there twitchin'." The boy's chin was quivering, though he struggled to control it.

Albert came to peer through the loophole. In the dwindling light of the torch, he could see a lax bulk, now motionless, lying on the pale dust of the yard. He laid a comforting hand on his son's shoulder.

"It's a bad feeling," he told Phil, "to kill a man. I'll never forget the first I shot. I was sick over it for a long time, and I was a full grown man. You try your best to put it out of your mind, Son. You did what was right, that's the main thing to remember." The boy gulped and nodded, and Albert hoped he'd said the right things.

He moved to the high window and stared through the chink in the shutter at the torch, which was now well up the slope. Dark shapes moved with it, and not one seemed to consider turning back after their wounded companion.

"I think we've discouraged 'em," he said. "But there's no knowing they won't come back."

Minutes crept past, as the Stoners waited, weapons ready, holding their breaths so they could listen more intently. Then from overhead Albert heard Jon's voice.

"Papa, they're firing the cornfield. I can see the fire running across the slope. Now they're up in the pea-field, and it's going up, too."

He was quiet for a long moment. Then, "The crops are going up in smoke, Pa. We've got to move, now. There's no harvest left to gather."

The baby, wakened by the shots, took advantage of the quiet to lift her voice in an angry wail. Her father, grimed with powder smoke, felt he would like to join his daughter in her protest. Instead he wiped his face on his sleeve and set aside his flintlock, without pulling the unexpended shot from his weapon.

"They may come back," he said. "Keep watch, Maryla. Mark, come with me to check on the roof. Jon couldn't see it all from the bed-loft window.

"Lizzie, you might melt some more lead. We'll be pulling out as soon as we can now, and we'll need the rifle balls, even if we don't use them all this time."

He dragged weary legs up the stair. In the long loft that served as bedrooms for all the children, he found Jon still kneeling at the unshuttered window, watching the red glare that lit the side of the mountain.

They had labored all year to raise the corn and beans and peas up there. Now they watched in silence as their sweat and toil rose in coils of fire and reddish smoke into the night sky.

"Tomorrow we'll finish packing. Then we'll go," Albert Stoner said to his sons.

They nodded, but they did not take their eyes off the glare that lit their fields. He understood. It was a peculiar pain to see things you had nourished and slaved to bring into being destroyed for no sane reason by men who made Indians look civilized by contrast.

CHAPTER FOUR

As she packed clothing and pots, tools and equipment for moving, Elizabeth grieved silently. This was not the life she had looked forward to when she married Albert.

Indeed, nothing they had done in their long years together had been what she would have chosen or expected. Yet it was her duty to go where he went and do what he decided upon doing, though it had required many long, silent struggles with herself to keep from complaining.

Albert's mother had been the first shock she suffered. The Merrihews, her own people, had strong feelings for social propriety, which seemed not to be shared by this tall, strong woman who put her hand to any task that came, even though she should have known, being in her forties when her son married, that such work was not proper for a lady.

Yet Albert's mother seemed to have no respect for the concept. She snorted when such notions were mentioned and went on her unconventional way, achieving mental and physical labors that would have taxed the powers of most men.

Used to his mother's ways, Albert had insisted upon his own wife going to the fields and forest with the rest of the family, although she was too small to do very much of the hardest work. It had almost been a relief when she became ill after little Lizzie's birth.

Worse yet, Albert's father did not object to his wife's unwomanly behavior. Indeed, he took unseemly pride in her abilities; he even boasted of her escape from her brother in England, wearing her father's clothing and pretending to be a boy. Perhaps it was his copper-red hair, unfortunately inherited by his son, that made him so different from other older men she had known.

The idea of a woman donning trousers made Elizabeth feel faint, but it was something she had to become accustomed to. Her own daughter insisted upon wearing the abominable items, and not only when she worked in the fields. Even now, as she moved around the house, reaching down things off high shelves or dishes from the cupboards, she was wearing cast-off trousers and a shirt belonging to her father.

Elizabeth sighed and folded her wedding dress, smoothing the full skirt, laying a bit of clean old sheet over the fragile fabric. It did not fit her any longer, for she was bony now, but she entertained dreams of seeing a daughter of her own wear it.

It would not be Maryla, she was certain, even if her big frame might fit into the narrow dress. The girl showed no interest in those few young men who had come to spend awkward evenings with the family. Maryla talked hunting and farming with them until she sent them away, never to return.

No, small Lizzie must be the one to wear the dress, if the silk Elizabeth's father had ordered from Boston twenty-five years ago did not shatter with age before the child was grown. Would she live to see the infant reach maturity? Elizabeth pushed the thought aside. That was for God to decide.

Around her the house buzzed with activity. She smiled as Philip dashed past with something his father had asked for. He was a dear child, if normally active and mischievous. Her sons were most satisfactory. Mark and Jonathan were delicate, as she was, but they were bright and brave, which pleased her.

Only Maryla was a disappointment, and Elizabeth had many an internal struggle because of that feeling. Her daughter was quiet, hard-working, quick to learn any new task, though she did not love books as her father did. She did nothing that should have distressed her mother and much that should have pleased her, but somehow the child could not manage to suit her.

What Elizabeth had dreamed of, as she carried her third baby, was a lovely, delicate daughter who would delight in curls and furbelows. What she had now was a young woman as big and strong as her grandmother, and as hard-headed. Helpful and loving as she was, she was certainly NOT a lady.

Elizabeth gave the dress a last gentle pat and laid it in the trunk with the rest of the extra materials. Both heavy woolens and homespun linsey-woolseys were there. She knew it would be a long time before she could find new fiber to card and spin and weave; she was taking enough, she hoped, to keep her people clad until she could make or trade for more cloth.

The rank smell of yesterday's burning drifted through the house, and Elizabeth frowned. If it had not been for those raiders, she might have found a way to dissuade her husband from this harebrained journey. But now it was inevitable...there were no crops left.

The night-riders had also burned all of the wood the family had been cutting and stacking for winter. To stay was to go hungry, at least, and to be forced to cut wood amid snow and sleet and rain, for there was not enough time before fall to gather another store. Burning green wood alone in a Missouri winter was not a comfortable thing, for you got far more smoke and sputter than you did heat.

When the last quilt was packed into the second of the trunks, she looked around the room, now bare and somehow unfamiliar. She and Albert, with his mother and father, had built this cabin, sliding the logs down the mountain with the help of the horses that had drawn their wagon from the east. She had lived so long with all their homely items in place that without them this was no longer the home she knew.

A faint glimmer of interest kindled in her mind. Would this be the great adventure the children celebrated? Would that new country be as rich and satisfying as everyone seemed to believe?

She sat suddenly on the lid of the bedding trunk, holding her hand to her chest. Her heart was racing, as it often did these days, with, now and again, a quiver as if it skipped beats. She said nothing to Albert, of course, for he would worry, but now Elizabeth wondered if she could survive this perilous journey.

The baby whimpered, and she turned to take up the small bundle. Lizzie was a dear; she would not have missed having her. Yet something about this last pregnancy had damaged Elizabeth. She knew that in her deepest instinct, for she had strange feelings that she had never known before, pains and weaknesses that were a constant worry.

She went into the back room, away from the activity in the big kitchen, and unbuttoned her dress to suckle the infant. Something about that familiar ritual soothed her, and she almost slept, sitting in the old rocking chair that must now be left behind with so much else that she valued and had intended to pass down to her children.

The heavy warmth of the baby against her, the pull of the small mouth on her breast made her drowsy, and she closed her eyes. Half dozing, Elizabeth rested, gathering her strength.

This was not going to be easy, she knew, and she must hold onto her control with both hands, in order to keep her family nourished and educated and disciplined.

* * * * * * *

Phil gave a skip and a hop, as he followed the big wagon along the dusty track. They were on their way at last, though for now they were alone on the winding road. In a week or so, his father said, they would arrive at Westport, where the wagon trains organized for the long haul west. Many others would be there, waiting for the journey to begin.

The boy found himself impatient at the deliberate pace of the oxen. Yet he was relieved to find them moving at last. It had seemed, for a while, as if the Stoners might miss the great westward adventure entirely.

He had been thrilled to think his family could help make the Oregon Territory a part of the United States. Pa had read to his family from the newspapers the circuit rider brought. The writers urged farmers to head west and make certain the English didn't keep their toe-hold on the northwestern frontier. It was a wonderful thing, the boy thought, to do something that was patriotic, at the same time you did something that was going to be fun.

From time to time he would catch his mother's eye, as she trudged along behind the left wheel, taking grim pleasure in breathing the fine dust it kicked up and coughing desperately from time to time. At least she wasn't carrying the baby, who rode in a basket behind the board wagon seat, as Pa drove the oxen.

Pa kept saying they'd better get used to walking, because there was no use to wear out old Pet riding back and forth while the oxen plodded along. And nobody who wasn't sick or injured got to ride in the wagon.

He tried to get Mama to ride, of course, but she refused. There was going to be too much weight in the wide bed of the vehicle to burden the animals with any more, and she knew it.

It took a lot of food to see a family across the dry country and the mountains beyond. As Phil approved highly of food, he made no complaint about the constant walking. The farming tools that also rode there were not quite as welcome, but he supposed they were going to be necessary, when the family again had land to till.

Pa's big trunk of books was something he didn't allow himself to think about. Might as well leave Pa behind as his books. And if he wasn't mightily mistaken, there would be lessons at night, if everybody wasn't too tired.

Phil knew his mother better than the older children did. He'd been with her more than the rest, after the baby was born and she got so peaked. Pa had assigned him to help her with the house work and the baby, being as Maryla was a lot more use in the fields and the woods. She wasn't worth a hang with a skillet or a broom, that was for certain.

He whistled, and Rags came panting up to his heels. Phil reached down to tousle the floppy ears and rub the dog's scruffy neck fur. He had been forced to plead for Rags to come west with the rest of them.

Pa had at first intended to give him to the deacon, but Phil couldn't bear that. It had taken everything he and the other Stoner young could say and do before Pa agreed that if Rags died on the trail, it was better than having him grieve himself to death at a stranger's house.

As soon as they set out, the old dog seemed to grow younger. He chased rabbits like a pup, dashing across the hills and hollows lying along their route. From time to time, he even brought in quarry that he'd run down and killed. Mama boiled the rabbits for stew, and it was clear that Pa was not regretting his decision to let the old boy come along.

Phil kept one eye on the horse, too. Petronius was tethered to the wagon on a long line, and from time to time he would try to stop and crop grass, only to be jerked along by the moving vehicle. Phil had to make sure the line didn't break and let the animal loose.

Baby work, he considered it. His brothers were walking ahead of the four-ox team, each carrying a rifle in case more night riders were about. He'd proved he could guard the family as well as anybody, but that reminded Phil of the last night they spent in their home.

He still felt a cold shiver down his back when he thought of sighting in on the man he had killed. It took something he didn't know he had to pull that trigger, and even now he felt sick when he thought of the way his victim jerked upright and then fell as if all his bones had gone limp.

Phil hadn't gone out in the yard, afterward, to see him up close. Somehow, the boy didn't think he could bear to look a man he had killed in the eye. Pa and Maryla buried him in the garden and pulled down the half-burned grape arbor over his grave to keep off the scavengers.

Pa had talked with him for a long time, trying to make him feel better, but he still woke in the night sometimes with tears trickling into his ears and the smell of black powder strong in his nose. Even Brother Sam, the circuit rider, who had come by just afterward on his regular round, told him it was all right to kill somebody who was going to do you harm.

Somehow it didn't seem to help all that much.

He had a sudden thought that lifted his spirits a bit. Surely there wouldn't be many boys on the trail who had killed a man before they were twelve years old! He'd have him a reputation, maybe, and that would help out. Bigger boys might think twice before beating on somebody who'd spilled blood.

The thought lightened his mood; he whistled to Rags and went off to gallop through a weed patch beside the dusty trail. Now it was summer; the grass was dry, and acrid dust puffed up as he leaped small ditches and prickly bushes.

A ground squirrel went scuttering away, raising its own little trail of dust, and Rags went yelping after it. Mama waved imperatively, gesturing for Phil to get back on the trail.

Drooping, the boy snapped his fingers and whistled again for Rags. The pair of them fell in behind Mama, in the pall of dust that hung always behind the big wheels.

Mama just didn't like this trip any way at all, Phil knew, and she didn't want anybody having any fun and ruining her misery. He sighed and trudged on, trying to keep the skip out of his step and the giggles out of his throat.

Rags, as if understanding everything, kept his head at his young master's knee and looked as solemn as Brother Sam in the pulpit. He understood a lot of things, that old dog.

After a while, Mama looked around at them. Phil saw her lip crinkle at the corner. "You can go romping again," she said. "I ought to be ashamed trying to keep you reined in like an old man. You go have fun, Philip, and take that idiot dog with you."

With a whoop, he shot off into a thicket beside the road. His brothers looked around to see what was happening, and Pa grinned at him from his position beside the wagon.

Maryla, marching along the other side of the oxen with a stick, winked as he skyrocketed past. He knew she longed to go running with him, though Mama would have had a fit if she tried it.

It must be hard to be a girl—and a grown-up girl at that. He could see how much his sister hated the things Mama wanted her to like and to do. Things like dresses and curls and mincy manners. He didn't blame her a bit.

A hawk flapped up out of the thicket, its skree of anger slicing through the hot air. Phil looked up to watch it out of sight; the sky overhead was clear and blue, without a cloud in sight. But from the next ridge that gave him a long view, he could see a low line of darkness lying along the jagged horizon to the northwest.

Weather up there, he thought, but he was soon lost in sniffing out the place and the day with those senses that only dogs and boys possess.

They traveled for what seemed like forever, the last two days of it in mud and wet fit to bog them down past ever getting loose again. The mess that was the staging area for the wagon trains was more than even a small boy could stand. Phil was glad Papa pulled way off onto the grassy meadow beyond the last waiting wagons before he stopped. At least, there wasn't any mud.

They had brought canvas enough to make a lean-to against the side of the wagon, and when everybody was inside, Phil sighed with relief. They were crowded in there, and the baby's foot was in his face, but that was better than being out in this weather.

He scrooched backward until he was flat against Jon, and his brother handed him a cold camp biscuit and a strip of raw bacon. Nothing had ever tasted better.

The canvas dripped slow trickles of water here and there. Still, after walking in the rain for two days and sleeping under the wagon in the mud for two nights, Phil would have been glad of a dry cave with a hungry bear for company.

They chewed on dry rations there in the damp dark, and he wondered if this was just a sample of what life was going to be like for the six months it would take to cover the distance between Missouri and the Willamette Valley. Then he shook his head in the dimness. No, it was going to be a Great Adventure, just like Odysseus or Hercules were always having.

It had to be!

CHAPTER FIVE

In the beginning, the journey was worse than Elizabeth could have imagined. When last she had traveled into new country, she had been a young woman, her first child only an infant. She had talked and laughed with Albert as they walked together behind the wagon where his father and mother rode, along with the baby and all their worldly goods.

She could still recall the songs of birds in the forest along the rude track, where low stumps scraped the wheels and tripped careless walkers. It had been a time of joy and good health, but now she had neither.

On this journey she trudged in the dust, hating everything about her, feeling her heart gallop and skip, her joints twinge with agony. She hated this departure with a desperate hatred that drained her even more.

After a while she realized that she was unconsciously punishing her family, even young Phil, for her own misery. Then she tried hard to keep a cheerful face, however much she felt like flinging herself down in the wagon track and dying.

Yet, after some days of travel, the exercise seemed to help her body gain new strength. Even her heart settled into a steadier rhythm. Then she began to feel as if this long trek might be worthwhile.

By the time the wagon crept into Westport, she was walking freely, sometimes even carrying small Lizzie. The seemingly endless encampment, with its many kinds of wagons and animals, multitudes of children, and busy women working about their temporary locations seemed promising. Surely there would be others here who shared her interests and who might become her friends on the long road ahead.

They made camp beyond the worst of the smoke and dust, beside a deep creek whose banks were thick with oak and willow and maple. She had not thought to find, in what had been described as prairie, such a wealth of trees, and she sent Mark at once to cut and bring a good supply of wood. Hot food improved everyone's dispositions.

As Elizabeth bent to arrange the firewood for kindling, she felt a sudden weakness that sent her onto her knees.

"Mama! Here, let me help you sit down. I'll do that. You just rest." It was Maryla, alert, as usual, to her mother's needs.

As her daughter put a careful arm about her waist and helped her to a pile of blankets, Elizabeth felt guilty for resenting this child who obviously cared so much for her.

She lay flat, stretching her weary legs and laying her head back while the world seemed to spin around her. "I'll be all right in a bit," she said. "But if you would make the fire, dear, and fill the coffee pot, I will be most grateful."

"I'll go get water out of the creek over there," Maryla said. "And I'll call Jon to make the stew. He's the best cook in the family, outside of you. Don't worry—I won't try to cook anything and ruin it. I'll just get everybody moving together."

After a moment, Elizabeth realized that the girl had placed the baby beside her mother, close and warm. That was good. She had no need to worry, now, just to rest...and she drifted into exhausted sleep. Nobody woke her, even when the night meal was ready, for it was obvious that she was exhausted.

She woke the next morning feeling rested and more fit than usual. Even cooking over a campfire wasn't the chore it usually seemed to be. Once everyone had eaten, she let Phil go about whatever business he could find, after he scrubbed out the long-handled skillet with sand and creek water.

Albert insisted that she lie down again, and as there was nothing much to do but wait she dozed again, only to wake to the sound of distant yells. Phil—that was Philip!

She struggled to her feet, holding to the side of the wagon as she fought off a wave of dizziness. "Albert? Albert, see to Philip," she called.

"Yes, my dear. You sit down again and don't trouble yourself. I am going at once," he said, his calloused hand guiding her down once more. "Care for the baby."

* * * * * * *

The morning dawned clear. The air smelled clean, for they were far enough away so the smokes from other camps carried away on the westerly breeze before they reached the Stoners. Phil stretched and yawned as he gazed over the trampled grass to thickets that clumped beside larger trees.

He found a clump of bushes and relieved himself. Then he gathered a bundle of dried branches and twigs to carry back for their own breakfast fire. Mama was already setting up the big coffee pot, and she smiled when he knelt beside her.

Before she could start the fire, she had to lie down, and Jon took over the cooking, which was all right with Phil. As long as somebody did it, he didn't much care who it was.

Soon bacon sizzled in the great camp skillet, which they could shift nearer to and farther from the coals by means of its three-foot handle. Flapjacks followed that into the pan, and Phil dug into his rations with gusto.

After cleaning that dratted skillet, he helped Maryla with rearranging the load inside the wagon. Pa was going over everything inside yet again, setting aside any item he felt they could manage without. After only a week of travel, it was already obvious that some treasured items would have to go.

Mama's carved oak sewing box, emptied of its reels of silk and cotton, its packet of needles, its fine steel shears, went out. The sewing supplies were necessary, but their container was not. Before Pa was done, every member of the family, even Phil, had seen some small or large treasure removed from the load.

Nobody wept, though Mama looked as sad as if she had been asked to leave behind one of her children. That box had belonged to her own mother and before her to grandmother Merrihew.

When they had things done to suit Pa, Phil looked up and asked, "Can I go see if there's somebody to play with? Over to those other wagons?"

Albert nodded absent-mindedly, and the boy went running before he could think of something else for him to do. As he approached the nearest wagon, a tall-wheeled one with a very long bed, he saw two boys standing beside it, staring at him.

One was tall, raw-boned, sandy-haired. The other, obviously his brother from their resemblance, was shorter, and his hair had a gingery cast. Both had cold gray eyes that seemed to light up at the sight of a smaller boy.

An alarm went off inside Philip. These looked like bad'uns, the kind that beat up younger children when they could get away with it. Phil gave a cheerful wave and kept right on going past the camp, heading toward the pair of wagons drawn up in a V beside a clump of persimmon trees.

A lanky man was cleaning an ancient Whitney musket. Phil

recognized it by the three bands circling its round barrel; Mr. Foster used to have one just like it.

The boy said, "Good morning, Sir. Nice musket—mind if I watch you clean it?"

The thin face looked up, and a snaggle-toothed smile greeted Phil. "You know a good gun when you see it, boy. I'm Jeff Hollings. You with that new bunch camped up yonder a ways?"

Phil hunkered down beside him. "Yessir. I'm Philip Stoner. My Pa's name is Albert. I used to know somebody back in Penderton that had a musket like that one."

"This belonged to my granddad, boy. It's kilt Injuns and Britishers and Frenchies and no-goods of all stripes and kinds. I keep it clean and ready to go."

Phil nodded solemnly. "We do the same. Good thing, too, because just before we come out here the night riders hit us. It took all of us to fight 'em off, and even then they fired our crops.

"I killed my first man, right then and there. Still makes me feel funny when I think about it." Phil found that he still got a cold feeling in his stomach when he talked about that night.

"That's not a thing sits light on a man's soul," Hollings agreed. "You're mighty young to carry such a load. Glad to meet you, young Stoner. You stay put and I'll call up my young'uns. Might be you'll hit it off.

"They been hankerin' for somebody to play with that's not mean and ornery like them Williams boys over there." He nodded toward the two Phil had avoided, who were now studying the Hollings camp with close attention.

Jeff whistled, and a small girl came around the wagon. Behind her was a boy quite a bit larger, but not as big as Phil. With these two, he felt sure he could relax and be comfortable.

They had obviously heard what he told their father. If he knew anything about children, word of his feat would find its way to the Williamses, who looked to be the kind to make trouble for anybody who didn't make trouble for them first. There had been a few like that back home, and he'd learned either to avoid them or to hurt them bad the first time they bothered him.

Phil promised himself to carry one of the big knives down his pants leg, while the camp was so close to those boys. He didn't particularly want to kill anybody else, ever again, but he'd a darn sight rather do that than be beaten to a pulp by boys who had the look of people who liked pain.

It wasn't to be that easy, though. As he passed the Williams camp on his way back to the wagon, the two boys came toward him, hands in pockets, faces split with mean grins. When they jumped him, he gave one loud yell to rouse his family and then, kicking and biting and hitting, Phil had his hands full.

* * * * * *

When Albert was gone, Elizabeth lay back, cradling Lizzie to her chest and listening intently as her husband's heavy footsteps moved away across the sun-crisped grass. Another, lighter step joined his, and she knew Mark was going with his father.

The yells had subsided into distant grunts and exclamations, now. Fighting off the dizziness, Elizabeth eased herself into a sitting position and stared toward the nearest wagon, which lay some fifty yards distant. Beyond it, there was a moil of dust and motion.

Even as she watched, a weary voice whined, "Thomas, you see to them chillen, y'hear? They makin' a racket agin."

Three figures tumbled into view as a chunky fellow ambled around from the other side of the wagon. "Gotch! Clem! What you boys doin'? I done told you to stay close and leave other chillen be, didn' I? An' here you are, hittin' on a young'un half yore size. I'm plumb ashamed of you."

By now Albert and Mark had also come into range and stood staring at the frozen group before them. A tall boy rose to his feet, his very movements filled with sullen resentment. One just smaller rose, too, and then her own Philip bounced up and went to his father's side in almost the same motion.

"Name's Williams," the man said, extending a hand. "Tom Williams. These here's my boys. Never had nothin' but trouble outen 'em since the day they was born, seems as if. Can't keep 'em from beatin' up on other people's chillen. Yore boy seems to've did a pretty good job on 'em, though."

Elizabeth squinted through the dust, trying to see, but it was too far. She could hear, however, when Albert said, "Looks as if he got in his licks. But it isn't right for two people to attack one, and if it happens again I will be forced to take a hand. I hope you won't object, sir."

"Object? Why I'll rightly welcome some help with them two young hellions," Williams replied in his rasping tone. "You whale the daylights outen 'em, if you take a mind to, and Caroline and me'll stand by and cheer you on."

Albert took Phil's hand, though the boy wriggled loose quickly. Then the three Stoners turned toward their own wagon, leaving the three Williamses staring after them.

Elizabeth gave a shuddering sigh and felt her heart skip a beat before it continued its rapid throbbing. They had hoped for so much, and here, the first thing, was trouble with the nearest neighbor in the camp.

She didn't like the look of those boys, either. Even from such a distance they looked tough and stringy and hard-edged. "Mean boys," she murmured to Lizzie. "I don't like this even a bit."

The baby slept on, her lips moving as if she suckled still. It would be a very long time before she would be at risk, but the other three—four, if you counted Maryla, which, sadly, you must—were old enough to face the world on their own. And that meant that the world might well follow them home, to the detriment of all.

CHAPTER SIX

NOTISBUCH, 1848, KATRINA HOLZER

I know, somehow, that I will never see my husband again. The revolution in which we have participated, even on so inactive and intellectual a level, has rent Vienna apart, and because of his direct involvement with the radical movement, it may have become a death sentence for my Guenter.

Our participation seems to have condemned him in the eyes of those now ruling the country. No sooner had Vienna surrendered and pro-imperial forces assumed control than the soldiers came for him. He is fragile, middle-aged, scholarly, unable to withstand hardship. They took him away secured between big men, as if he were a violent criminal.

This morning, I watched him march, back straight, white hair drifting about his shoulders, as they hustled him into a black carriage and clattered away down the street. My intuition, decry such matters as he and his peers may do, tells me that I will not see him again in this life.

NOTISBUCH

It has been almost a year. I have only now received a carefully worded communication from our friend, Herr Professor Glanznacht, that tells me my dear Guenter died of pneumonia during the winter, locked away in that dreadful prison.

He also reminds me, though so subtly that anyone who does not know us both would never suspect, that I, too, was involved in the movement that rid us of Metternich. Although to the casual observer it may seem that a more liberal government will result from the rebellion, Glanznacht warns me there may well be many dangerous possibilities.

He does not feel confident that the present regime will last, and he warns me, in a line from Guenter's favorite poet, to "cross the mountains, despite the snow, and flee the wolves that follow."

He is a wise and thoughtful man. I shall follow his advice and hope that no wolf will be quick enough to follow me.

Our sons, *Gott sei Dank*, took flight to Amerika before the revolution; wherever they may now be, they are certainly not in danger from the political situation. I shall convert my grossmutter's jewels into gold, sell the most valuable of Guenter's books, and escape from Austria. When I arrive in their new homeland, surely I may find some way of locating and joining our sons.

We have always been very close; indeed, it was I who urged them to leave home, though the older had not yet reached his twentieth year when they left.

NOTISBUCH

I am not one to sit meekly and wait for doom to come upon me. I have found a friend who was not known to be associated with our movement, and he has arranged for the sale of my goods. He obtained a sufficient sum for passage and more. I shall not be destitute when I come to those alien shores.

I have hired a carriage, Guenter's own having been seized, along with his considerable accounts with the Jewish bankers. Only because this house belongs to his Cousin Alphonso was it left untouched.

NOTISBUCH

I have set off for Marseilles, using a Travel Permit obtained for me by a friend of Guenter's, who kept his freedom and position because of his discretion. He used some means I feel better for not knowing. What I do not know, I cannot betray.

NOTISBUCH

From Marseilles, I have set sail for England; from there I shall find passage to the New World, a place called Charleston in a state called Carolina. I now regret my former lack of interest in that new country, even after my sons departed for its shores. I now realize that one can never anticipate one's destination in life. I should have learned geography, along with mathematics, literature, languages, and art.

NOTISBUCH

We departed from Southampton weeks ago. Our ship, after an initially easy voyage, now plunges and rises with a motion that makes my stomach quease.

The voyage seems incredibly long. Fortunately, I managed to afford a tiny cabin and do not have to share quarters with strangers. I have not been to sea before, and the continuous heaving makes my stomach rise and fall with the waves. This is a sickness worse than that I suffered when carrying my babies.

I can hear others vomiting beyond the thin partition, with occasional soothing words from someone who comes regularly to help. I refuse to ask for aid, preferring to remain alone and retch into a basin.

It is best to keep my presence quiet and unobtrusive. Anyone searching for Katrina Holzer must not find an easy trail to follow... if, indeed, that trail does not end in a watery grave, as my present condition seems to suggest.

I have paused to retch again, but I find that writing distracts my mind from my nausea. I have been careful to attract no attention and, so far, have spoken with no one unnecessarily. No one aboard has taken notice of me in any way. Indeed, why should anyone notice this middle-aged widow traveling alone?

NOTISBUCH, SEPTEMBER, 1849

The vessel at last reached Charleston safely. I find this to be a city more attractive and less primitive than I had expected, although to one who has never before set foot in a house built of wood, it has elements that come as something of a shock.

Stone buildings, solid underfoot and meant to stand for a thousand years, are what I know. The slight movement of the floor of a frame building beneath my tread is startling, although I am beginning to get used to it.

Charleston is the port for which our sons took passage. I had hoped to find here some trace of them, for they carried letters of introduction to merchants known to their father and his friends among the bankers and merchants of Vienna.

I went first to the ship chandler, to whom one of the letters referred Karl and Franz. Herr Walther, I find, is now a stout man, not the thin youngster I knew when he was a youth in Vienna.

He did not, of course, recognize me as I came forward with

some trepidation. "Do you recall, Georgi, the lady who used to visit your mother when your family lived in Vienna?" I asked. "I used to bring you sweets, when you were tiny, but then you became older and scorned to take them. I would give them to your sister Trudi, pretending that they were all for her, and you would then share them."

He stared at me for a moment, his pale eyes widening with wonder. "Frau Holzer? *Gott in Himmel!* Can this be? I had thought you and your good man would be still in Vienna, safe at the University. How came you here?"

"I ran away, after they took Guenter. He died in prison, Georgi." For the first time in months I felt tears gather at the corners of my eyes. There has been no opportunity for me to grieve properly, for my own danger and my efforts to escape have been immediate and compelling.

Walther moved to take my hand between his own massive ones. "The revolution, yes? And the new Emperor...I see. Come with me, *gnädige Frau*, to meet my Johanna. We will talk of the old times, *nicht wahr*? And I will, if you permit, offer you lodging in this strange city."

"Then my sons did not come to you with letters?" I asked, my heart sinking. "They set out for this place last year, and I had hoped they came to an old friend like you."

"They did not, and I regret that. Sons of my mother's friends would have been welcome to my heart." He beamed at me, leading me out to the street, where a trim carriage appeared at his hail. It was driven by one of the many black-skinned people who seemed to inhabit this place, and to one who had never seen one of his kind, he seemed strange and exotic.

"Now we come to meet Johanna, and to see *mein Haus*. I am not without vanity, dear lady, and I long to show you how well I have succeeded here in this young country. You will remain with us, I insist, until we find a proper place where you may live comfortably."

Away we rolled, through mud and over occasional stones, and as we left the area immediately about the docks I realized there were impressive houses already in place here, along with others in the process of construction. New buildings are something with which I am not familiar, for Vienna is a very old city with little room or need left for new buildings.

This, it is clear, is a young, prosperous, and growing one. The idea of an entirely new city interests me a great deal. I had never considered the possibility, sealed as I was within the unvarying sameness of the University.

"Only in a new world could such building take place." I gestured toward a spanking new building. "In the old country, there is no space, no need. We have built, long ago, everything we require. Perhaps that is a pity—it makes for a certain lack of originality."

The dark-skinned driver reined up before a tall iron gate. At once a small black boy darted out of the shrubbery and swung open the lacy-patterned halves to let the carriage enter.

The house that now faced us is built of wood, but that does not detract from its effect. The grace of line and curve, of porch and steps, of roof and windows is most pleasing to the eye. Stone, I suddenly realize, must always exhibit a quality of heaviness, whereas this is airy and seems almost to hover above the ground. I have grown used to this new style of building, now, but even then it impressed me favorably.

I drew a deep breath of pleasure. "It is so different from those I know!"

"Here there is not the stone to build with, as in Europe," he said. "And the climate, it is very hot and damp. We build high, you see? To allow the air to circulate. That is why the veranda is so far from the ground, requiring so many steps to approach. We have much pride, Johanna and I, in our dwelling."

He alighted without waiting for the driver to help and handed me down with a flourish. Before I could settle my skirts and turn, a bustle of motion approached.

This was Johanna, without doubt. Small, slight, yet strong-looking, she was alight with excitement. "Do you bring company, Georgi? And without telling me? Yet that is good, for the unexpected is often the best, I think."

Her cheeks bloomed like roses, and her pale blonde hair shone in the brilliant sunlight as she took my hand. Nothing but the friendliest interest shone in her round eyes.

"Frau Holzer, this is my wife Johanna. She speaks much, but often she makes excellent sense," Walther said. "Come, we will go in and refresh ourselves. It is long since I have seen Frau Holzer," he said to his wife, "and much has happened in the Homeland since I left it."

The Walthers took me in as if I were kindred of their own. For that and many other favors I shall always be grateful. Though their large house is crowded (or so it often seems) with their three sons and daughter, they insisted that I take up residence with them, for the time being.

The customs, the streets, even the names in this new city confused me. Without Georgi's help and guidance I would never have been able to find those who could set me on the track of my sons. Indeed, he himself made the inquiries for me among those to whom other letters had been addressed.

Feldmann, the goldsmith, had been one; he had spoken with Franz several times, sending him with a reference to his friend Carter the merchant. When Walther came home with that news, the entire family rejoiced with me as if this were one of their own kinsmen.

Carter had taken him on as a clerk, and he had also known Sullivan the banker, to whom he sent Karl. Sullivan smiled when I visited him to ask about my son.

"What a nice lad he was. Indeed, I recall him well, though he remained with me for only a short while.

"I lost more than one good lad when word came that gold had been found in California. A round dozen left from my neighborhood alone."

He chuckled, and I had the feeling that he was amused by the foolishness of the young.

"This is the sort of wild adventure that draws young men like a magnet, and I have no doubt that Karl and his brother are, this moment, traveling westward. Better let the young do it, I say! Not for me the dust and dirt and dangers of that journey!"

Carter confirmed Sullivan's guess. Franz, too, had determined to go west to make his fortune. However, those bright sons of mine did not intend to dig for gold but to take with them goods that would be needed by those who did. They pooled all they had earned, plus the generous sums we had given them when they sailed, and invested their cash in a variety of useful things, which Carter had obtained for them at excellent prices.

"They bought coffee, tea, sugar and flour. They piled up pots and kettles, blankets and rope, axes and spades, weapons of all descriptions, along with powder and lead.

"Good heads those youngsters have on their shoulders," Carter said. "They will, I suspect, realize more gold from their enterprise than anyone who hopes to pick it up from the ground or pan it from a stream."

NOTISBUCH, 1849

Now I face still another great decision in my life. Should I wait for a while in order to allow the boys to settle in some location that might be found easily? Or should I set off at once to follow them, while the trail is still warm?

The Walthers insist that I wait until the spring before making a decision at all. "Travel in winter is miserable, muddy, and wet, without comfortable inns along the way. This is not Europe, *gnädige Frau*," Georgi insisted. "Even when I travel to Boston on business, it takes many days to make the trip, and I am exhausted when I arrive, particularly if it must be done in winter."

Johanna nodded vigorously. "I traveled only to visit my sister, a day's drive from this spot, and I arrived as cold and wet as if I had tried to swim the river. Only her need for me to attend the birth of her child would have taken me to her, I insist."

I have retired to the small room that was a box room until turned into a private space for my use. This is a hard decision. My first impulse is to go at once, trying to follow those who have gone to California from this area. Yet now I understand what it might have been difficult for me to comprehend before—this is not Europe.

Conditions here are unlike those I knew, in every way. If I had recently descended here from the moon, I could not feel more alien and unsure.

If I should become ill along the way, I might die on the road and no one would ever know what happened to me. The thought is frightening, that my sons would never know.

NOTISBUCH

When I went down this morning, I said to Johanna, "I have decided to spend the winter in Charleston. But I cannot crowd you so with my presence. I must find lodgings and perhaps some student who needs tutoring in mathematics or languages, in order to make a bit of money to finance my trip west, when the time comes."

"But we like having you here, *Liebchen*!" Johanna protested. "The children will be forlorn if you leave, for no one tells tales as you do, and no one is so effective at kissing bruises or giving hugs.

"Surely you will remain with us! Indeed, you might tutor them, for you are far more qualified to do that than anyone here in Charleston."

It is most gratifying—and yet I feel the need for independence. All my life has been spent among other people. Though I adored my parents and my brothers, loved my husband and sons intensely, I now seem to need space and time to learn who I am and what I might be able to do alone.

It is an odd idea, and yet I now understand that I shall travel alone into that perilous West. It is never too soon to learn how to do other things alone as well.

This new world, I am learning every day, demands every skill, all the strength, and all the wit that anyone can muster, whether they be male or female.

I shall find my sons, or I shall join my dear Guenter in death. That is my decision.

CHAPTER SEVEN

Marta Hirschorn heaved her plump bulk into the wagon and took her seat behind the patient oxen. Beside her, Klaus, her youngest, held the long whip in chubby hands, eager to begin their long journey. She smiled down at him, although it wrenched her heart to leave her home.

It was no longer their home, however. The Cathers had paid her for it, and that modest sum would mean the beginning of a new life for her sons. If her Klaus had lived, it would have been different, of course, but she did not quarrel with fate. Death was the lot of everyone, and it was now left to her to rear their eight sons to manhood as best she could.

Free land—rich land—in Oregon would help her accomplish that huge task. Perhaps there would be some learned person among those who settled there who could teach her sons the things they must know as well.

Her own parents had not been able to read the great German Bible that even now rode in her trunk in the wagon. Klaus had taught her to read English, bless him, and to write and cipher, but she knew only enough to make certain she was not cheated in trade. She wanted far more for her sons.

Mrs. Cather came out of the sprawling cabin that Marta and Klaus had built with their own hands. She was carrying a big basket, a jug, and a bag.

"Mrs. Hirschorn, I fixed a bite for you to take with you. And Paul makes the best corn whiskey in this country, so I thought you might need a jug to take along, in case somebody gets sick." She handed the things up to Gustav, who was hanging out of the back of the wagon, despite his injured leg.

"Besides that, I gathered you a bunch of herbs from your garden. I figured maybe you didn't have the time to think about such things, and with so many children, it's almost certain you'll need some medicines along the way. Horehound and comfrey and such can come in handy, as I know too well. I've doctored neighbors and family for years, and your herb garden was one reason we decided to take up this place."

Marta leaned down to take the woman's hand. "It is kind, Frau Cather. Ve haf the long journey to go, and to take vith us the kindness of a new friend, that is a comfort, *nicht wahr*?"

As the woman stepped back, Mama Hirschorn cracked the whip, while Klaus jumped down and prodded the slow beasts into motion with the stick peeled for that purpose. She kept her face forward, for she didn't want her sons to know that her eyes were filled with tears.

She had come here as a bride, straight from Franconia, after working and saving for years until she and her affianced husband had the money for her fare. Once they were wed, she and Klaus had come westward to Kentucky and camped under the trees, while they hewed and trimmed and notched the timbers for their home.

Almost every year there had been a baby, and new rooms were needed soon. The house had grown only a bit less quickly than had her family.

There her *geliebte* Klaus had breathed his last, in the winter just past, gasping out his life as bright blood stained his lips and chest. Broken ribs had pierced his lungs and his chest wall when a tree, caught by an unexpected shift of the wind, fell onto him.

With all the skill she possessed, she had worked to save him, but it would have required the services of a surgeon—or of God—to mend what was torn inside. She still felt that in some way she could have saved him, when she was ill or depressed. Yet she knew it was impossible.

And now she alone was responsible for their brood. They had worked hard to give them the manners and the ways of the Old Country, and it was now her task to make certain they were not contaminated by the rude Americans with whom they would come in contact.

Again she cracked the whip, and Klaus prodded the beasts until they moved more quickly. At her nod, the boys piled out of the laden wagon, in order to lighten the load.

They had the time to amble along at a very leisurely pace. That would not have been within boy nature however. No, they flitted ahead and behind, to dart into the wood after rabbits or skylark among themselves. They had no difficulty in keeping up with the deliberate gait of the oxen. She knew they would walk most of the way to the new land, for that was what she had learned from those few who had traveled west and returned.

Marta gazed ahead along the dusty track that wound through deep forests and among steep hills. It was as well that she had made her decision quickly and started at once for her goal. Even at this oxen-slow pace, the weeks they must travel would find them arriving at the emigrants' gathering place in Missouri well before the last wagon train started for the Oregon country.

She hoped no unforeseen accident or illness would delay them. There were frightening tales of the dangers of traveling across the mountains, if the snows began before wagon trains arrived. Trailmasters would not form a train too late in the year, fearing they might be trapped in the mountains by deep snows that might well wipe out an entire group.

Word of the disaster to the Donner group had come even to her remote home, and she shivered to think of those starving people, surrounded by snow, with their companions dying before their eyes. She refused even to think of the more gruesome tales told about the survivors.

Surely, human beings could never bring themselves to consume human flesh! She pushed that thought away and touched the lead ox with her prod stick.

Marta knew she must not hurry her three spans of oxen. She had purchased the extra animals with part of the money from the sale of the farm, and the Scotsman who sold them had seemed concerned that she intended to take such a journey without a man to help.

"Be sartain," he said, his weathered face earnest, "to care for t' beasts proper. A dead ox will pull no wagon, y'see, and the strong backs o' these beasts will stand between the nine o' ye and disaster, if ye dinna hurry them."

She had worked their own oxen beside Klaus in their fields, of course, but that was far different from taking them upon a journey of over two thousand miles. There would be no lush riverside pastures where they were going, to keep the animals fat and active. From what people told her, she knew that even water would be hard to find.

The boys, of course, were more excited than sad to be leaving the only place they knew. Tall Andreas, who was now eighteen and felt himself the man of the family, walked at the head of the lead span. Ernst, Benedikt, Franz, and little Klaus popped into and out of the wood, playing with their dog, Bianca.

Tagging behind the wagon came Ludwig and Walther, faithful to their promise to keep a watchful eye on the younger boys, though they were even more likely than the small ones to get into mischief. The bigger they became, the more difficulties they were able to cause, she had learned as her sons grew.

Marta turned to look behind her, into the wagon. Fifteen-year-old Gustav had sprained his ankle badly as they prepared for the journey; now he gazed out of the rear opening of the canvas, his very shape longing to be out there with his brothers. It hurt his dignity to have to ride in the wagon like a baby.

She sighed. They were very lucky he had not broken his leg, when the great supply trunk shifted unexpectedly and came down on him. A twist of the ankle and bruises to the knee and thigh would heal soon, with rest, but a broken leg would have been an injury that might have delayed them for too long to catch the last wagon train of the season.

The sudden rainstorm that caught them in mid-afternoon did not damp their spirits, she realized with relief. The rain was warm, and the boys simply shed their homespun shirts, rolled up the legs of their breeches, and waded gleefully through the deepening mud.

She, perched on the board that formed the driver's seat, was drenched quickly, but she didn't complain. The oxen seemed not to care whether they walked on dry earth or trudged through slush, for their pace neither slowed nor quickened.

When they reached a village, just before dark, there were three wagons camped in a clearing just beyond the inn. She heaved a sigh of relief. Perhaps from this point on she would have company on this greatest journey of her life. Her sons were bright and steadfast, but it would be a comfort to have other adults to consult, if anything went wrong.

She pulled to a halt beyond the last campfire and whistled shrilly, signaling to the boys, who were trailing some distance behind the wagon, to unhitch and set up camp. While the eight busied themselves with the formerly unaccustomed chores that had now become second nature, she climbed down from her hard seat and stretched her legs. She was getting old, she knew, for her body stiffened and her back ached after the long day of driving.

A man, a woman, and two young girls were moving around the first camp she passed on her way to the inn. She greeted them, and they looked up to nod and smile. The other campfires were unattended, though there were indications that potatoes had been set to roast in the ashes at the edges of some of their fires.

The inn was long and low, built sturdily of logs, with loopholes drilled through the walls and also through the heavy shutters, which were already closed for the night despite the warmth of the season. A stagecoach stood beyond it, and she could hear the stamping and snorting of horses beyond the corner of the building. The stable stood there, she was certain, and the coach had arrived earlier in the evening.

Perhaps there were travelers inside, with word from the East. Even, she might hope, traders returned from the West, with news of the trains that had already undertaken that journey.

She pushed the half-open door wider and stepped into a big room, low-ceiled and filled with cooking smells, tobacco smoke, and the rumble of talk and laughter from the principally male customers, who sat on rough-split benches arranged along two long trestle tables.

The smell of their food almost dizzied her, and Marta realized for the first time how ravenous she was. How much hungrier her sons would be! But first she must inquire as to travelers to Westport.

The boys were willing and eager, but they were also young and inexperienced. She was knowledgeable about many things, but not such travel as this. They must go in company with someone who understood the difficulties and dangers of their route, if they were to reach their distant goal and the wide, free land she envisioned as the heritage she must give her sons.

A withered old fellow, stumping on a wooden leg, came to meet her. "How-do," he said. "You wanna set down an' eat?"

She shook her head. "I haf my own camp, out there vith the rest. Vhat I need is to find someone going to the Oregon. To travel vith, you see?"

Before he could reply, one of the half-intoxicated young fellows at the nearest table rose and came toward her. His face was flushed with drink, and he was grinning in a manner that warned her of trouble to come.

"Nice plump lady," he said. "Need nice plump lady...keep me warm. Hic! Come wi' me, sweetheart." He made an inaccurate grab for her, and Marta spun out of reach.

She kicked him behind the knee, and he went down, hurt and surprise on his face. *"Teufelsbraten!"* she growled. "I am old enough to be *ihr Mutter*, you fool! I haf the eight sons and am too old to trouble mineself vith another."

There was a stir in the farther corner of the great room, and Marta saw a woman working her way around the crowded space, heading toward her. A lady, she saw at once, well though simply dressed in dark brown wool. She gestured for Marta to wait.

Stepping near the door, Mama Hirschorn waited until the lady was within hearing. Then she nodded toward the door, and both went outside, where they could hear themselves speak. To her astonishment and joy, the lady spoke to her in German.

"I could not hear what you said, after you called that one a Devil's roast," she began. "Yet that one round term told me that you understand my own language. That alone is enough to make me glad to meet with you in this coarse and uncivilized place." She brushed her skirt with both hands, as if to shake off the dust of the inn.

"It has been a journey...a journey that even after warnings from trusted friends I did not quite believe. I have needed someone to talk with, and if you have no objection, I will come with you and we will speak together."

Marta smiled and replied in German, "I have the wagon and the camp. Food should be ready soon, for my children are skilled at cooking over the open fire. Come with me, and we shall speak. I think we may do business together—I have that feeling, also."

CHAPTER EIGHT

Jostling along in the heavy coach, smothered in dust or spattered with mud, according to the weather, Katrina realized that she had not truly believed what Georgi told her about travel in this raw country. She had been moving for weeks now, staying at night on the floor of some isolated farmhouse or in some rude inn set up just to milk money from such travelers as herself.

Worst of all, she was usually the only woman in the coach. There was no overt problem—in this new world it was evident that women were more valuable and better regarded than in the old. Yet the men who shared the cramped space, lurching onto her lap or receiving her on theirs when the coach swerved in the opposite direction, were dirty, often drunken, and seemed to have no conversation other than obscenities whose meanings she could only surmise.

This last inn was the worst, smoky and dirty. There was no private room; she would have to stretch herself on a pallet in the corner of a big chamber in which six men also rested.

She felt she could not bear it. Better to go outside and sleep beneath a tree, if it were not for the mud and the occasional rain!

She found a bucket and a bowl on the side porch of the inn and managed to wash some of the filth off herself. When she went into the main room, where food was being slopped onto tin plates and ale was being consumed in unsafe quantities, she moved as far against the rear wall as she could. She felt it safer to stay out of the way of these rowdy young men who had arrived just before the coach.

"Gold!" That was the tallest, drunkest of the lot, raising his cup. "Gon'er pick it off the groun', out there in Californy. Every one of us'll be rich 'nough to buy the best whores in Boston!"

His companions banged their cups on the table in agreement, and the innkeeper, a wrinkled whitebeard with a wooden leg and a cast in his eye, squinted through the smoke and snorted.

"Gold, ye say? Young fools! Nothin' comes without a price, and you'll learn that hard lesson before ye make it over the country betwixt here and the far ocean. I been there. It's no place for towns-men or weaklin's, and that's my final word." He stumped away to-ward the kitchen, mumbling to himself.

Making a mental note to try to speak with the man before leav-ing, Katrina settled to eat her portion of greasy stew and to drink her bitter coffee. She had chewed the last of her gritty bread and was preparing to rise when a woman entered the inn. She was a round, pink-faced little body, neither old nor young, but strong-looking.

When one of the would-be gold miners accosted her, she took him down so quickly that Katrina had no idea how she did it. Only when she heard the accent in which the newcomer dressed down the boy, along with the somewhat scholarly epithet she aimed at him, did Katrina Holzer realize that this, too, was a native speaker of German.

Going to Oregon? Had she said that? Even to travel partway with her, until the trail forked toward California, would be better than being stifled in that coach. To have a respectable woman, and this was a very obviously respectable one, at her side would be a comfort whose value she had never before suspected.

She rose and began working her way around the wall toward the doorway. When the woman looked up, she made an emphatic ges-ture—"Wait!"

Once outside, they quickly found that though Katrina spoke High German and Marta spoke Low, they communicated very well. There was no question of parting at that point, and Katrina willingly followed Frau Hirschorn to her camp, where a gaggle of boys of all sizes tended a fire, stirred a pot of stew, and sat about waiting for their mother to return.

Over their supper, the Hirschorns listened to her story. "But you cannot go into that dirty place to sleep!" Marta said at last. "You sleep here vith us, on the ground perhaps, but on clean bedding and vith safe company, ja?"

A tremendous relief filled Katrina's heart. "I will stay with you gladly. If you have the room, I will travel with you, as well. I have the money to pay for my food...."

Marta Hirschorn waved a plump hand. "Not to vorry about that so soon! Ve vill take you, yes, though there vill be much place vhere you must valk, along vith *die Kinder*. The load, it is heavy upon the beasts, *verstehen Sie?*"

Katrina nodded. "I would far rather walk than ride as I have been doing. My husband and I, in the summers, would sometimes climb mountains. I am not a weak person, though it may take time for me to regain my elasticity."

She looked around at the circle of boys, who seemed to come in every size possible. "It will not trouble your sons?"

"My sons vill be most happy to velcome the *gnädische Frau*," Marta said, her tone firm. There was no sign of disagreement from the eight sons themselves. "There vill be supplies at the end of this part of our journey, and then ve vill think about such things. For now, ve haf enough to care for even so many.

"Now ve go und get your things from the inn, eh? I do not trust those *jungen* to care for the luggage. Andreas, you come vith us. Walther, tend the animals. Gustav, you see to your brothers...get them to bed. Ve haf a very long day tomorrow, I think."

Her orders were given in a soft voice, but her sons sprang to action instantly. Before Katrina had followed the woman out of earshot, she knew the sons were obeying without question. There was no doubt of it; this was a self-respecting family, reared to attend to duty and to care for one another.

She sighed with relief. Perhaps her journey would begin anew, among people more compatible and civilized than those she had encountered thus far.

By the time they arrived at the inn, most of those who had crowded the room had gone to their rest, wherever that might be. The innkeeper was stumping about, wielding a brush broom and muttering under his breath. He recognized Katrina and leaned the broom against the wall, coming to meet her.

"Herr Faulkner, I'd like to get my trunk," she said. "I've found a family going in my direction, and we intend to travel together for a time."

He nodded, his whiskers twitching. "Better that way. A lady don't need to bunk in with the sort of rough customers we git here. I set yore bag in my back room. Pat!" His screech was enough to deafen you, Katrina thought.

In response, a skinny youth came out of the back, his arms wet to the shoulders. "Yes, Pa?"

"Git the lady's bag outen the back there." He turned with a satisfied air and headed for his broom again, but Katrina put out a hand to touch his sleeve.

"I heard you tell those young men that you had been west to the ocean. My sons went to California last year. They were supplied with trade goods to sell to the miners. I must find them, if possible, but I have no idea how to go about that. Is there any advice you might give me?"

He squinted at her, his forehead's furrows deepening. "Yore sons? Two of 'em, talked German like you? Hair like yourn? Got a mule string loaded to the gunnels with practical stuff like likker and tools and weapons?"

She felt suddenly breathless. "It might just be...were their names Karl and Franz Holzer? They are still very young—Karl is twenty-one, now, and Franz is twenty. Very fair, with dark blue eyes. They are, like their father, most intelligent. They decided there was more gold to be had from supplies than from digging in the ground."

"Them's the ones!" Faulkner's pale eyes brightened. "Polite little cusses, they were. Thanked me for every little thing.

"They come through...oh, must be midsummer of last year. Looked to be in good shape, and I made certain they understood they had to keep their pistols in their belts and their rifles handy. There's folks that will rob you of the dust on your coat-tail, 'twixt here and the Pacific."

Katrina controlled her emotions, though joy filled her almost to bursting. "Where would they be likely to go?" she asked.

"Might be they'll stop in the mountains, right there where the miners will be. Or else they might make for San Francisco. Gettin' to be a big place, all of a sudden, I hear. You'll never find 'em by wanderin' around all by your lonesome, I tell you.

"I'd advise you to go on to Oregon with the lady, here, and send word that you're lookin' for your sons. There's a lot of goin' and comin' up and down the coast now. Word should get to 'em in a year or two. Then they'll come to find you, I'll bet."

She thought for a moment. Already she realized that communications here were far different from those in Europe. It seemed that more was done by way of personal word passed among travelers and innkeepers than by letter.

Faulkner's advice made good sense. Once she had passed over the mountains and the deserts, Katrina felt she would at least be on the same side of the continent with her sons, and that might make the task of making contact easier.

She glanced down at Mama Hirschorn. The round face smiled up at her reassuringly. "Ja, Frau Holzer, I think this is a good vord to heed. Ve go together beyond the mountains, und there ve see what vord can be sent to find your sons.

"It pleases me vell to haf another voman to talk vith along the vay, also. You vill go vith us, und all vill be happy together, *nicht wahr?*"

Katrina found herself smiling back. She had not even hoped that it would be easy to locate Franz and Karl, though she knew she must make the effort. Now there was the promise of congenial company, at least, along the harsh journey.

If a message found its way along a tenuous route, borne by guides and travelers and suppliers and others whom she could not even guess at, then the boys would, indeed, come to find her. Until then she would have useful work to do.

It was with a far easier mind that she settled, that night, into her nest of blankets under heavy canvas. The mud had dried around the big fire the Hirschorns kept burning, and the rain remained only a sprinkle, easily turned by the sheet that she propped up on sticks to cover her bedroll.

She did not sleep with one ear open, as she had been doing. She woke the next morning warm and relaxed and rested as she had not been since leaving Georgi's home in Carolina. The sounds of movement, the crackle of fresh wood piled onto the fire, the good smell of coffee brought her out of her bed, stretching and yawning.

"Do not trouble yourself," said Marta, when she offered to help with cooking breakfast. "You vere so tired—ve let you sleep long. Now ve eat and harness the oxen once more. It is still a very long vay before ve join the train."

"If you will not allow me to help with the work, perhaps you will allow me to give the children lessons, as we walk together," Katrina offered. "My husband was a teacher all his life, and I studied with him and tutored students at the university in Vienna."

The woman's face brightened like sunrise. "You can teach *meine Kinder*? I am not a learned voman, though *mein* Klaus haf teach me to read und to cipher a little. I vorry that they grow up ignorant, in this new place. Unless the parents know, they cannot teach the young, is it not so?"

"You are very wise, Frau Holzer," Katrina said. "I will be honored to teach your sons, and any others who may travel with us along the way. With something to hold our interest, the journey should not seem so long, after all."

She only hoped that would prove to be true. She was beginning to feel that this quest had been undertaken in ignorance and might include disaster along the way, if she were not extremely cautious. Her good fortune in finding the Hirschorns did not entirely remedy that intuition.

CHAPTER NINE

Of all the strange journeys Katrina had made since fleeing from Vienna, her time with Mama Hirschorn and her brood bade fair to be the strangest. It had never occurred to her how different the lives of rural people, particularly those living in a primitive environment, might be from her own comfortable and intellectually challenging existence in Vienna.

The self-sufficiency of even the smallest of the Hirschorns amazed her. The strength of the plump little woman was surprising to one who had never had need for physical exertion except for her husband's mountain climbing expeditions when they were young. Marta seldom called upon her tall Andreas, even when something heavy needed to be moved.

She was also able to run very fast, for one of her age and weight, when one of the children called for help. She would go leaping over bushes and crashing through tangles as surely as a young man might have done. Her vigor and determination were refreshing after the vapors and languidness of the few socially prominent ladies of Katrina's acquaintance and the wives of academicians she had known.

Any qualms Katrina might have had about changing from travel in a coach full of men to a wagon accompanied by a woman and children soon dissolved. She found herself lending a hand when the wagon wheels sank deep into mud or threatened to slide off the edge of a precipice. The constant walking made her feel younger as they moved into the Missouri country.

As they struggled over the almost nonexistent roads toward their goal at Westport Landing, she found that small Klaus had adopted her. He ran circles around her like a puppy, as she moved steadily after the wagon. He insisted upon sitting beside her on the high wagon seat, when she took her turn at driving the oxen.

Indeed, her first lesson in driving was directed by Klaus. "You hold the lines so, and tie them around this. See?" He looped the leather reins around the brace holding the wagon cover.

"You poke 'em with the stick to make 'em go faster. If they start off the road, you yell like this...."—and he gave a shriek that sent the blackbirds in a nearby treetop rocketing into the sky.

The oxen flapped their ears and continued their steady pace down the middle of the track. "But they don't listen to you," she objected.

"Oh, they don't care what we say. That gets me or Ernst or Walther here with our sticks. Then we poke 'em and make 'em straighten out. And if they go too slow, you yell again, and we'll help you punch 'em up." His ruddy cheeks creased in a grin. "There's nothin' to driving oxen. You just keep a lookout, mainly."

His yell had brought Andreas to find out what was needed. He looked up at Katrina, his blue eyes merry. "That Klaus—he makes me walk a lot of extra miles, just to see what he's yelling about," the young man said. "And he keeps Mama on the move. Don't let him bother you, Frau Holzer."

She was impressed with the Hirschorn boys, even the two middle and mischievous ones. Ludwig, at twelve, and Walther, at fourteen, were inseparable, and seemed to attract troubles without even trying.

One afternoon as the weary group trudged along a steep slope between tall ranks of oak and ash trees, there came a startled cry. Ludwig had been walking beside the trail to avoid the worst of the dust. He now stood frozen, while a blur of insects buzzed around his head.

Marta looked back, saw what was happening, and gave a groan. "He haf stepped into the hornet nest," she muttered. "Now he vill be stung und he vill get sick. I know from of old—if there is a nest or a hive vithin miles, mein Ludwig vill find it."

She ran forward, tying her light shawl over her head, and lifted the boy bodily out of the debris about his feet. Then she dropped him onto his own feet, shook him hard to detach the insects that had stung him, and pushed him ahead of her through a thick tangle of huckleberry bushes, which effectively brushed off the clinging hornets and discouraged those following the unfortunate boy.

The rest of the sons backed away to avoid attracting the notice of the furious insects, which darted about, buzzing, until they began to settle down again. Andreas came at a trot, carrying a bucket of water from their reserve barrel.

Evidently the Hirschorns had devised a method for dealing with Ludwig's frequent stings, for Mama began bathing the angry bumps that were rising on his face and neck, forearms, and bare ankles. The boy bore it stoically, but he turned very pale around the red circles. Andreas lifted him, once the cool water had been applied, and put him into the back of the wagon beside Gustav.

"Ve stop early," Marta said. "I must find the plantain to put on the stings. I haf the dry plant, but for this purpose I must find the fresh. That vill help him to get vell more quick. I make, too, the comfrey tea, to cool his blood, *nicht wahr*?"

To Katrina, used to calling a trained physician for any illness, it seemed strange and primitive, but there was obviously no alternative to the use of such remedies. Even in the few villages they'd passed she had found that no doctors existed. Midwives and those who understood the uses of wild plants seemed to be the only source of healing for the settlers in this wild country.

They pulled off the track at last, into a small meadow. There a creek had cut a deep ravine leading down the slope of the small mountain they were descending.

"Plantain, it like the damp spot. I vill find it there, I think," Marta said as they loosed the oxen and began gathering wood for their nightly cooking fire.

As soon as the boys were about their evening tasks, their mother headed down the slope toward the creek. Katrina, curious, hurried after her.

"May I go, too?" she called. "I know nothing about herbs, and I anything I can learn along the way will be helpful, in the country to which I go."

"Surely," Marta replied. "Vhen you look for the plantain, you go to the low place, ja? Here is the game trail that vill take us down to the creek, I think. Yes, there go the little prints of the deer, you see?" She pointed to sharp impressions in the dusty groove leading down the steep bank of the creek.

Katrina picked her way down carefully, watching for the snakes that she had learned from experience were often to be found near water. Serpents were not something she had encountered in Vienna, and she had a healthy fear even of those that were not poisonous.

Before they were quite at the level of the water, Marta gave an exclamation. "There, you see? The long mottled leaf, in the cluster, vith the tall stem and the little vhite flowers at the top? That is the plantain, most useful for many things."

The two moved to kneel beside a patch of some three or four plants, whose strongly ridged leaves rayed outward from a flower-bearing stem. Marta took from her apron pocket a small knife, with which she cut the larger leaves.

"The small ones, they vill vork, but it is the great ones that are best." She gathered them into her apron and turned to go up the hill again.

Katrina looked back as they climbed, imprinting in her mind the distinctive look of the leaves. This would be a valuable addition to any family's pharmacopoeia, she thought. I must remember.

Poor Ludwig was desperately swollen by the time they reached the camp again. He obviously had fever, and his face, usually long and thin, with high cheekbones, was round. His eyes were slits, his cheeks puffed, even his forehead was swollen. It was plain that without some treatment, the child might become desperately ill. Even die?

Katrina shuddered at the thought. How did one dare, she wondered, to risk having children in this place, amid dangers that were forgotten in Europe? Then she remembered the revolution, as well as the wars that Napoleon had carried across the continent.

Worse things than stings and bites occurred in the old world. Children had died there at the hands of soldiers and looters, which seemed somehow worse than dying of perils supplied by raw Nature.

Then Marta looked up, her eyes filled with anxiety, and Katrina forgot her musings. There was work to do.

"Pound the plantain, vill you, Frau Holzer? The boys, they are too impatient. The vooden tray in the vagon is gut for that."

Ernst ran to the tailgate and grubbed about until he came up with the required vessel. Already Katrina was spreading the thick leaves on her lap, making certain that no mud or dust adhered to them.

When she had the tray before her, she began squeezing the leaves between her hands, reducing them to a pulpy mess that she pounded in the tray, using a heavy iron spoon. Walther gathered batches onto a pewter dish and ferried them to his mother for plastering onto his brother's distended face, arms, and ankles.

There was a lot of plantain to crush, and before Katrina was finished Marta nodded. "*Das ist gut*. Ve save the rest for aftervard, I think. He is covered now, and the fever, it is already sinking."

To Katrina's amazement, the chilly mess seemed to have begun reducing the swelling. When she touched one of the few clean spots on the child's forehead, the fever was noticeably less.

"This is amazing," she said. "Are there other such herbs in this new country? It would seem that physicians back home might study them with useful results."

Marta grimaced. "There are many such things, ve learn from the Rothäute who used to live near our old home. They doctor their own people for many centuries before ours come here. But no Doktor who ever came there vould ever listen vhen ve tell him about the plants in the voods."

It didn't surprise Katrina. She had encountered the arrogance of medical men in Vienna on more than one occasion. Her dear Guenter, possessed of a sharp and unoccluded mind, had commented more than once upon the lack of open-mindedness among some of his fellow academicians. He had even less patience with physicians and surgeons, which his increasing frailty, in late years, did nothing to improve.

She had, in her own small circle, seen real miracles performed by old women who dosed their families with chicken soup and familiar herbs. More than once the Herr Doktor, called in by concerned relatives, had bled a recovering patient to the point of death, while the grandmother wept in a corner to see her loved one taken when he might have been saved.

"That does not surprise me," she said, scraping the last bit of plantain from the tray and wiping its damp-streaked curve with a bit of cloth. "I have learned a valuable thing today.

"Now we should cook, for the children are hungry. We might give Ludwig a sip of broth, do you not think? The rabbits Andreas killed this morning should boil tender, if he might manage to chew."

Andreas had already skinned and gutted the rabbits, and soon the pot was simmering over the campfire, filling the air with a rich aroma of rabbit and wild onion. Various green plants that Marta had picked beside the road were dropped into the stew, along with mushrooms found at last night's camp.

When it was ready, Katrina found it excellent. Even Ludwig drank some broth, though his face was too painful when he tried to chew. He seemed to be improving now, much to her relief.

Sitting in the flickering red light, Katrina Holzer thought with some amusement of her former self. I would have been shocked to think of sitting on a baulk of wood beside a fire in the forest, with people I have known for only a week, she mused. Even I must have been contaminated by the rigid thinking of those proper people about me. Poor Guenter—he would have loved this life, if he had survived.

Tears filled her eyes as she thought of that slight shape moving away from her between two soldiers. He was so frail and so brave, her beloved husband. It was, perhaps, best that he had not lived through that winter in prison, for he would not have consented to flee with her to the new world.

No, Guenter would have remained to fight, and another winter would have seen him again in prison or standing before a firing squad. She would never cease to love him, but her life would be far simpler on her own. She found to her astonishment that she liked being responsible for herself.

She found that she wanted to be like Marta Hirschorn, strong and determined and afraid, it seemed, of nothing at all. She smiled, set aside her pottery bowl, and went to check on Ludwig. It was good to be a part of this family, able to lend a helping hand when it was needed.

Already she was thinking about things she had been told of the trail west. Far along the way, it would fork, and one part of the expedition would turn toward California, while the rest would go on, with the Hirschorns, to Oregon.

More and more, she was inclined to accept advice from those who had heard her story. The sons would find her, once she sent word by those going to the gold camps. She would go on with these people and find a place for herself in the new land of Oregon.

Perhaps she might remain with the Hirschorns, helping Marta with her many tasks while the boys staked a claim of land and began the work of readying it for the plow. Before they spread their bedrolls for the night, she approached the resting woman and sat beside her.

"I would like to go on with you, Frau Hirschorn," she said, "when you go to Oregon. I feel that I may be of help, and I am learning to regard your family highly."

Marta looked at her with firelit eyes, and her lips quirked into a smile. "I haf hoped that you vould," she said. "It is gut to have one who speaks my language, and it is even better to become fond of her. Ve vill go on vell together, I think."

So Katrina turned to her place amid the sighing and stretching children, and gratefully laid herself on her bedding. She now had a place and a family. It was very good to be a necessary part of a group, rather than a dependent to be cosseted like a child.

"I must preserve these things that happen to me," she mused, half aloud. "The notebook in my luggage will become my *Tagebuch*, in which I will write each evening, if not too weary, the events of the day and the things that we see as we travel. Then when the children of my sons ask me of this time, I shall be able to turn to the correct pages and read them just what occurred."

Smiling, she rolled herself into her blankets and closed her eyes, feeling more confident of the future than she had for a very long while.

CHAPTER TEN

At last the wagon train was ready to set off, having organized the traveling arrangements, elected the leaders, and accommodated the huge number of travelers headed for the California gold camps. The train numbered some two hundred wagons, and the confusion and dust arising as the animals were hitched was enough to fill any youngster with excitement.

Phil was no exception. He had a hard time staying by the Stoner wagon, for he wanted to go and see the tenderfeet from the East try to wangle their mules or oxen into harness and get them headed in the right direction. Those who had farmed for years had no trouble; under experienced hands, their teams fell into place without so much as a twitch.

Others were having billy heck, and the boy's ears turned toward rich sources of new cusswords. Mules bucked and hee-hawed, and oxen grunted gruff objections and milled in slow circles, putting wagons into precarious predicaments. Here and there a wagon-tongue cracked under conflicting pressures, and the unlucky wagon-eer had to make quick repairs, to be reinforced at the first stop along the way.

The train, under the urging of Jesse Gunter, their former mountain-man guide, was going to start right now, while there was time to get across the mountains. Any remaining behind would not get to their destination until next year, unless they set off on their own, which was a perilous project.

The terrible fate of George Donner's group some four years before was fresh in the minds of anyone attempting the westward journey through the Sierras. Though many of those now entrained were not taking the California route through the Sierras, a number intended to. Besides, the guide said the mountains the Oregon emigrants must cross were tough enough on their own.

Phil leaned against the big wheel and gazed with delight at the confusion about him. This was a real adventure. Even after tangling with the Williams boys, he hadn't truly believed in it until now.

Anything that could begin with such action and drama had to be worth doing, he decided, as he watched a young mule go bucking and twisting down the narrow space between the ranked wagons, upsetting the teams already in place and braying its lungs out. The animal's owner, red-faced and sweating, came panting after it, and it turned out, to Phil's great amusement, to be the Williams boys' father.

"Stop that gaw-damned mule!" Thomas yelled.

Gotch and Clem came behind him, taking their time and letting their father do all the running. They were snickering at him too, and Phil felt sudden anger. Didn't they know what a big step this was, and how much nerve it took to leave everything behind and start off for a new place? He had no use for the boys, but he came near to liking Thomas Williams, because he was so honestly stupid and well-meaning.

A bunch of dogs came ripping along behind the trio, and Rags, at Phil's heels, raised his hackles and drew back his lip. The old dog didn't quite understand this new situation, and strange dogs had never been to his liking anyway. If he'd been just a mite younger, he'd have lit into them like a grizzly.

Phil reached down to ruffle his tattered ears. "It's all right, boy. You just stay by me and watch the show. I never in all my born days saw anything to match this. Must be a thousand people and a million critters churnin' around here, tryin' to get goin'."

Maryla, coming up behind him, laughed. "I never saw such a mess," she said. "You'd think somebody intending to travel for six months behind a team would learn how to manage his critters before he set out, wouldn't you?"

Elizabeth, waiting in the shade of the wagon-cover, made a shushing gesture. "Don't be rude, dear. They're doing their best, I know. Not everyone can be good at everything, remember."

Phil winked at Maryla, who grinned. Mama would find something nice to say about a rattlesnake, the boy thought, even if it bit her.

He wondered how well she would get along with the strange mixture of people he had already spotted among the wagons. Some were coarse and foul-mouthed, and he knew she'd avoid them and expect him to do the same. There were, however, two ladies with more boys than he'd ever seen in one family. He thought she might like them.

Their wagon was three up and one over from Pa's, and they managed their oxen quietly and easily. The tallest son, really a man,

Phil thought, at least seventeen or eighteen, stood beside the lead ox, a long stick in his hand, watching calmly while the wild mule bucked past.

The smallest boy, up on the wagon seat for the time being, was giggling, though the sound couldn't be heard above the din. He was younger than Phil, but he seemed like somebody who would keep things lively, given the chance.

Phil decided to bring him to meet Mama and Pa, when the train was well on its way and things settled for the first night. He needed someone besides the Hollings children to pal around with, though they were all right for little 'uns.

The mule had trapped himself between two oxen up ahead, and Williams managed to rope him and turn him back down the line of wagons. The animal was tugging backward at the halter, making Thomas even redder than usual as he hauled on the rope. Only when he yelled at his sons did they lend a hand, and among the three of them they dragged the mule back to the starting point and got him hitched in tandem with his partner.

Phil amused himself for a while by checking on the many different kinds of wagons and the teams that were to pull them for two thousand miles across the country. They were mostly oxen, hitched in pairs, sometimes as many as eight for the biggest wagons, often in fours.

The Hirschorn family with all the boys had six, which seemed a sensible number. That was how many Pa had decided would be needed to pull their own heavy vehicle. He chalked up another plus mark for them. They seemed to be the right kind of people.

About a quarter of the teams were composed of mules. Nobody used horses, because everyone who ever advised on traveling west warned against that. They couldn't live on wild grass and sagebrush while working at top level, as the oxen and mules managed to do. They had less stamina than either of the other kinds of animals, but they could be ridden when necessary and would follow the train with other spare animals, for use later at the end of the journey.

Behind the last of the ranked wagons was a dreadful confusion made up of those spare animals. Oxen, mules, milk cows, steers for meat, young bulls for breeding—you could have started off farming in a big way right here, Phil thought. They balked and bellowed and raised dust and dropped dung until it looked like pure confusion back there.

His father appeared around the wagon, spitting dust. "This is sheer chaos," he said to Elizabeth, and the boy almost laughed aloud. "I think Phil and Maryla should take you and the baby off past the edge of the train so you can breathe some decent air. You'll both be sick if you keep inhaling dust mixed with cattle dung."

Mama sighed and nodded, wiping her dusty face on a corner of her apron. She was coughing hard, and it was a moment before she caught her breath.

"You're right, Albert. Lizzie is gasping like a little fish. Here, Maryla, you carry the baby, and Phil can help me get through this confusion." She coughed again, and the boy saw her heart jumping like a small trapped animal beneath her calico bodice.

He put his arm around his mother's too-thin waist and half carried her as they worked their way around wagons, past teams, through yapping batches of dogs and small children, to the area beyond the last of the train. Here, too, the ground was trampled and covered with drying manure, but at least the prairie wind carried the dust away from them.

Phil settled his mother beneath a big oak tree, and Maryla laid Lizzie in her lap. They stared at each other over Elizabeth's bonnet. She looked bad, Phil thought, and by her expression he knew that his sister had realized that as well.

Mama's face was splotched red and white, and she was breathing with difficulty. For the first time the boy realized how hard this journey was going to be on her. She hadn't been well in months now.

He felt a knife of fear in his stomach. Life without Mama and Pa was something he'd never considered. Now he was filled with a horrible feeling that she just might not make it all the way to Oregon and the new land where they were to live.

He leaned against the tree, his legs suddenly feeling weak and shaky. Maryla reached to touch his shoulder reassuringly, and he tried to relax. Surely God wouldn't let Mama die on the trail, even though earlier travelers had suffered a lot of losses. Many besides the Donners had laid down their bones beside the wagon road.

Jesse Gunter's words came back to him: "When I come along the trail on my way east, I seen whole patches of prairie that was covered with skulls and arm bones and hanks of hair with bone hairpins still in 'em.

"It ain't no easy job you're takin' on, moving whole families across this country. They got to walk—walk, mind you—for nigh onto six months, the better part of two thousand miles. Not many men in the prime of life would set out to do that in cold blood. A little sprat and a pregnant woman got no business tryin'.'"

"But, Gunter," Trailmaster Netherbee had objected, staring at the man with chilly little eyes, "Others have gone ahead of us. Others have got there and homesteaded land. We can too."

Gunter spat into the fire and grimaced. "Some can. Some can die on the trail, some can drown in the Kansas or the Platte or the Snake, tryin' to wangle cattle and wagons and such foolishness across. It's up to you. But I warned you."

Phil recalled clearly the trailmaster's next question. "How do you explain taking your own wife along with you, then?"

Gunter had laughed loudly and spat into the fire again. "Swift Water is a Cree. The Injuns know how to live out here. They're tough and strong and understand what to do in a tight spot. Man or woman, they're able to handle whatever comes along. Injuns don't teach their women folks to be useless.

"I can't say the same for most of yore folks in them wagons. Hell, they're goin' to have a high-heeled old time when they try to hitch up their own teams, some of 'em."

He had been dead right about that, and Phil wondered now if he was right about other matters. The talk while the wagons waited had dealt with frightening things the traders and guides consistently found in the wakes of earlier wagon trains.

Phil, too, had heard about the woman—dead of cholera and dug up by wolves—who had greeted the next lot of wagons, lying beside the trail in her shroud with her posy of wilted flowers still clutched in her dead hands. He shivered against the rough bark of the tree.

Not Mama, he thought. Not Maryla or Pa or Jon or Mark. Not Lizzie. Lord, not me!

He reached around the tree and caught Maryla's hand. She might not be a lady, his tall sister, but she was a mighty comforting person to have around in a pinch.

After a long time filled with cussing and barking and whinnies of horses and mules, not to mention the painful lowing of the cattle, the first wagons began to move. They were so far out in the flat that it was hard to tell, but in time those nearer began moving as well. When the motion got all the way along to the wagon where Pa waited, Phil and his sister made their way back with Mama and the baby.

They were actually on their way at last!

Phil had looked at the map while his father and Gunter studied it; their present route angled north and west until it met the trail from Kanesville. There would, the trailmaster assured the men, be more wagons that would join them there.

Phil felt a bit odd about this trip, now, for he knew his father thought the trailmaster was a fool. Malcolm Netherbee was red-faced, loud-voiced, opinionated—everything, in fact, that Albert

Stoner detested.

Pa made no secret of his feelings about Netherbee. He had disagreed with him more than once as the families signed on, got their assigned positions, and began to realize that their fates were in the hands of this blustering fellow.

The most frustrating thing, according to Pa, was the fact that Netherbee kept arguing with their guide, who knew the country and the Indians. Something about the old mountain man seemed to stick in the trailmaster's craw. It might be the fact that Gunter was the kind of man who never had called anybody his boss.

Or maybe it was Jesse Gunter's Cree wife, Phil thought, although he and the other boys were awed at having a real live Indian traveling with the train. Every time the trailmaster looked at her or Gunter, his face drew up like he'd been eating green persimmons.

Already there had been sharp disagreements. Despite the horrible example of the Donners, Netherbee had wanted to wait for any stragglers who might come in the next few days. That had been argued hot and heavy, with Gunter shaking his grizzled head and spitting tobacco juice at weeds with vicious accuracy.

"You wait another day, an' it could mean the difference between makin' it over the mountains before snow flies or bein' stuck someplace you don't want to be," he'd growled at Netherbee.

"If you want to git to Oregon, then by God you better move. If you want to kill yourself, then take your handgun and do it the easy way, without killin' a bunch of women and children along with you."

Netherbee had turned even redder at that and started yelling. At that point, Pa had taken Phil by the arm and walked away, along with almost all the other men. They were almost certainly going to have to change leaders, the boy thought. If Netherbee was a fool, then they were all fools for letting him boss the train. Why not hand it over to the guide?

Gunter, when asked, didn't want to be the trail boss. He preferred to scout ahead, find water and good grazing for camps, and stay free and easy. He made no secret of it.

"If I'd wanted to boss a bunch of tenderfeet around, I could of stayed in Kentucky and done it without takin' so much time and trouble along the way," he told Albert Stoner.

"I'll do my best for the lot of you, but I won't put my neck in a halter for nobody, no way." He spat so fiercely that he flattened a yellow flower.

So Netherbee still led the train, and now it was on the move, angling up the country toward the intersection of this leg of the trail with the one coming down from Kanesville. Phil grinned fit to split his face and gave an irrepressible skip.

They'd all get to Oregon in fine shape. They just had to.

CHAPTER ELEVEN

Once the train was well on the move, Phil ranged far to the side, to avoid the worst of the dust while keeping an eye on the family's milk cow and their horses. There was so much brush and woodland along the many creeks that it would be easy to lose strays.

The Stoner animals were with the mixed herd that tagged along behind the last wagon. His father had made the safety of his saddle horse Petronius, the milk cow, and the spare ox Phil's sole responsibility.

That meant he had to stay well back, keeping the animals in sight and close enough to chase after, if any of them strayed. He was altogether out of yelling distance, if he needed help, he decided on the first day. As the trail moved up and over the low hills that began to break the flatness of the land, it was impossible to see more than the last segment of the line of wagons.

When the Williams boys drifted toward him from their place beside their father's wagon, the boy's neck-hair bristled. What did those two want?

They'd kept their distance while the wagons were in camp, though they watched every move he made with squinted eyes and thoughtful expressions. Now that he was on his own, they seemed to be eyeing him like wolves on the prowl.

While camped, Phil had kept his promise to himself to carry a knife. Once on the trail he felt safe enough to leave it behind in the wagon. Now here they came, and all he had was his sling.

He bent and picked up a conveniently shaped pebble. He kept searching, locating good ones, and they went into his pockets. Better to have something than nothing, he thought, as Gotch and Clem came nearer and nearer, angling toward him all the while.

When they were near enough to be heard, Gotch yelled, "There's the mankiller. I just bet mankiller. Baby-faced ninny's what I call him."

Phil ignored him. It was bad enough to kill somebody. He

wasn't about to brag about it to somebody like Gotch Williams. But his hand closed tightly around one of the stones in his pocket.

He didn't spare them a glance, keeping his gaze turned toward the herd. When Clem came near, dashed up suddenly and pushed him off-balance, Phil caught himself, turned, and looked down his nose, though he had to cock his head up to manage it.

"You children need something?" he asked. Inside his pocket, his right hand gripped a good-sized rock.

Gotch turned scarlet, his ears standing out like red flags from the sides of his freckled face. "You little bastard, I'll punch your lights out!" he growled.

Clem sidled off one way while his brother came face to face with Phil. "I'll cut your ears off, you give me any back-talk," the big boy said. "I have my knife right here...."—and he took from inside his linsey shirt a rusty blade that he held in a businesslike manner, blade forward, level with his waist.

Phil swallowed hard, though he tried not to let it show. The last wagons seemed a mile away, instead of a thousand yards; the bawling of cattle and the barking of dogs made any call for help useless.

His father's wagon was far ahead in its assigned position, and nobody would think to look back to see how he fared, and they couldn't see him for the dust if they did. He had to handle this himself, one way or another.

Turning the other cheek, whatever the Deacon or the Circuit Rider might say, was not going to work. Phil backed away, gaining throwing room, while Gotch paused to see what he was doing and Clem stared stupidly.

His sling slid out of the back of his pants, and in one fluid motion he placed one of his rocks in the leather patch and whipped the weapon around. There was a solid thunk.

Gotch reeled back, his hands covering his face, while blood trickled down his chin. It was evidently a painful blow, but it didn't put him out of action. He gave an inarticulate roar of rage and caught up the knife, which he had dropped, while Clem came surging toward Phil like a charging buffalo.

The boy fumbled another rock into the sling. Before he could let fly, Clem was on top of him and Gotch was coming fast, bent, it was clear, on sticking that knife clean through his body.

Phil gave a strangled yelp as Clem bowled him over. He landed and rolled under the bigger boy; then he came up onto his knees, ready to fight for as long as he could.

There was a yell of alarm and surprise. Gotch rose into the air and flew some distance, landing with a thump amid a puff of dust.

Clem looked up from his proposed victim and Phil shouted with relief.

His sister Maryla stood over them, reaching for Clem's collar with one hand, while drawing back her other fist. With a fruity spat, it hit the boy squarely in one eye, and she let him drop. He lay stunned, nursing his eye and gasping with pain.

Gotch was getting up, his bloody face twisted with rage. As he came toward them, Maryla bent, lifted Clem, and flung him at his brother as if he weighed nothing at all. With a thud and a double grunt, both went down.

Then she stood over them, kicking whatever showed signs of disentangling itself, until both lay flat, covering their heads with both hands and groaning whenever a booted foot landed on a tender spot. She was pale with rage, he noted, glad that he wasn't the one on the receiving end.

"You all right, Philip?" Maryla asked, without taking her gaze off the subdued Williamses.

He grunted. As he got up, he shook the dust off, felt himself over, and said, "Seem to be all right. Clem just hit me hard when he jumped me. Kind of knocked the breath out of me. Old Gotch never got his knife into me, but I got him good. You ought to see his nose."

"Oh, I saw it," she said. "But you take a gun with you from now on. Mr. Gunter says there'll be Indians, before long, who'll want our livestock. He says if we don't trade our critters off to them, they'll take 'em anyway, sooner or later. We have to keep a close eye out.

"If you have to shoot one of them"—she glanced contemptuously at the prostrate Williamses—"go ahead and do it. I don't think anybody's going to mind, including their folks.

"You can't run off Indians with your bare hands, or a rock either. And these two wouldn't have the nerve to bother you, if you had your musket. I'll tell Pa, and Mama will just have to understand that we're not in Missouri any more. Out here, we've got to take care of ourselves."

She backed off and said to her moaning victims, "Get up, you two. Head for the train. I'm about to turn you in to Mr. Netherbee— or maybe to Jesse Gunter. And if you ever set your sights on my brother again, I'll really hurt you."

Gotch sat up, and Clem rose to give him a hand. The boy's face was streaked and splotched with his own blood, and his nose was bent at a strange angle. Phil thought with some satisfaction that his rock had done better work than he would have expected.

Given the time, he thought he might have handled both the Williamses without the help of his sister. Then he thought of their relative sizes and the fact that he was beneath one of them when Maryla took a hand. And maybe not, he conceded.

Still, he felt a warm glow. Maryla had somehow known he was in trouble and she'd come a'skiting, without asking anybody else for assistance. Mark or Jon might have come, but either of the Williams boys could have licked them both at once, because they weren't big enough to handle them.

Not Maryla. He had a feeling she could tackle a grizzly bear and give him the first two bites.

He looked around for Rags. If his dog had been there, he might have come off better, but the old hound preferred to tag along with the wagon. He was just too tired to run off into the tall grass with his master, any longer.

"You come with me," Maryla said, as she fell in behind Gotch and Clem. "I need for you to tell Pa and their own daddy what these two did. Then you can come back and keep an eye on the stock."

Phil wiped his nose on the back of his sleeve, tucked his shirt tail into the rope that served as his belt, and picked up his pace. Anybody who kept up with Maryla better have long legs.

Before he got his wits in order, they were beside the last wagon, and from there they worked their way forward to that of Thomas Williams. There Maryla called to the woman beside the wheel, "Mrs. Williams! Your boys have been making trouble for my brother. Where's your husband?"

Caroline Williams squinted through the dust. "He's gone up a ways to talk to somebody. You keep callin' an' you'll find him. Beat them rascals, if you want. I done give 'em up long ago."

Her sons walked past her as if she wasn't there at all. Phil felt a bit sorry for them. As sick as his mother was, if he'd done something bad, she'd find the energy to whale him good and proper. He had a funny feeling that Mrs. Williams just didn't care enough to bother.

He scuffed along, barefooted, behind his sister, dreading what was to come. He hated to have to talk to the trailmaster. If it was Mr. Gunter, now, he wouldn't mind so much. He hadn't any hope at all that Netherbee would do anything but yell and cuss and let the Williamses off scot-free.

CHAPTER TWELVE

As she jostled her captives along, Maryla wished that her own problems could be solved as easily. Gotch and Clem were only children—almighty big ones, but with the minds and reactions of boys. There was nothing to handling them, if you didn't show them any mercy and were strong enough.

Leo Freeman was another matter. She hadn't mentioned him to Mama or to Pa, because they had enough to worry about. She understood better than any of her siblings just how concerned they both were about Mama's health.

She stayed close at night to help with the baby. The boys just dropped their bedrolls wherever they pleased, so they couldn't hear the whispers from the wagon where her parents slept. Only Phil suspected how serious things were getting.

It was clear to Maryla that her mother was far from well, and the trip wasn't making her better. That was why she hesitated to make any fuss about her personal problem.

Leo Freeman had put his hands on her as she passed by his wagon, both her own being dragged down by buckets of water from the creek beside which they were camped. She'd dropped the right-hand bucket on his instep, and when he bent over with the pain she dumped the other bucketful over his head.

It would have been funny, if he hadn't made the wild threats he shouted after her. Old as he was, his mother would have stopped him if she'd heard, but she was visiting another wagon at the time, and his father was as deaf as a rock.

Freeman was big, and he was no boy, being at least as old as Maryla. He had narrow gray eyes and a cruel mouth, and she wanted nothing to do with him. That didn't mean he wouldn't find a way, over the next months, to make problems for her, if she gave him the tiniest chance. She wished she could corral him as easily as she had the Williamses.

Gotch turned his head to look back at her. "Gaw-damn bitch...," he began.

Maryla jerked his collar tight, and his face turned gobbler-red, while his throat gurgled a pretty good imitation of a turkey. "You keep still until we get to your Pa. I want no foolishness out of you; you hear me?" she said in her sternest tone. "I'll lick a quarter-section of hell out of you if you give me good cause to."

She let him back down, for she'd pulled him up onto tiptoe; he hawked and spat and glared at her. He didn't, however, dare to say anything else. Almost at once they came to the group of men walking along together beside Malcolm Netherbee, who was leading his horse.

Maryla grinned to herself. The wagonmaster had trotted his mount up and down the line of wagons at first, looking important. She'd bet anything that by now his butt was one mess of blisters, because it was clear Netherbee wasn't a practiced horseman.

The way he was walking made her think of Phil, when he was younger, after a particularly bad spanking. She hid her smile, however, as she shepherded the Williams boys to catch up with the men.

"We've had a problem," she said. "These critters took out after Phil while he watched the cattle. He was way off to one side, out of the way, and they deliberately went out and tackled him. Pulled a knife on him, too. Here, Phil. You tell 'em."

Her brother swallowed so hard she could hear him gulp. "Gotch came after me with a knife in his hand," he began, "and I hit him in the nose with a rock. Then Clem dived onto me, and if it hadn't been for Maryla comin' to help me they'd have beat me real bad, I think. She flattened 'em both." He sounded proud, which rather surprised her.

Thomas Williams turned to glare at his sons. "You whelps! You been at it agin. By hokeys, I dunno what me'n your ma are goin' to do with you two. You ain't worth a puddle of spit to work, and you keep makin' trouble, wherever we go.

"I thought for sure you might shape up on this trip, but looks as if you're just doin' your same old stuff. By damn, I wish I knowed what to do."

"Let me take care of it," said Jesse Gunter, who was striding along beside Netherbee, leading his roan gelding. "I've got my own way with boys, seein' as how I raised my two brothers while I was back in Kentucky. They was too ornery to profit from a lickin', but I found other ways to deal with 'em."

He flicked a glance aside at Thomas, who gave a grave nod. "Long as you don't kill 'em, I guess you kin do as you like," Williams said. "Me'n Caroline done give up a while back."

Gunter gestured to the pair, who moved more briskly than usual as they came to stand before him. Clem looked stunned, still, but Maryla knew that was his usual expression.

Gotch was trying to look repentant, but his narrowed eyes showed the desperate working of his devious mind. He'd try to get around Gunter, if he could, she was pretty sure. I wish him luck, she thought.

Jesse Gunter was shrewd, and his Cree wife had eyes in the back of her head. What he missed, she'd catch. If the Williams boys tried anything nasty, she felt sorry for them.

Netherbee, as usual, put his oar in where it wasn't needed. "You need any help with them boys, Gunter, you just come to me," he said. "I've raised four, and believe me it wasn't easy. Anybody who can get four sons growed up and takin' care of families can do most anything."

Jesse just grunted, though Pa gave a muffled snort. Maryla wondered at Pa allowing someone else to assume responsibility for something that affected one of his children. Yet as she watched him and Gunter glance at each other and nod, she realized that the two had a good understanding. Without exchanging a word, they'd hatched up some plan to keep those two so busy they wouldn't have time to get into trouble.

She wondered for the first time if she might approach Gunter about her problem with Leo. Or, better yet, his wife? Swift Water was silent, strong, and watchful. Maryla felt certain the woman understood a lot more about her white companions on the trail than most of them understood about her, and she just might have some Indian trick she could teach.

Gunter was moving away, shepherding the Williamses before him, and she forgot, for the moment, about her own problems. She began to smile openly, for it was plain the two weren't going to have time to get into trouble.

Gunter was pointing, gesturing, talking quietly but with such effect that even from a distance she could see that Gotch and Clem were wide-eyed and a bit pale. She would have given her eye-teeth to know what they were saying.

Phil tugged at her elbow and she looked down into his gleeful eyes. "They're goin' to get every dirty job he can find to give 'em," the boy whispered. "You just watch!"

Albert turned and surveyed his son. "You get back to watching the herd. We're not far out enough to tempt Indians yet, but you need to get into the habit. Skedaddle!"

Phil bounded away, and old Rags, who had been supervising

Pa, decided to follow him. As Maryla watched her brother depart, she felt someone grasp her arm. It was Pa, staring down at her sadly.

"It is not the work of a lady to discipline hooligans," he said. "To have my daughter accused of trouncing those two is humiliating."

But Maryla was no longer a child, to be thrown into a misery of guilt by such words. She was grown, or all but, and she knew that she was the equal, in both strength and wit, of most of those on the train, including many of the men.

"Pa," she said, "Would you really have me leave Phil to be bullied by the Williamses while I have the ladylike vapors and run away to get help, giving them time to do a really good job of hurting my brother? Besides which, I didn't hear one word of blame from anybody except you."

Albert sighed and loosed her elbow. He stared down at his boots as they walked along beside Netherbee and his horse. He didn't answer, but Maryla hadn't expected him to. It wasn't easy to be a non-lady in her family, but she realized that she was beginning to learn how to deal with that.

* * * * * * *

Jesse Gunter was straining a gut not to laugh in the terrified faces of the two boys. They were a kind he had known back in Kentucky, big and strong and bully-ish, yet not used to meeting anyone bigger and stronger and more bully-ish.

It was clear they thought they understood his qualifications in that department, though he knew that even their worst imaginings couldn't come near his actual knack for brutality. He had survived nearly thirty years among mountain men, Cheyennes, Crow, Blackfoot, Cree, Arapaho—the list of tribes was nearly endless.

He had bested Frenchmen at wenching and wrestling, Spaniards at knife-work, Englishmen at marksmanship, and Americans at brawling and tobacco-spitting. His plans for the Williams boys were simple but aimed at complete submission on their part.

"You run over to that clump of trees—see it?" he said to Gotch. The clump was a good half-mile distant.

"Take Clem here with you. When you get there, take off your shirts and tie your galluses around your waists. I intend to whip the daylights out of you when I get there." And that was no lie.

Gotch opened his mouth, and Gunter laid his hand on his knife suggestively. "You want your tongue split? Makes a man stop to think before he talks, and that might be a good thing with you."

Gotch's mouth snapped shut and he began running toward the distant trees. The grass, so late in the season, was beaten down and grazed off by the earlier trains, so he and his brother stirred up puffs of dust as they went. When they were almost at their goal, Gunter mounted his roan and kicked him into a leisurely trot.

The boys were red-faced and panting when he arrived. That suited him fine, for he had taken more bruises and bumps than he wanted over the years. He didn't intend to have any problem with the Williamses.

He dismounted and slipped off his shirt. He wore, under its long tail, a breechclout and leggings, and when Gotch saw that Indian-like get-up, he gave a shuddering gasp. But he came in anyway, fists flailing, which Jesse considered to mean the boy must have good stuff in him someplace. At least he wasn't the coward most bullies tended to be.

Reaching out a sinewy left arm, Gunter held Gotch well clear of his body, letting the windmilling fists run down. Then he cocked his right and popped the boy neatly on the chin, snapping his head back.

Gotch's eyes rolled back, and he fell flat when Jesse released his grip. He was out cold.

Clem gave a sort of growl and came at the mountain man without fear or caution. Jesse reached for him, caught his right wrist, twisted it behind his back, and dropped him to his knees. Then he clipped him behind the ear and laid him out beside his brother.

Sighing, he put his shirt back on, straightened his leggings, and led his gelding closer. He lifted Gotch onto the animal, laying him on his belly across the saddle. Clem went behind the saddle in the same position. Then, leading the roan, Jesse Gunter took his unconscious charges back to the wagon train.

In the distance, a small shape trudged along beside the train, watching the cattle. Jesse knew Phil Stoner had been keeping an eye on his activities; before he was too near the train he raised one fist into the air in a signal of victory.

Phil returned the gesture, and Jesse chuckled. That was a good boy. Had his problems, of course, but he was laughing his head off right now, he'd bet anything, to think of the Williams boys being brought in dead to the world. He'd keep an eye on that boy, Jesse thought, as he sauntered toward the Williams wagon, which was halfway down the long line of vehicles.

Thomas had been watching, too, but with all the dust and the distance he evidently hadn't been able to see much. "You hurt 'em much?" he asked, as Jesse came within earshot. His tone seemed more hopeful than concerned.

"Not much. Give 'em a bit of their own medicine, I think. Here, let's heave 'em into the wagon. Can't leave 'em behind to be et by critters, and they certain sure ain't in any shape to walk. Or crawl," he added, seeing that both were still completely out of it.

"When they come to, you send both of 'em back to trail the herd. Better not be an ox or a mule or a milk cow missing, you tell 'em. Young Phil better not be molested, either.

"Tell 'em if they have any objections to come see me. And tell 'em that I'm goin' to see they do every mean job I set 'em, all the way to Oregon."

Thomas nodded, and Jesse mounted the roan and turned toward the spot where Swift Water rode, leading their pack horses behind her. She kept clear of the dust, and he pitied anyone, red or white, who thought she might be vulnerable so far from the train and tried to meddle with her.

He had a notion Gotch and Clem might try to get even with him by tackling her. The thought almost made him bend double with laughter. God have pity on them if they did, he thought, taking his place, with suitable gravity, beside her.

* * * * * * *

FROM *DIE TAGEBUCH* OF KATRINA HOLZER

Already this has been a longer journey than any I ever thought to make. Yet in a strange way it has been both interesting and entertaining. These people of this new land have their own ways, which seems odd in a culture so young.

The independence of character demonstrated by almost every adult and some of the children appears strange to me. Here there are no masters, I am beginning to understand, and those born and bred here have no concept of subservience. Perhaps those who remain behind in more settled places may be more like Europeans, but these among whom I travel would come as a shock to almost anyone at the University, although Guenter's peers consider themselves to be open-minded to almost any idea. My traveling companions would indubitably dumbfound all those I know in Vienna who consider themselves to be of the nobility.

I am used, I suspect, to the subservience of those of low social position in Europe. Here, it seems that no matter how humble one's origins or tasks, an individual retains a certain dignity and self-worth. They call no man their master.

From *Die Tagebuch* of Katrina Holzer

We have at this point given thought to our companions on the road. Marta and I have made friends with several families. The Hollingses are not bad. The Fairchilds exhibit a certain amount of integrity and a great deal of determination. The Freemans are solidly honest people who do not dream that their son is going to pose a problem for them in time.

The Stoners, several wagons back, are quiet, disciplined, and intelligent. Albert, the father, is well read, and we share talk of books, on the few evenings when we are not too weary to do anything except eat and fall asleep.

The mother, Elizabeth, is frail. Marta and I have said nothing, but I see in her eyes the knowledge that this well beloved mother may not arrive at their destination. The older sons seem unaware, but young Phil, closest to his mother, and Maryla, the grown daughter, understand. They remain close to Elizabeth, when they can, taking every possible task out of her hands.

We watch, Marta and I, all those about the fires at night. With the darkness shut away by the curves of wagon canvas, we shiver as strange beasts wail and bark and shriek in the distance. But we do not miss anything that happens. We are two older women whose eyes are quick.

That is why I worry about young Maryla. The Freeman boy is watching her even more closely than I, and he means her no good. She is big and strong, yet it is possible for someone to surprise her, I fear. Leo is even bigger than she, and though he is lazy, it is obvious that he is strong.

Andreas has an eye for the young women in the train, and I have seen him also watching Maryla. I shall hint that he should keep an eye upon her. He is a good-natured young man, and that will not be a difficult or unwelcome task for him, I strongly suspect.

CHAPTER THIRTEEN

We have traveled through countryside so flat that if it were not for the many streams and trees it would seem that we might see all the way to our destination. After angling toward the north for some time, we passed an eminence, rising from the flat country, that seems completely out of place. The guide calls it Blue Mound, and many took the trouble to climb it and survey the way we have come.

At the end of the day we came to the crossing of the Wakarusa River. The names of places here, being of Native origin, sometimes are difficult, but that is my best effort at spelling it. That stream is very crooked, and the men had to dig new ramps down which the wagons must roll to reach the water.

Those ramps left by earlier wagon trains were washed out by rain, leaving the approaches too steep for wheeled vehicles. Luckily, at this time of year the water grows shallow again very quickly, and we crossed without difficulty.

The crossing was slow, however, and we camped beyond the stream. The next day we traveled easily and camped early in a cove of trees beside a small stream, the wagons halting in a long line along its curvature. Herr Gunter called this Coon Point, saying that it was a popular camp site for such travelers as we. It is a natural place to rest, with plenty of shade and water.

Young Philip Stoner shot an actual raccoon out of a tree and showed it to us; the creature was most interesting, having a black-banded tail and mask across its eyes. It looked something between a dog and a cat, at least to me. Herr Professor Langfeldt would have liked the skin for his natural history lectures, I assured the boy, and it seemed to please him. He is a bright child, one to be watched in future.

Not long after breaking camp the next morning, we passed beside the sod hut of the Frenchman Goulet. He came out to walk beside our wagon for some time, finding that I understood his French. He said that he plans to create a town on the site of his tiny settlement, and such is his enthusiasm that I suspect he may do as he intends.

We have traveled for weeks, now, and the country changes only slowly. For some time we moved along a low ridge above long flats. Still we had streams and trees, although many of those have been reduced to stumps by earlier wagon trains needing firewood.

We have now crossed so many creeks, toiled up so many slopes, and passed so many graves, that they are mingled in my mind. The dreaded word Cholera is mentioned in connection with too many of those lonely burials, and I begin to wonder if we, too, will suffer its ravages.

This night we camp in a most congenial spot called Alcove Springs. At the edge of the water a rock thrusts out, and upon it are carved several names, some of which were those of people involved in a tragedy that I have only now encountered. In the evening, Herr Gunter told me of the ill-starred Donner train, which camped here, even as we do, and which all but perished in the heights of the Sierra Mountains of California.

What terrible things can occur in this raw and fascinating country!

* * * * * * *

It had been a hard trip from Pennsylvania. Although his mother was strong and managing, Andreas had felt all along that, as the oldest of her sons, he was in some way responsible for the well being of his family and their wagonload of supplies. Just keeping his brothers from killing themselves, or accidentally damaging each other, seemed to be a full-time task.

Gustav, the next oldest, could have helped a great deal, if he had not been confined for so long to the wagon with his injured leg. Even now, he was much slower on his feet than was needed for keeping up with his brothers. Walther was only fourteen, and he and Ludwig seemed to get into much more trouble than their younger siblings—indeed, more than all the other boys added together.

Sometimes Andreas missed his father so desperately that real pain filled his chest and welled up in his throat. Klaus lived still in his memory, big and burly, his pale hair shining in the sunlight as he followed the plow, chopped wood, or supervised the harvest.

Life without *Vater* had become more and more difficult on the farm, but once the family left that familiar place it was, to Andreas, chaotic. The journey was far longer than he had expected, for one thing. They had already spent a month on the road when they met Frau Holzer.

He had to admit that she made things easier, for she seemed to have a gift for controlling the younger boys. Mama had made no mistake inviting her to join them on their journey.

Now she sat beside a cottonwood tree, watching little Klaus, who was rummaging among the weeds beside the camp, arousing startled crackles of insects. Pretty soon he'd roust out a snake, Andreas felt sadly certain. He always managed to do something like that.

Every night when she was not too weary, that lady wrote in a fat book with metal hinges. She was making a record of their journey, and Andreas hoped she would allow him to read it, some day when there was time for such luxuries.

Now the people waited in the dawn for the signal to start their morning's trek, their teams in place, the wagons in line. As he ranged up and down, checking his own wagon and others nearby, Andreas watched their neighbors on this months-long trek.

Some his mother would not allow her sons to become close to. Although she had no pretensions above her station, Mama did not take kindly to cursing and vulgarity. Others had become good friends along the way.

There were several girls, too, though Andreas always avoided staring at them. Instead he watched them from the corner of his eye as they followed their fathers' wagons or moved about the campfires at night, the swirls of their calico skirts fascinating to a young man who, as yet, had not even dreamed seriously of young women.

One he found particularly interesting, though not at all romantically intriguing. One of the Stoner family, four wagons down the line from his, she stalked about in trousers, hard to distinguish from her father and her brothers. She was pretty, too, in a sunburned, strong-backed way, and she moved like a cat, with grace and litheness.

He would have liked a sister, and one resembling Maryla Stoner would have been his choice. The pretty girls, with their giggles and curly hair, were wonderful, but he thought of them as children—or as toys.

He would like to find a chance to get to know them, there was no doubt of that. Yet he looked forward just as much to finding more opportunities to talk with the tall, trousered girl whose bright hair was worn in a severe braid, just like that of their guide, Jesse Gunter.

The hail came down the line as the sun rose. Andreas trotted to the lead span of oxen and waited for the lethargic snake of wagons to begin moving. Long before the section in which the Hirschorn wagon was included began to roll, a pall of dust rose behind the wheels of those already in motion, obscuring the clear prairie sky. Frau Holzer had already arrived with Klaus to join the boys beside the wagon, and he lifted his small brother onto the seat beside his mother.

Andreas spat and grinned up at Mama and Klaus. The wagon ahead surged into motion, the noise of yells and whip-cracks drifting back as the driver pushed his team to move. Then Andreas tapped the broad backs of the lead oxen with his stick, and Mama urged them on. They were on their way for yet another day.

* * * * * * *

The long line of wagons rumbled and clanked, creaked and jingled its way over the tan grasses and tough weeds, which were now trodden flat with passing wagon trains and studded with dried tumbles of cattle droppings. Mostly it was very dusty, as the train came into the middle reaches of the plains, but when it rained it was much worse.

At Rock Creek they had struggled through deep mud, cutting ruts so deeply into the soil that Maryla wondered if they might not last longer than any of those who had helped to make them. She felt as if she breathed pure dust, most of the time, and when she blew her nose something like mud came out. When it rained, the soil turned to muck that stuck to wagon wheels and boots with equal tenacity.

Within a dozen paces, anyone walking (and that was almost everyone) gained pounds of weight. Even Phil, barefooted as a goose, had thick soles of mud caked to his tough feet.

There were many young people with the train, and often she struggled along beside Tina Littlefield or one of the Hirschorn boys, trying to keep up their spirits with occasional talk or jokes. Today she walked wide of the mucky trail and was disgusted to find herself joined by Leo, who for weeks had been a constant thorn in her side.

He was even bigger now than he had been early in the journey, seeming to grow by the day. His temper was uncertain at its best and brutal most of the time. He had not forgotten his earlier harassment, though why he tried to dog her steps so much of the time mystified the girl.

With Leo the less said the better. Although he was almost as old as her brother Jon, he left the work of tending stock or assisting his mother, who walked with a stick and had rheumatics, and his deaf father to his little brothers.

Any girl caught alone with him either returned flushed with anger or in tears. She did not intend to allow him to do the same to her.

His talk was filled with obscenities and his hands tended to wander where they had no business being.

Maryla wouldn't worry Pa with her troubles, and she scorned to go to her brothers for help that she was more than able to attend to on her own. She was caught in a trap, now, which her own stubborn pride had created.

She stalked along silently, avoiding the muddy wake of the wagons and the soaked and slippery dung left by the last train's livestock. Her ears automatically screened out the stupid conversation going on beside her, for Leo never stopped talking, although he never expressed any idea worth listening to.

Maryla stepped up her pace over the soaked mat of grass, overtaking and passing the wagons, one by one, as they struggled along the muddy ruts. Leo kept pace, talking all the while, nudging closer and closer to her as they moved.

The girl kept an eye on him, trying to locate someone within calling distance, if she should need help. Far behind, watching the livestock at the rear of the train, was Phil, but he was too young and too small to deal with a big fellow like Leo.

Far ahead, out of sight, rode Jesse Gunter beside the trailmaster. They, too, kept clear of the mud on their horses and were much too far away to hear any cry she might make. Pa was a half-mile behind, with Mark and Jon flanking the wagon, ready to give a shove if it showed signs of sticking in the occasional runnels that crossed the trail.

She felt a bit breathless as she realized that Leo was grinning widely and moving very close to her, his hand extended to grab her. Although she had veered sharply to get nearer to the wagons, she was still too far away.

Maryla turned to face him squarely. "You keep your dirty hands off me, Leo Freeman," she said in a grim tone. "I don't like you and I don't want you touching me like you do the other girls. And don't laugh. If I have to hit you, I'll hurt you."

The words were braver than she felt at the moment, and they didn't slow him at all. He leaned again to catch her, but she turned and ran toward the wagon train. Something hit her in the back, pushing her down onto her face. Hard hands caught her shoulders and twisted her, face up.

Leo was holding her legs down with his own, and his grin was now closer to her face than she could bear. She butted upward, bloodying his nose; he jerked back, surprised. Drops from his nose began dripping onto her upturned face.

"Bitch!" His right hand loosed her and drew back into a fist.

She closed her eyes and heaved as hard as she could, hoping to keep him off-balance. If he knocked her out, that sorry fate peculiar to women that Mama talked about might happen to her, here and now.

He was big-boned, heavy, impossible to budge. He caught her braid with his free hand, jerking her head up and slamming it down again against the hard-trodden ground. "Teach you to try that with me!" he growled under his breath.

Again she bucked, and this time the left hand, which was holding her shoulder down, came within reach of her teeth. She sank them into his grimy flesh and bit as hard as she could. He kept banging her head into the ground, cursing steadily and trying to make her let go.

His curses rang in her head, but she held on like a turtle, determined to keep biting even if it should thunder, which it showed signs of doing any time now. Then, to her amazement, Leo was jerked upward, freeing her from his weight, only his hand remaining between her teeth.

She opened her jaw, letting him go free. Blinking grit out of her eyes, she stared up to see Andreas Hirschorn turn Leo toward him effortlessly. The younger man's mouth was set in a stern line, and his pale eyes were furious.

"You leave this lady alone, do you hear me?" he said, shaking Leo for emphasis. "You won't touch her again, or I will whip you within an inch of your life, *Schweinhund*! You will go to your wagon and help your mother, and you will not trouble Miss Stoner again."

He gave Leo another shake, dropped him, and prepared to knock him down if he showed fight. Freeman got to his feet and backed away, cursing even more luridly than usual; then he turned to run toward his family's wagon.

Maryla was sitting up now, still staring with awe at her rescuer. Andreas was taller than she, true, and strongly built, but he looked so fresh and innocent, with his cornflower-blue eyes and scrubbed pink skin, that she had never suspected him of being able to handle himself so well against a person so much bigger than he.

Andreas bent to help Maryla to her feet. "You are not hurt?" he asked. He looked distressed, even pale.

"No, no, I'm fine. He just was too big for me to handle, and I didn't realize I was too far from the train to holler for help. I do thank you, Mr. Hirschorn, for your assistance."

She found, to her horror, that she was sounding like one of the proper young ladies she scorned so fiercely.

Andreas looked relieved. "I am happy to help. My mother has spoken to me about you. She enjoys your visits to our wagon in the evening, when Frau Holzer teaches the young ones. She considers you one who is capable and strong, as she is. She has said that she will always be happy to talk with you, if you feel the need, while your mother is ill."

Which was a very tactful way, Maryla realized, of saying that she might need to learn how to avoid such incidents as the one she had just escaped. She grinned at Andreas, feeling suddenly close to the quiet young man.

"Thank you, Andreas Hirschorn. I think I'd like to talk with your mother. You tell her I'll come see her when we camp." His answering smile was filled with relief.

She accepted his offer to escort her to her father's wagon, and all the way she berated herself for getting into a position where such a thing could happen. She, of all people, had never dreamed she might need rescuing. And this visit from Andreas would, if she learned about it, make Elizabeth all bright-eyed and hopeful, thinking that Andreas was a suitor instead of a friend.

Maryla found herself suddenly tongue-tied. She had talked with Andreas many times before, discussing everything from the care of livestock to speculations on the career of Jesse Gunter.

Now she couldn't think of a thing to say, and he seemed equally shy. It was as if this sudden encounter, under such unusual conditions, had made them strangers, and she didn't like that.

As they approached the noisy line of wagons, squishing and splashing through mud and water, she turned to the young man. "You don't know how much I thank you, Andreas. But if you don't mind, I won't tell Pa about this. He and Mama will make a big fuss, and they might not let me walk alone any more. That would be a bother."

He nodded, understanding instantly. He, too, had a mother who tended to worry about her brood. "You fell, out on the grass, and I saw and helped you up, yes?" he said. "It is not entirely a lie—we just will not say why you fell."

Maryla grinned. Jon waved, and she hurried to fall into step beside him.

Andreas said, "Greetings, Jonathan. I found your sister fallen down on the grass and came back with her. But now I will go. Walther is not to be trusted for long with the oxen." He trotted up the line of wagons and was soon out of sight.

Jon stared at Maryla's muddy trousers and torn shirt. "You look like you tangled with a wildcat," he said. "Better get another shirt out of the wagon—if Mama sees you like this she'll have a fit. You've got skin showing."

She sighed and dropped to the tailgate, climbing up and over to rummage in her bag of necessaries that she kept beside the clothing trunk. Another shirt, once her father's, came to hand and she shrugged off the torn one and slid into it. Now she could continue her day as if nothing had happened.

For three days the sun rose clear and burned down until afternoon. Then clouds rolled up in the north and west, black and threatening. The family learned to tie down anything that might blow away in the blustery winds that accompanied the storms.

The train generally didn't stop, unless they sighted a twister in the distance. Halting made wheels sink deeper into the mud and meant that getting started again was more difficult than need be. Maryla pitied the oxen, who dropped their broad heads and plodded forward with the big raindrops and pellets of hail pounding their backs.

She and her brothers walked close against the leeward side of the wagon, escaping some of the blast, while her mother and the baby rode, as usual, under the wagon cover, not much dryer than those trudging along outside. Pa, leading the oxen, just hunched his back and seemed as stubborn as the beasts beside him. That didn't surprise her at all—she was the same way.

Every time one of the rainstorms rolled over the wagon train, Maryla hoped it would be the last. While the dust and grit borne by the prairie wind were irritating, when it rained so hard she felt that she might almost drown while standing straight.

The sight of those black tornado tails lashing the prairie, miles distant, terrified her. Thinking of being whirled away amid black cloud and thunder and roaring wind made her shiver with apprehension, as she clung to the wagon wheel to keep from being blown off her feet, even so far away from the path of the storm.

The only good thing about the weather was the fact that Leo stayed close by his family's wagon and ignored her. Yet when the weather cleared at last and they traveled, once more, on a broad and sun-baked sea of dried grass and hard-packed earth, she realized he was watching her. She took to carrying a knife in her boot, though she hoped he wouldn't make her use it.

No longer did she range wide of the dusty track without company. Phil sometimes walked beside her, and they both kept a sharp eye on their animals.

Sometimes she found one of the Hirschorn boys willing to go, but not Andreas. They both seemed to feel strangely shy, after that incident with Leo, and, somewhat to her distress, they tended to avoid each other.

Mama Hirschorn noticed, Maryla knew, for she caught the woman watching her from time to time. Frau Holzer also seemed to take particular notice of her.

That lady seemed so bright, so graceful, and so informed about many matters that Maryla was determined to make an even better friend of her. She was learning a great deal about the world beyond the sea from the Viennese lady's talk.

When Mrs. Holzer read from the big Shakespeare belonging to Pa, Maryla sat spellbound. She had never before dreamed that such magic might lie among the pages of those dreaded books. Some day, when she was old and had the time, she would borrow some of the fat volumes and read them for herself, she decided.

Until then, she was too busy, too restless to bother. It took enough time and energy just to walk with the wagons and to dream of what they might find at the end of their long trail westward.

CHAPTER FOURTEEN

FROM *DIE TAGEBUCH* **OF KATRINA HOLZER**

We have left the Blue River, which has supplied our stock and ourselves with water and whose banks have provided firewood for weeks now. It is somewhat disturbing to leave behind such a reliable source, although our guide assures us that soon we will find ourselves beside the Platte River, which will accompany our trail along much of its length.

The train is moving well, although we have had two deaths from cholera within the past few days. This is a terrifying disease, obviously caused by the lack of clean water and of sanitation as we move. Those who went before us left some taint of the disease along the trail, I am certain.

Herr Doktor Levensohn would be interested, I think, for he has for years proclaimed the necessity for cleanliness, both in patients and in their physicians and surgeons. The practice among those who deliver infants of wiping their hands on their lapels until they are stiff and shiny with filth is a thing that the Doktor blames for the frequent deaths of new mothers from childbed fevers.

I am certain that he would connect cholera with equally filthy conditions along the trail. Not only are we moving through the wastes of our own train but of all those who have gone before us, although they have been reduced to dust and mud by wind and weather.

Because I feel it is so important, I have insisted that my own party take extraordinary pains to wash, no matter how weary we may be when we camp. I have also spoken with Albert Stoner and with the Hollings family of such matters and both groups are imitating us in this.

The others laugh and cannot be troubled to try to maintain their own health and safety. I fear there will be more deaths before we reach the Platte. To cheer us all, I try to read a bit aloud, each evening when there is time, from one or another of Herr Stoner's wealth of books. Those precious volumes travel in his wagon and cannot be discarded, no matter what difficulties we encounter, he assures me.

We have reached Fort Kearney, a raw, new fort built here of logs two years ago and set near the wide and shallow Platte. Here there are supplies, although most of us are still well stocked at this point. Yet there are unexpected needs, always, and finding a pot to replace a cracked one or leather to repair worn-out harness is a luxury.

There is a blacksmith, sweating in his faded uniform, who remains busy most of the time repairing wagon wheels, shoeing horses, and making the air ring with the sound of his hammer. Never having seen such work done, I have tried to watch several times, but my presence inhibits the language of the soldiers who tend to loiter at the door of his shed. Unfortunate—I would like to observe more.

We will rest the animals here and wash our clothing in the river, which is absolutely teeming with tiny insects that must be strained out before one can drink the water. I have persuaded Frau Hirschorn to pull our wagon to the side, clear of the noise and dirt of the main camp. The thought of cholera is in all our minds, and she agreed readily with my suggestion. Indians are less to be feared than disease, I begin to believe.

We have left behind the relative security of the fort and now move through country that is higher and dryer than that through which we traveled before. The grass, which had been fairly green from the regular rains, is now short and dry, despite thunderstorms almost every afternoon, and the land itself rises and sinks in long, increasingly deep undulations. The guide calls these swells, and I agree that the contour is not unlike that of the ocean.

We cross, I estimate, some ten to fifteen miles almost every day, although at times we must pause while some family battles cholera and inevitably loses. We have left behind at least a dozen graves, although they will never be noted or tended. The thought fills me with sadness, when I recall the eager anticipation and hope with which most began this journey.

Much to my shock and surprise, the dead are buried on the trail ahead of the lead wagon. As we pull out, every animal and every wagon crosses it, eliminating all trace from the earth. This, they tell me, is in order to hide the corpse from marauding animals and from Indians, who might otherwise dig it up to secure its scalp. The thought makes me shudder, but I do understand the necessity.

We have crossed the river in order to follow the North Platte. We used, I am told, the Middle Ford, and it involved much cursing, splashing, and the loss of the Stoners' milch cow and several spare oxen.

The shallow stream is more swift than one would suppose, and its bottom is treacherous. Broken legs are an immediate death sentence to any injured animal, although the meat provides a welcome change in our diet of salt pork, beans, and skillet bread.

Yet the terrain before us is terrifying. Instead of the gentle swells of the other shore, we now face higher and higher hills, deeper and deeper declivities. The grass is golden tan, though it is not yet fall, and the sky is a glaring blue that is shocking to one used to the more misty weather of Europe.

We have descended a hill so steep and dangerous that we were forced to use a device called a windlass to lower wagons and some livestock down its bosom. There was a tremendous straining of ropes and backs, along with groans of effort; shrieks of despair rose as more than one vehicle crashed to the bottom when the ropes failed.

At the bottom of the declivity lies a veritable graveyard of shattered vehicles tangled amid the bones of lost animals. Shattered ambitions and expectations lie there as well, I am most certain.

Yet, after such effort and pain, we now find ourselves in a place that might be called a sort of Eden. This is a hollow guarded by a high cliff of sandstone (Herr Professor Schildkraut would be fascinated by the formation, which contains a sort of rude shelter used, I am told, by primitive Indians who also rest here).

There are several streams, plenty of grass for the livestock, and fine trees enough to supply firewood to a much larger party than ours, even though numbers of raw stumps bear witness to the wood cutting of earlier wagon trains. The shade is grateful to us, who have been baked by the relentless sun and dried by the dehumidified atmosphere.

Here we shall rest again, mending what is broken, and wondering, I am certain, why we have undertaken this grueling and sometimes unbearable trek.

The land through which we are now moving is incredible to one used to the more civilized contours of Europe, where soil is decently covered with grass or with crops. Here stone seems to master the landscape. Weird formations rise on the skyline, some like chimneys of lost castles, some shaped like castles themselves, all of reddish-gold stone, turned on the lathe of time.

If I did not know better, I should call those distant shapes the ruins of some lost city, weathering away in the constant wind. Today we began to see, in the distance, two mountain-like protuberances....

Two Days Later

Lying on the horizon somewhat to the west of our route, they have grown, day by day, until their contours come clearly into view. Today we passed most closely to them, and so strange are these formations, rising sheer from the level plain, that many walked the distance to examine them more closely.

The guide calls them Courthouse Rock and Jail Rock, and indeed, they do look much like elaborate civic structures. With young Klaus, I went part of the way, although I did not dare to squander the energy to clamber about them as nimbler members of the party did.

I am continually amazed at the Stoner daughter. Maryla is as agile and daring as any of the young men, and more so than most. Her own brothers are no matches for her in size or strength, and while she works beside them uncomplainingly, she never fails to take advantage of a chance to see new wonders along our route.

That is a young woman with much potential, although in Europe she would be considered a shocking oddity. Here, however, I can foresee a useful and perhaps even important future for her.

It is this sort of women, to greater or lesser degree, who evidently have enabled their men to spread civilization across so much of this vast continent. I must talk with her more, awaken her obvious intelligence to its fullest extent, and encourage her to follow her unique abilities as far as possible.

What a challenge!

For several days we have seen another tall shape on the skyline. Herr Gunter assures me this is the famous Chimney Rock, rising like some Egyptian obelisk from the dust of the plain. Although at this point it alone is visible, he says that other formations flank it, and we will see beyond it other fanciful sculptures of wind and weather.

I have wished that I possessed artistic talents, since coming into this part of our journey, for it would be pleasant to capture these shapes upon paper for further study when we reach our destination. Think what a wealth of detail to remember in days to come! Sadly, my studies in the field of art pertained to the artists of old and the historical background of the great masterworks of the past.

We have passed the trading post established last year by the Frenchman Robidoux. It was good to replace fabric that has worn to tatters, pots whose bottoms have burnt out, and other minor items for which no spares could be brought with us.

He assured us that Fort Laramie, our next landmark, is less than a week away, if we are lucky enough to avoid breakdowns and sickness. I, for one, am more than ready for a rest from the grueling dust and effort of the trail.

Although singularly unrefreshed by our stop, we are once again upon the way. So exhausted have we found ourselves upon camping at night that this is my first opportunity in several days to write in this book.

However, writing was done by several of our company. As we passed the cliff upon which names of many travelers are inscribed, they marked our passing with names and other inscriptions. Given the dry weather here, I suspect those names may well outlast us all.

Much to our astonishment, the sand-pale soil over which we have traveled for so long has become reddish. The presence of iron might be suspected, although the rosy hue seems to hint at some element with which I am not familiar.

Herr Professor Schildkraut would know. When we are settled in our new home, I must write to him and describe this phenomenon. Perhaps my letter may find its way to him, when the time comes.

CHAPTER FIFTEEN

Jesse felt his knees creak as he dismounted inside the wide circle of wagons. It had been a long day on the trail, and his butt was numb from the saddle; he had ridden half again as far as the train had traveled, scouting ahead, making certain the trail was clearly marked and free of hazards.

He'd been this way more than once, but never before as a guide to emigrants. Now that earlier trains had marked the plain so clearly, it might be guides wouldn't be needed much longer, and that was fine with him. Farmers heading for free land were as different from his old trapping companions as Kiowa were from Cree.

He was getting old, and that was the fact of the matter. The wind, cooling fast now that the sun was down, would make him ache when darkness came, too. Nights out here in the wide lonesome were cold.

Besides that, his patience wasn't near as long as it used to be. He could get red-faced mad at the idiot who ran the train, if he let himself think about the nonsense Malcolm Netherbee pulled.

If they could have found somebody dumb enough to take his place, he'd have been voted out as trailmaster long ago. But nobody was quite that much of an idiot, and so far things had gone pretty well, considering they had such a gaggle of farmers to move.

It might be true that such a big group, all traveling together, had to be organized in military fashion, with a single leader whose word was final. That was up to them, and if they wanted to put up with Netherbee's shouted commands it was their choice.

He wasn't any soldier, and he didn't take orders from anybody, much less a pipsqueak like Netherbee. The next time that bald-headed blowhard gave him an order as if he'd bought him on the auction block, Jesse felt certain he was going to flatten the son-of-a-bitch, and that was no lie.

At the very least, nobody was having any trouble out of the Williams boys. He'd squashed them pretty well flat, it seemed.

Swift Water was already arranging their bedrolls fairly near the spot where the central campfire was being kindled. If he couldn't stay young and spry and even-tempered, at least she'd keep him warm and well fed. A wife was a comfort that an old man needed more than a youngster did, that was sure and certain.

He grinned at the thought. Most of his fellow trappers had come to that conclusion, as beaver dwindled and they grew older; those who survived tended to marry competent young squaws. Women from the Plains tribes knew how to take nothing much in particular and create a comfortable home out of it in no time at all.

He sighed as he heaved down his saddle and pad, the rolled pack behind it, and his heavy rifle. It was a long time since he had trapped the Rockies; most of those young men he'd known at Rendezvous, drinking and wrestling and wenching and topping each other's tall tales, were dead now.

He, who had been as successful as any and luckier than most, was reduced to guiding eastern farmers to the Promised Land, like some left-over Moses. It wasn't the job he'd have chosen, and he knew that after this trip he was going to find himself some remote mountain valley and settle there, clear of the annoyances caused by easterners and their foolishness.

Around him families were watering oxen and horses and loosing them to graze on the grassland around the wagons, under the eyes of watchful boys who were too young to count as men but old enough to be responsible. When darkness fell, their places would be taken by their elders, well armed and watchful. Their owners hobbled the horses, but the oxen were considered too slow to wander far enough to make any problem.

These folks didn't altogether understand that they were now in a country where stealing horses and cattle was the favorite sport of adventurous young men of the Plains tribes. When some of the farmers' precious draft animals or riding horses came up missing, they were going to be wild with anger.

They'd want to take it out on the first Indians they saw, whether or not they were the right ones. They couldn't get it into their heads that these people were as different as Frenchmen and Germans or English and Dutch.

They might just think they could hang cattle thieves out here the way they did in Indiana or Missouri or Pennsylvania. That would make big trouble with the tribes, whatever the variety, and he had to figure out some way to prevent it.

It seemed to be impossible for farmers to understand that Indians didn't have any particular love for property, just for the sport of raiding. What they took they'd give away just as quickly and even more cheerfully.

"Mr. Gunter!"

There was Philip, running right through the middle of the confusion inside the circle. As Jesse watched, he leaped over a pile of bedding, ducked under a horse that had been tied to the tailgate of a wagon, and bumped into Mama Hirschorn, who was trudging toward the fire, kettle in hand.

"*Gott in Himmel*," she muttered, giving him a motherly swipe on the bottom. "Take care, young Philip! You vill upset me yet."

But the boy was gone before her hand touched him, still darting toward Jesse. Sometimes, the guide thought, it was a pain to be a hero to a bunch of children. Still, he grinned as the boy panted to a stop beside him. There was something about the young'un that appealed to him mightily.

Maybe it was partly because Phil kept asking for his stories of the old days in the Rockies, as the travelers sat around the fire and nothing but the howls of coyotes broke the stillness of the vast night around them. Jesse had to admit that he enjoyed it, too, reliving those wild and dangerous times while sitting, warm and secure, in a circle of firelight.

He grinned at the boy's immediate question. "After I get through talking to Baldy Netherbee, I'll be ready to talk my snaggly teeth out," he said.

Philip gave a skip of pleasure and darted off toward his family's wagon. Jesse watched him go, feeling slightly sad. He could recall being that young, having the energy to whip the world before breakfast every single morning. But then he thought of all the terrible mistakes that lay before the boy, errors that, whatever the pain of learning, were behind him in his own past.

The fire grew bright as children brought buffalo chips and brush from the surrounding plain. Swift Water was now stirring an iron pot, her greatest pride, which was set on rocks at the edge of the bed of coals. Rich scents of meat and sage and wild onion began to make his mouth water.

Beyond his wife was the Stoner girl, who was sharpening a butcher knife on a narrow stone. She was watching Swift Water closely, and he'd bet his last set of moccasins that she'd remember every move the Cree made. That was a sharp one, and strong.

She'd have made a good Indian, and there weren't many white women he could say that about. It was a pity her folks didn't really appreciate her, but he'd learned early in his youth that, back East, folks hadn't much idea of the difference between proper and just plain stupid.

Later, full of stew and skillet bread, he leaned back against his saddle and looked into the ruddy faces of the youngsters circling the fire. Maryla, he noted, was back in the shadows, but she was listening hard as he began his story.

"The worst winter I ever spent, I calculate, was either Thirty-two or Thirty-three or thereabouts. Didn't keep no calendar up in the mountains, and the beaver didn't either, so it made no never mind. I was way up in the Yellowstone country, camped with six horses and God knows how many traps.

"No partner, though—Josh Sowell got snakebit back in the summer. Rattler got him on the cheek, and he swole up like a turnip, till his eyes plumb disappeared and he couldn't hardly breathe, even through his mouth. Had to make a sort of tunnel of his tongue and whistle his breath through that."

He was watching Phil Stoner out of the corner of his eye, and he could see the youngster's question coming before it got out of his mouth. "How'd he eat?" Phil asked, leaning forward and watching Jesse's face.

"Couldn't. Drink, neither. It strangled him when he tried to swallow, because that little tongue-hole was all he had to get air through.

"I tried every way I could think of to get somethin' down him. Taken turkey-feather quills and dripped broth through 'em, but nothing helped. He lasted near three days.

"Then he grabbed me by the leg and felt up it for my skinnin' knife. Shook it hard, and I knowed what he wanted. I put it in his hand and went off to check the traps. When I come back, he'd cut his throat. Poor cuss—he was a first-class trapper and a friend. I hated to lose him."

The boy had been holding his breath. Now he let it go in a long sigh. "He killed himself? And you let him?"

Jesse shook his head. "You got to look at it straight, young Stoner. Would it of been better to let him starve to death? Or even to smother if the swelling kept gettin' worse? That's a miserable death for sure. No, he ended it clean and certain. Way I'd of done in his place."

He could see that handsome foreign woman...Holzer? Yes, that was the name...sitting on a keg at the rear of the circle of firelight. She looked pale, even with the red glow of the fire on her face.

It was plain to see she was from a country that was civilized—that always meant people got things wrong-end-to. Seemed as if civilized folks thought dying was the worst thing that could happen.

He'd like to give 'em a chance, one day, to choose between doing them the kindness of shooting 'em, once they'd been entertained by Blackfeet, or letting 'em take a long time dying with their skin flayed off and their eyeballs dug out.

"Anyway," he continued, "I got the horses and the traps up to a little valley we'd spotted the year before. Two creeks come together and run off along a deep channel through solid rock, with good aspen and alder and fir on either side. Couldn't hardly tell the place was there, but there was beaver dams makin' a series of ponds along both sprangles. Big lodges, too. Lots of beaver, and by then choice trappin' was getting a little lean."

He shifted his back, stretched his long legs toward the fire, and remembered that valley with a twinge of regret. "It was pretty high up, and the snow was fallin' when I got there, which was good, because it meant the beaver would have their full coats. I set me up a tipi.

"Now I know most of my friends in the business built shanties, but I learned that a tipi squats down over you like a old hen over her chicks. It holds the heat down, and the hot air circles round between the outside hide and the lining and usually carries off the smoke pretty well, too, without gatherin' all the heat up in the corners to waste. When the wind's right, the smoke goes up the smoke hole neat as anything."

The Stoner girl asked from the shadows, "Doesn't the cold get through the sides? I've seen tipis along the way, and they don't seem to be made out of real heavy hides. The light shines through."

"Buffalo hides will turn most any wind that blows," he replied. "And I learned a trick or two after I had to live alone. If you fix your tipi right and then make a good nest for yourself with deer hide to pull over your blankets, it keeps any draft that comes wanderin' in from getting to you. No, I was warm enough. I just near about starved to death."

He grinned, thinking about the blizzard that snowed him in tight as a tick before he had a chance to set a single trap. He had jerky, of course, and pemmican that he'd traded off a Crow and his wife. But that blizzard seemed not to intend to quit.

"I got snowed in so deep that not much but the top poles of my tipi stuck out. I had to go out and clear away the drifts, or they'd have caved the thing in on me. There was no way in hell to set traps, and I'd depended on beaver to provide a lot of meat. I hadn't packed in near enough to last a winter, and nobody can live altogether on coffee and beans. Not in weather that cold, he can't. Takes a lot out of a body, just stayin' warm."

He shivered, recalling the deep chill that penetrated even the buffalo hide walls and his deep layers of furs and deer hide. "You can't keep warm without meat and fat in your belly, and that's the truth.

"I kept still and quiet for a week, and then I knowed I had to get out and hunt or I'd be too weak to do anything. I bundled up in every stitch I could put on and dug my way out like a badger coming out of his den.

"The snow had slacked off by then, but it was as cold as hell's toenails. The forest was more than knee-deep, even where it was sheltered by big pines and spruces, and there were no tracks that I could see.

"Not even a rabbit had risked gettin' out in the weather we'd been having. But I had me a serious hunger, by then, and I knowed I'd not be able to make another go at hunting, if things didn't warm up. In November, at that altitude, that ain't likely." He toed a disarranged buffalo chip into the edge of the fire, seeing in his mind that snow-hushed forest, hearing the slither and slip of burdened branches and the soft hiss of wind.

"I knowed better than to go far. If it'd begun to snow again the way it had been, I'd never of found my way back. So I made a big circle, and when I got around on the lower slope, there was a moose with its leg broke, froze to death in the blizzard.

"If I was a religious man, I'd of said that Providence was lookin' out for me. Maybe it was, too. I dunno.

"There was a lot of meat on that critter, but it was hard as a rock. Couldn't cut it up and sure couldn't drag a thousand pounds up through the snow to the tipi.

"So I decided to gather up a great big pile of dead wood, dug from under the snow, and put on top of that a lot of the green branches that had broke off the trees in that storm. I'd build me a fire close up to the critter so as to thaw him out right there on the spot.

"Which I did, and pretty fast, too.

"By then it was almost night, but I had me a fire goin' that lighted up the woods like sunshine. I made me a deep trail up to the tipi, so as to make it easy to carry up the meat as I chopped it loose.

"Then I got to work. With such a big blaze, it didn't take all that long to get most of the meat off that carcass, either, once it begun to thaw. I marched up and down that slope 'til my legs felt like mush, but finally I was done, and only the useless parts was left there in the snow.

"I didn't want to draw hungry critters so near my lodge, so I hitched the carcass around, got it laid over so's it would slide without diggin' into the snow, and just shot everything off down toward the bottom of the mountain. I figured it'd attract all the wolves and such and leave me unmolested up on my little flat spot."

"That was mighty smart!" Phil said. "You think I'd do that well, if I was trapping in a winter like that?"

"You would if you had to," Jesse grunted. "It's mighty interestin' how slick you can operate when your life depends on it."

The girl leaned forward into the firelight, her eyes shining. "But how did you manage to keep all that meat? You couldn't have it inside, because it'd spoil, if you kept the fire going. And if you let your tipi get cold, you'd freeze right along with your meat."

"Oh, I hung most of it in the top of some good-sized trees, not far from my lodge. I roasted a bunch, of course, right off, and kept it with me. The rest I figured would last long enough to get me through the worst of the winter, if things didn't lighten up so I could trap.

"But I didn't figger on other folks bein' as hungry as I was. Things rocked along and rocked along, with wind fit to slice you in two and snow gettin' deeper all the time, and I went out to get some more of my moose meat. Went trompin' over to my trees, and now the snow was up to my hips.

"When I got there I looked up and there, hanging onto one of my bundles, was a wolverine." He shivered, remembering the flat head, the sharp snout, the black, beady eyes regarding him from above.

"If you never tangled with one of them critters, you never want to. Before I could think, the bastard jumped off right on top of me and begun clawin' and chewin'; if I hadn't been wrapped in ten layers of fur and leather he'd of dug a hole clean through me.

"I never messed with anything as strong and mean as that 'un, I tell you. Seems as if wolverines are just purely born mad at the world. Finally I rolled over on top of him and smothered him to death, because I outweighed him something like twenty times.

"I made a winter hood out of his hide—best there is, because yore breath don't freeze to ice on the fur. Swift Water's still got it, back with her folks in the Bitterroots."

There was a concerted sigh around the campfire. Phil Stoner stretched and yawned, and Jesse knew it was time to send the young'uns off to bed and turn in, himself. Tales was fine, but they didn't make it any easier to get up in the morning, when his joints were stiff and his bones felt every lick and injury he'd done to 'em in a lifetime of hard living.

"Time to sleep now," he said. "But remember, don't tangle with no wolverine, whatever you do."

He could still feel, as he made his way to his blankets some of those old bitten places in his arms and hands. Seemed as if a man carried old hurts with him all his life, he thought, as he stretched out beside Swift Water and dropped into dreamless sleep.

CHAPTER SIXTEEN

The summer wind carried scents that seemed almost new to Running Fox's nostrils. As a child, he had not noticed such things much, but now he was a man, and the feel of the air on his skin was different from that of years before.

It seemed as if the sap that rose in the past spring had risen also in his young veins, filling him with vigor and ambition. Now, in full summer, he seemed about to burst with the pressures of his new maturity.

Two Crows, only a year older than he, had already counted coup in a raid on the Pawnee. He owned two horses, stolen from the Piegan when those traditional enemies traveled near the Cheyenne's hunting grounds. When he had stolen or traded for four more, Fox knew his friend would speak with the parents of Bright Green Beetle and, because she looked warmly upon him, Two Crows would marry. Perhaps as soon as next spring.

As yet, Running Fox had no mind to marry, but he coveted those horses. He, too, must find a way to begin acquiring his own herd. There had been no raids, this year, though Pawnee ponies were fat and their camps were not terribly far from the lands of the People.

Strange concerns filled the minds of the old ones in the Council Lodge, and they had turned their thoughts away from the usual pursuits of their young men. The Elders were watching the passing of the many pale-eyed men and their families along the distant wheel-road. Already there had been trouble between his own people and a few of those newcomers who came hunting or simply prowling about the lands belonging to the Cheyenne and the Arapaho.

Running Fox had also watched those white-topped wagons, like clouds sailing against the wind across the plain. Behind them came cattle and horses, and before each moving lodge went the great slow oxen that pulled them along.

Why had the old men not realized there were horses there for the taking? Cattle and oxen were good eating, as well, and far easier to kill than buffalo.

He had slipped close to the wheel-road himself many times, after hiding his pony along a willow-grown creek or behind a clump of brush out of sight. The whites seemed to have no eyes at all. He had lain in scanty cover not a four-handful of paces from the track they walked, and not one had noted his presence.

Now the season grew late, and fewer of the wagons traveled. Soon the last train would pass, and the opportunity for gaining a horse of his own, instead of one allotted him from his father's string, would be lost for another year.

The youth was weary of waiting. If no other warrior suggested a raid on the animals of the whites, then he would go alone, steal a wonderful horse, and even, if he were lucky, count coup upon a white warrior.

It was too late to start the two-day ride toward the wheel-road, of course. This was a thing best undertaken after a good sleep, with a belly full of his mother's young dog stew. He would not pause to eat until he returned, and he must be as strong as possible when he set out.

He rose from the spot where he had been lying beneath a cottonwood. Nearby the little river, now all but dry, ran soundlessly, only a trickle along its sandy bed. Above, almost too high to see, a hawk wheeled on the wind, and the echo of its cry sounded dimly over the grasslands, where shadows crept away from the westering sun.

When Running Fox rose, his own shadow stretched out beside him, turning him into some giant spirit with endless, spindly arms and legs and an impossibly long body. The boy grinned.

When he was a fully grown man, he would have two double-handfuls of horses and four wives. He would be as tall as that shadow and stronger than Bear-Claw, the best hunter in the clan, whom his mother had chosen as his role model when he was a tiny baby.

He would have sons, and if their mother had no brother, perhaps his sister Broke the Tree would allow them to trail her husband and to imitate his hunting methods. There would be girls to gather plants and seeds and trap rabbits and help their mothers with the many tasks of keeping a family alive. He would be kind to them all, generous to his parents and his fellows.

He felt a surge of warmth inside him as he thought of this. It would all begin tomorrow, when he set out on a daring one-man raid against the last wagon train that would travel the wheel-road before winter set in. He must sing the proper chants, paint himself in the correct manner for raiding, and then he would take the trail.

He would return with horses that would make the old men suck in their breaths and say "Ahhh" with astonishment. The women would pretend not to notice, but there would be bright-eyed girls who would peep around the curves of their lodges and admire his courage and skill.

Again he smiled. When the time came to marry, he would have many horses to trade for the wife of his choice.

He slept dreamlessly, after retiring to a private spot for his ritual preparations, returning to his family's lodge after all were asleep. When he woke, he wondered for a moment why there was a knot of excitement in the pit of his stomach.

Then he remembered, and he rose silently to creep among his still sleeping kin. When dawn broke, he would be out on the plain, riding swiftly toward his goal.

He prided himself upon the stealth with which he caught the best pony from his father's herd and led it away without even the dogs detecting his presence. Once well clear of the sprawl of lodges, he kicked his heels into the animal's flanks and turned its head toward the south, where the great shallow river guided the whites on their incomprehensible westward journey.

All the hunting and raiding trails ran from north to south. Why should these strangers want to go west?

It was good to have the freedom of the horse herd, to be allowed to go and come as he would. The summer before, he had been a child still, but now he had traveled his medicine journey, found his totem, and seen his vision. As the prairie rolled away beneath the hooves of his mount, Running Fox thought of that quest.

He had been fortunate, he knew, for often it required many days of fasting and long journeys to arrive at one's final destination. He had gone north into the dark hills that flanked the Bad Gods' Tower, in Dakotah country—the danger made the quest even more daring. The forest had greeted him with the whisper of pines and the sigh of wind across huge cliffs of stone, and he had known that he was one of those to whom a vision comes easily.

There had been no threat, no difficulty, no danger, and that was in itself a hardship. Better to conquer such matters in perilous circumstances than to have one's manhood come so easily that it seemed to make no difference, he had thought at the time.

Yet that vision, when it came, was strange enough to make even the old women and the medicine chief frown with bewilderment. He had sat upon a narrow lip of stone that thrust out from a cliff top. He had chewed the herbs sent for that purpose, and he had fasted for two days. His mind had dimmed at first with the herb, and then it had sharpened to terrible intensity.

He seemed to look down from very high, as if he sat on a cloud or a mountaintop. Below there had been a blur of motion, as if a herd of buffalo moved on the plain. Beside him an eagle dipped a wing and curved along the air, as if guiding his gaze toward something important, and suddenly Fox found himself floating lower and lower, as if he rode within the body and mind of the bird.

Dust rose to meet him, as the herd traveled along, not running but moving quickly and steadily, as if heading for some well understood goal. The eagle was gone, but still he descended, and he began to wonder if a buffalo was to become his totem.

That did not seem correct, however. There was something else there, among the trampling hooves and tossing horns, that compelled his attention.

He wondered, even as he sank nearer and nearer to the animals, why they did not sense his presence. Would those wickedly curved horns catch him and toss him when he came close?

But he continued to float downward, and when he came to the level of the heaving herd, he realized that his body had been left behind on the height. He was all spirit, moving along like the dust raised by the buffalo.

And then he saw the thing that had seemed strange from so high above. There was a glint of red, down in the thickest of the dust. A brushy tail whisked in and out of sight, and the boy focused upon that shape, that color, amid the confusion of the migration.

Then he saw his chosen target was a fox, running desperately along with the buffalo, avoiding being trampled by the narrowest of margins, yet never looking back or seeming to hesitate. What did it carry in its mouth? He tried to see more clearly, bending forward in his spirit-body to stare.

This was a female, and she carried in her mouth a ball of fur that squeaked and squirmed. Her neck strained, her head rose painfully to keep the infant from dragging on the ground. She was saving her young from the herd, it was clear, and so intent was she upon that purpose that she was unconscious of anything else.

The boy wondered. What did he see? A running fox. And yet why did she carry a young one? What could that mean for his own life and future?

Always the totem beast appeared to be aware of the one who came seeking for it, and yet this one ignored him completely. Should he look elsewhere? And yet he could not turn his gaze away, for the animal's danger, its determination, its speed and strength and persistence compelled his eye and his mind.

This was the animal he had come to find. He would return to the village and describe this strange vision to the elders, and perhaps they would know what it meant.

Yet when he did that, not one of the old men or the wise women could quite understand its meaning. He was to become Running Fox, that was clear. There would be some task that he must accomplish, but no one could think what it might be.

Now, on his second day of riding toward his first raid, the young man thought of that small creature of his vision. He must be quick, brave, and determined, it was clear. Whatever result might come of his solitary endeavor, he would deal with it as he could, without fear or hesitation.

That much he had learned from the fox running amid the herd, carrying its furry burden in weary jaws. He could almost feel the desperate throbbing of the animal's heart, the stress of its muscles, the squirming of the small one it carried.

He shivered and looked ahead. A clump of willow marked a stream of water, and he halted his mount in the shadows and looked for the creek. It had been a wet summer, and the trickle was clear and cool as he quenched his thirst and let his pony drink.

Then the boy lay flat and put his ear to the ground, listening to the sounds of the earth. Beneath the creak of willow boles in the wind and the purl of water there was another sound, steady and strange.

It was, he knew without question, the grinding of those metal-shod wheels on the wheel-road, the tread of many hooves, the pacing of many feet across the prairie. The white-topped wagons were coming, and he would shadow their route until night fell, when he could capture horses to fulfill his dream.

Keeping below the swells that now hid the wheel-road, he led his pony forward, knowing exactly the spot where the wagons would camp for the night, as others had done before this. They would not know he was there until he chose.

The wheel-road followed the shallow river faithfully. That meant Fox could take shortcuts to save distance and time, so he would arrive at the spot he had chosen much earlier than the wagons.

A stream ran down to join the Bug River, as his people called the Platte. He went far up its winding course and hid his horse among the willows and cottonwoods growing along its bank.

Then he crept down again and hid among a cluster of rocks in a spot amid lush grass. The last wagon train had camped there only a hand of days before; the grass was still trampled, but the rains had made it grow again. Surely the herds of the white men would come here to graze, while the wagons circled and the fires burned and the people talked and sang and fought.

Running Fox would choose his opportunity and his animals with care. When he took them away, not one of those careless people would know their livestock had been stolen.

He might miss the chance of counting coup, but as one alone against an entire group of the alien people, that was a matter of good sense rather than a lack of courage.

CHAPTER SEVENTEEN

The days on the trail strung out endlessly, beginning at dawn and running, sometimes, to well after sunset. Phil found his job of watching the livestock so boring that he walked, sometimes, in his sleep until he stumbled into some hole or fell flat into a cowpat.

However, he had made friends with a few of the other children in the train. Annie Hollings was only six, and a girl to boot. Her brother Fred was eleven, almost old enough, but so backward that Phil found him tiresome. Neither of the Hollings children could even read, which shocked the boy mightily. Fred knew a lot about hard work, and he was a willing companion at the tail of the herd, when his father didn't have other things for him to do, but he wasn't one bit interesting.

For the first time, Phil realized that having a scholar for a Pa meant that your family talked about things that most folks never heard tell of. He also found that most of the farmer-boys traveling with him found it highly suspicious that someone their age could read, and he determined to keep his beginning Latin and his aptitude for arithmetic a dark secret. Avoiding the Williamses as far as possible, he ranged around the nightly campfire, adding to his list of acquaintances.

Though the adults and smaller children all but dropped in their tracks, most evenings, the boys of his age usually still had a bit of ginger left. His new-found variety of friends had heard the rumors that he had already killed his man. They were wide-eyed with awe at his prowess.

These boys, some half-dozen in all, formed a fairly compatible group who, without mentioning it to their elders, kept each other company and sometimes offered a hand when help was needed. Today they were scattered along the other side of the herd, watching, he supposed, but beyond any chance of talking.

Now, trudging along, his bare feet too toughened by travel even to feel the prickles and sharp stones in his way, Phil was thinking with satisfaction about the night before. They'd gone out into the dark grassland beyond the circle of wagons and the bawling clutter of animals and played Injun until they were ready to drop.

They'd seen Indians along the way, it was true, but those in the villages seemed too tame somehow. He'd dreamed of counting coup on a Cheyenne warrior, after hearing some of Jesse Gunter's stories, and it looked as if they were going to cross the entire width of the Plains without so much as spotting one.

Pa's horse, Petronius (nicknamed Pet), was lagging farther and farther behind the herd, reaching out to crop occasional tufts of grass. Phil sighed and grumbled every time he had to drive him back to the other horses, for today not one of his friends had been able to walk beside him. Even Rags just panted along in the shade of the wagon, neglecting his oldest friend.

After a while the boy just dreamed along, his feet automatically finding the way. Lost in a daydream, he stopped noticing what Pet was doing.

He was riding a paint pony, galloping toward a battle where war cries mingled with the sounds of moans and gunshots....

And then he heard the thud of hooves, a startled whinny. When he roused himself and turned, a mounted man, naked to the waist, was driving off Pet and two other horses that had fallen behind the rest.

Phil stared around, looking for help, but he had dropped far behind the last wagon and the other boys were almost out of sight. Dust clouded everything, and he could see nothing but the rumps of the plodding cows and oxen ahead of him.

One of Gunter's spare horses was nearby; he tucked a toe behind the animal's knee and climbed onto its back. Long-legged and rangy, the animal tried to sidestep, but Phil had learned, by now, to mount anything with four legs.

He caught the skinny back between his knees and leaned forward to catch the lead-rope that Gunter kept attached to the hackamores he favored for his horses. Using the free end as a whip, Phil slapped it against the beast's rump, kicked his heels deeply into its sides, and they took off after the horse-thief.

The cows would follow the train. The other horses might stray, but he'd round them up when he got back.

He was almighty glad his Pa had insisted he carry his rifle, after the trouble with the Williams boys. Otherwise he'd have been forced to tackle that redskin with only his knife.

The red horse stretched out, seeing the fleeing animals ahead of him. He seemed to relish a race, which was handy. Phil felt sure the critter could catch up with just about any horse in the herd, though he didn't know what kind the Indian might be riding. It was fast, though, he thought as he pounded along. Even moving back and forth, keeping the stolen mounts together, it was holding its distance.

"Come on, Red!" he shouted into his horse's ear. "You can catch that red-tailed son-of-a-bitch!" His mother would die if she heard that, he thought with some satisfaction.

It seemed to be language the red horse understood. He picked up his hooves and fairly flew across the short-cropped grass toward the line of trees for which their quarry was heading.

The last stolen horse disappeared among the cottonwoods. Phil kicked his mount through a gap between two deeply creased gray tree trunks and found himself following a game track toward a thicket along the stream. Once in the trees, he slowed the animal and checked his rifle.

He had one of the cap-and-ball weapons, which was a blessing. Maryla's old Hawken took forever to load and prime.

He could hear horses stamping, whinnying, splashing into water somewhere close at hand. Leaving the red horse tied to a branch, the boy slipped cautiously through the skimpy brush toward the noise. His bare feet made no sound, even among the dried debris under the cottonwoods, as he moved like a shadow over the leaf-dappled ground, sinking to his belly behind bushes at intervals in order to listen hard.

At last he lay flat and slithered through the bushes. He could now see Pet, snorting as he shook water from his nose. The other animals were close to him, still drinking. Where was the Indian?

A pair of hard hands caught him, pulled him backward by the hair, and he found himself staring upside down into cold black eyes above twin stripes of red paint. The edge of a knife was touching his scalp, and Phil realized for a stunned moment that this was it. The end, and he hadn't got back Pa's horse!

* * * * * * *

Running Fox had watched for days for the white men's wagons to arrive at a convenient place. He remained beyond the river, screened by its big cottonwoods, low willows and scrub growth, as he learned the habits of those he was stalking. The spare animals came behind the last wagon, in a long straggle attended by children, with a single rider far behind out of the dust.

It was plain that the watchers were weary of their tasks, and as days passed, the Cheyenne knew he would find a chance to take horses.

After a hand of suns, they came to the spot he had chosen and his opportunity arrived. The rider at the rear stopped to relieve himself, allowing the herd to move so far ahead of him that nothing happening amid the dust would be seen or understood.

The boys tagging along in the distance were talking and laughing, and the one on the river side was almost asleep.

It required only a daring dash, quick work with his horse, and three animals fled with him toward the trees along the river. He did not expect so small a boy to follow a warrior, and it was only after he reached the river and was concealed among the growth there that he realized the sleepy youngster had come after him.

He left the horses to drink and slid into the bushes. Behind a thick clump, he waited for the boy to track the horses; he was surprised at how silently this white-eye youth was able to accomplish that feat. He was almost at hand before Running Fox heard a sound.

The Cheyenne remained quite still as he waited for the boy to pass by, on his way toward the river. When he rose onto his elbows to examine the horses, Fox had him, and only when he looked into the youngster's eyes did he realize that this was one fit to be called a warrior, no matter how young he might be.

Even with the knife at his throat, the boy blazed with defiance. His skinny body tensed into an arc, trying to shake off the iron grip holding him.

Such spirits were not to be wasted, Running Fox thought, as he flipped his prey onto his face and bound his hands and feet with thongs. Yet he could not wait to examine his captive now—others would realize, in time, that both horses and boy were gone and then they would track them all to this spot.

Fox heaved the struggling child onto the big black, roped the entire string together, and led them across the shallow river and up a long draw beyond it. Only when he reached a branch and followed it up into a maze of broken land did he pause and set his victim on the ground.

He was sharply reminded of something—something dreamlike—his vision that gave him his totem! This small, desperate creature was much like that bundle of fur the mother fox had carried amid the stampede.

Had that vision been a kind of signal that he would also be burdened with saving a young one from destruction? The ways of the spirits were strange, yet Running Fox had the conviction that this was exactly what had happened.

Now he must find a way to return the child without relinquishing the horses or losing his life. As he drove the herd before him through the confusing clutter of ravines, he was thinking very hard, and when he stopped at last, he thought he had found the answer.

CHAPTER EIGHTEEN

FROM *DIE TAGEBUCH* OF KATRINA HOLZER

There has been much excitement and terror among our group. Yesterday four horses were taken, along with little Philip Stoner. Although measures were taken to seek out a track that might show where he had gone, so confused is our trail that even Herr Gunter could not find the spot where they might have left our route.

As no one knew exactly where or when they disappeared, searchers would have had to go back for many miles to locate any trace. Unfortunately, by the time the loss was reported, darkness had fallen, making such a discovery impossible until morning.

Frau Hirschorn and I went to attend Frau Stoner. We feared for her, for her heart was most painful. Only a tea that Marta made of dried hawthorn berries eased her and allowed her to sleep. Thank the good Gott for the herbal knowledge of my friend, for otherwise we should be at the mercy of illness, altogether without recourse.

This dreadful dilemma was solved in a strange and unexpected manner, at dawn this morning. Those guarding the camp detected a distant figure on horseback, approaching our great circle of wagons.

There was much alarm when we saw this to be a Cheyenne, who was painted for a raid, Swift Water told us, and riding a painted pony.

Behind him, eyes shining, rode Philip Stoner. Before drawing too near to our encampment, the warrior stopped his steed and motioned for his captive to dismount, which Philip did with alacrity. Then his captor wheeled his horse and sped off into the dimness of dawn, leaving any thought of pursuit behind.

We could not know if there were others hidden beyond the river. No one was willing to risk life and limb for four horses, and Gunter advised against pursuit. As we had the child back, all felt we would be wise to ignore the other losses and to pursue our way as if nothing had happened.

Although Albert Stoner regretted the loss of his horse, he was so relieved at the return of his son that he agreed this was the best course open to us. When he spoke with Philip, the boy's story made us glad of the decision.

Evidently this young warrior was unlike others of his kind. He returned the child to us, unharmed, and for that we must be forever grateful, whatever his other transgressions may be.

* * * * * *

Running Fox led his string of stolen horses through the hills, sticking to the familiar tangle of ravines. He didn't feel the white men would pursue him, after he returned their child, but he was going to take no unnecessary risks. These horses, one of them an unusually strong animal, would give him his place in the band.

He camped the second night in the shelter of cottonwoods beside a stream. In the distance he heard thunder, but he knew he walked a charmed path and no rain would dampen his night.

The horses, tied on long lines to prevent their escape, munched bits of grass beside him as he rolled into his blanket and closed his eyes, listening to whispers of wind among the leaves and to insects crickling among the grass and pebbles nearby. A great satisfaction filled his mind and his heart...

He floated above the plain, as he had done long ago on his medicine journey. Below him, the grassland was thronged with animals: elk and antelope, mule deer and small clumps of darkness that marked the presence of bison. He smiled, thinking of long years of hunting that lay ahead of him.

He descended slowly, watching the creatures graze, their young gambol about the herds. Their mothers were at peace but watchful, and the bulls and bucks, seemingly careless of danger, were ready to flee any threat or to defend their herds against any attacker.

Among the larger animals he could see, once again, the flick of a red brush as a fox danced forward among the hooves of those much larger than she. This one did not carry a young one. As Running Fox drew nearer, she lifted her head and looked at him. He touched the ground beside her, though he could not feel the soil beneath his intangible feet.

The dark eyes gazed into his, as if asking a question. Then the fox barked gaily, only once, and danced away to disappear amid a group of antelope.

Running Fox sighed, and instantly he was again inside his own body, hearing the night sounds of the wind and the horses. A thought sprang into his mind, and he knew it had come with him out of that dream vision.

"I will have a young one of my own, one day," he said aloud to the night and the dozing horses. "And because I spared the young one of the whites on the wheel-road, my own will be spared in turn. That is what this dream has told me." A strange and yet triumphant feeling filled him.

He rose, though it was not yet dawn, and urged his horses toward the Cheyenne camp, now only another day distant. He had begun to acquire his herd, and when he had enough, he would go to the father of Pale Gray Dove and offer six as a gift. He was not yet ready to marry, but when he became ready, it was Dove whom he would like for his first wife.

When he rode into camp, proudly erect upon the back of the biggest and most beautiful of the horses, she was watching around the curve of her mother's lodge. When he dismounted before his own mother's lodge, she was there among those who came to exclaim and admire.

He had obeyed his medicine dream, and in obeying it he had achieved the goal he set for himself. Could any man do better?

* * * * * *

Now the wagons ground mercilessly along over pale soil, beside pale rocks that seemed to suck all moisture from the body. There wasn't any way to drink enough water to quench that thirst, no matter that the river still ran near the trail. Animals and people alike felt their nostrils clog, their faces parch and peel, and their lips crack.

Maryla's nose began to bleed, and Frau Holzer told her it was probably because of the altitude. That made sense, but the girl had no time to worry about it. Her mother was growing worse by the day, and small Lizzie was getting weaker along with her mother.

The loss of the cow was not the disaster it might have been, for Mrs. Jeffries, six wagons behind the Stoner vehicle, had lost her baby crossing a river some weeks back. She had supplemented Elizabeth's diminishing supply of milk ever since, and now she took over the task of wet-nursing the infant.

Still the baby dwindled, grew fretful and big-eyed. It seemed that her small life was somehow linked with that of her mother, and as Elizabeth's life waned that of her infant did too. It was painful to watch the two of them wither away.

Now Maryla walked behind the wagon, watching her mother as she lay on the pallet Pa had made for her atop his huge box of books. A thin shift was all Elizabeth could bear against her skin, and her daughter could see her heart jumping erratically beneath her collarbone. Mama's ragged moans, just audible to someone very nearby, tortured Maryla, and she knew they were tearing her father apart.

Cold fear filled the girl, for she knew with an unalterable conviction that she was about to lose her mother and probably her sister as well. Albert would not speak about this with anyone. She could see that he was filled with guilt for bringing his wife on this journey, and he could not face her approaching death. What would he do when she died?

Not one of her brothers except for Phil would talk about that. Only he, the youngest, smallest, perhaps brightest of them all, understood, as she did, that their lives were about to change completely. At night the two of them huddled close together in the chill of the high country darkness, whispering comfort to each other as they listened to the ragged breathing of their mother.

They crossed the Platte using the Mormon Ferry, and headed south and west toward Willow Spring. All around them now was country that seemed made for destroying rather than sustaining their lives.

As they moved, tortured shapes came into view among the mountains edging their route. Devil's Gate came into sight, after they passed Independence Rock, where several young people left the train to leave their marks.

Maryla felt she had outgrown such childish matters. The very shapes of the stones seemed to her the embodiment of evil. Or perhaps that was only her mood of depression, as she followed her mother's labored breathing and tried to comfort her sister's thin wails.

Split Rock seemed even more forbidding, twisted and somehow devilish in shape. She wondered if these forebodings were caused by her mother's illness, or by something inherently wicked in the country and its unending succession of stony giants.

Whatever the cause, she felt as if she had aged decades in the past months. She seemed older, when she considered the situation, than her father, who would not consent to discuss her mother's condition.

Now they had left the Platte behind and were crossing and recrossing the Sweetwater River, traveling sometimes through deep sand that wearied even the oxen and wore the walkers down to the bone. Here beside the small river, which would at least supply water while they waited, Albert Stoner at last admitted that Elizabeth could travel no more. The jolting of the wagon was wrenching from her the sort of sounds that tortured his heart.

Every lurch of the wagon, every drop of a wheel into a hole or bump over a rock brought from her groans that became too painful for those who loved her to bear. Every one of the family agreed they must halt. Others had dropped out along the way, because of illness, and now it was their turn, dangerous though it might be.

Elizabeth said nothing, for she lived now in a sort of daze that held nothing, it seemed, but pain. Albert felt it would be kinder to put his rifle to her head and end her suffering, but that was an intolerable thought. No, they must leave the train and take their chances on catching up again or meeting them in Oregon at the end of their journey.

There were cottonwoods, skimpy ones by contrast with those back in the plains, to shelter the wagon from the sun. Now, however, it was late in the year and at that altitude it became imperative to build a fire early and to cover Elizabeth well. The chill came long before the sun was down behind the cliffs marking the way into South Pass.

"She will get better here," Maryla's father insisted, and she didn't disagree. She thought he looked almost as ill as her mother, now, his flesh worn down, his hair, because he had lost his hat while crossing a river, faded to a pinkish shade by the sun.

"Of course she will," she told him, though both knew it was a lie.

Mark and Jon and Philip stood with them, staring at the passing train. Hands waved sad goodbyes to them from the wagons of those they knew well. Mrs. Holzer, Mrs. Hirschorn, and the boys pulled out of their position to pass near enough to call last farewells.

"We shall pray to the good God that you will be safe and that Frau Elizabeth will improve," Andreas told her as he gazed down at her. "We will meet in Oregon, you will see." Then he moved abruptly to rejoin his wagon. He did not turn again.

Maryla felt unaccustomed tears welling in her eyes. Never in her life had she felt so alone, even though her father and brothers stood beside her. There would be no other train this year, Gunter had warned them. Even if Elizabeth died on the trail, it would be better for those of the family who survived if they kept on with the others.

But not one of her family could bear those pitiful moans. They had to stop, come what might.

When Maryla climbed into the wagon to see to her mother, small Lizzie, in a basket beside her mother, was stiff and cold. Without speaking, for Elizabeth's eyes were open and for once she seemed aware. Maryla took up the basket, climbed out of the wagon, and handed it to her father.

"The baby...she died while we pulled out and set up. Maybe before. She seemed to be sleeping." Her sobs overcame her, and the girl leaned against Jon and wept bitterly.

Albert straightened his shoulders and looked at the tiny shape in the basket. Lizzie had not grown on the journey. Indeed, the baby had seemed to shrink, and now the little body was almost lost amid the soft blankets in the hickory splint container.

"We'll bury her beside the river," he said. "Don't tell your mother. She doesn't need any more....," he choked, and Maryla knew that he, too, wanted to cry until tears washed away the pain in his heart.

Above them the leaves of the cottonwood seemed to whimper, too, as they dug that small hole beside the river and set Lizzie Stoner in her grave. As she knelt there, Maryla could not weep any more. She seemed to be wrung dry of tears.

The time for weeping was past.

CHAPTER NINETEEN

FROM *DIE TAGEBUCH* OF KATRINA HOLZER

Two days past we left behind the Stoner wagon. This lies as a weight upon our hearts, for all of us had a great fondness for Maryla, her father, and brothers. We know, Marta and I, that Elizabeth was a dead woman long before we reached our parting, and the infant, too, was marked for death. What a tragedy!

And yet each day we pass more graves, fresh ones marked by piles of stones, old ones revealed by bones and scraps of clothing scattered by animals. This is a road of death indeed, and as we travel I ponder the strange ways of humankind. We cannot rest at ease with things we know, familiar places, peaceful pursuits.

As my own Vienna proved, peace is not our natural state. Our eyes are always upon something apart, something forbidden, something unattainable. Even the Philosophers could not answer that conundrum. I doubt that my own dear Guenter would have had a sensible solution to offer.

So we found ourselves committed to a terrible trek over deep sand. Strangely enough, one can find water beneath this seemingly arid waste, and we have added our own share of wells to the mole-like depressions along our way. Though unfit for humankind, the water can be used by the animals, who suffer greatly from thirst.

We traveled for what seemed a great distance over flat plains covered by the dusty gray of sagebrush. When we paused, it was at the point at which the trails diverged, one going south and west toward California, the other toward Oregon.

We have forded the Green River, and our guide assures us that though we yet have weeks or months of travel, we are at last upon the final leg of our journey. As we approach Fort Bridger, I cannot but wonder what has befallen the Stoners. Of all those with whom we travel, Marta and I felt closest in heart and spirit to that family, and we both pray nightly that nothing terrible will befall them. Perhaps they will be able to find a place sheltered from the weather, in which to pass the winter, if they are caught in the mountains.

And yet I have had dreams that wake me in the night, visions that seem to foretell some further disaster for those people. I devoutly hope these are merely the protests of a weary mind and an exhausted body.

God be with us all!

* * * * * * *

Maryla stared at the ground, shoulders slumped in the way that Mama would have deplored, if she had still been alive to see it. "Yes, Pa," she breathed to the scatter of tan grass and pebbles at her feet.

"And just you remember that!" he snapped once more. "Your Ma may be dead and gone, but no daughter of mine is going to be anything but a lady! It's all she ever wanted of you, and you never gave it to her."

He glared at her for a moment. She didn't look up to see, but she could feel his furious gaze on her skin like the heat from a fire. But what was so terrible about asking to go hunting with him and her brothers? He was more harsh with her now than he had ever been before Mama died.

The boys were waiting quietly in the shelter of the wagon. They knew better than to call attention to themselves—Pa was firm with his discipline always, and every one of his children knew it. Now, with Mama gone, he seemed like someone else, bitter and harsh and unbending.

Maryla shook herself. That was not the sort of thought a lady should have, she knew. She should be respectful of her elders, no matter what.

Yet she had suffered along with the others. She, too, was left without Mama. Why did her father regard her as somehow at fault?

The long-barreled rifle was in Pa's hand, and the boys carried caplocks, while young Phil had Mama's blunderbuss. Her brothers were excited. A hunt was fun, whether or not there was any need for meat.

Old Rags, sensing their excitement, wagged away after them, turning once to look back at her before they disappeared into the trees. She found herself wishing the dog had remained behind with her. This was a lonely spot, she thought, as she began building a fire to cook the beans for supper.

Maryla knew there was enough flour and meal and bacon and

beans to take them all the way to Oregon, if they'd content themselves with it. They all just wanted to get away from the wagon and the oxen and roam the mountainside, where they might forget their grief for a time.

They had found this nice little valley to make camp in, with a deep creek cutting across one corner of a clearing. The wagon fitted into the space between two clumps of fir as if it had been measured for it, and there was a cluster of white rocks nearby, just right for building the cook fire without endangering the grass or the bushes.

They'd seen a deer, when they pulled in, and Pa decided at once to stop here for the night. That had set them off, Pa as much as Jon and Mark and Phil. Now they'd go skitting off through the trees and up the mountainside to the west, leaving her here to pound their clothes clean in the creek and cook beans and flapjacks to go with their wonderful venison.

Her time of freedom from most woman-work had died with Mama. Now everything from cooking and washing to mending the clothing was left to her, and she had never been a handy woman with such things.

She watched the four stride into the fringe of trees and begin climbing the easy slope up the mountain. Pa, strong and square-shouldered and red-headed, dwarfed both his grown sons. Jon and Mark looked so much like Mama from this distance that tears came to Maryla's eyes.

She sighed, pinned her thick braid of coppery hair on top of her head, and piled the family's stinking heap of dirty clothing beside her on a rock at the edge of the stream. She had a bit of Mama's homemade soap left, but she didn't waste it on big jobs like this.

She took the first sweaty shirt out of the pile and began beating the wet cloth against the smooth rock with Mama's wooden paddle, turning it over and over, letting the water carry away the dirt. It took a long time. Lucky they had decided to stop just after noon, else she would never get finished before dark.

From time to time, she rose and went to stir the beans in the iron pot that sat over the coals on three handy rocks. The beans would be done by dark, and she could fix flapjacks in the long-handled skillet, when she saw them coming. Pa hated cold food.

Washing finished, she peered up the long slope, trying to see if they were coming back through the thick timber. Nothing moved, however, except the wind in the firs, as the sun set behind the height. After a time, long shadows pooled in the valley.

She brought more wood from a tangle of fallen aspens that slanted into the creek. The evening was cooling quickly, and she got her blanket-coat from the wagon and huddled it about her as she hunkered beside the fire, waiting.

There came a long wail from above. Not a coyote, but a wolf. Back in Missouri she might not have known that, but she had learned a lot of things as they crossed the prairie country and the mountains.

She could handle the oxen as well as Pa and better than either Jon or Mark. She could chop down a tree, if there was one to hand, as easily as anyone, and she could build a fire in a blowing rainstorm. Not to mention her shooting abilities!

So why didn't they want her to come with them? What mysterious man-things did they talk about that she wasn't allowed to hear? She shivered and spat into the fire, knowing rebelliously that this wasn't ladylike, either.

It was dark now. The sun had left a red wash across the west, behind the dark peaks, but it was fading fast. The sky above the clearing was black, studded with brilliant stars that looked close enough to touch.

Pa would see the fire for a long way, and it'd guide him back to the wagon. She piled on more of the dead wood, keeping the blaze leaping high.

By the time the patch of stars she called the Sisters was going down into the west, she knew they'd had trouble and camped for the night. There was nothing she could do...except maybe signal them? If they were lost, which Pa would never be, why, a shot might guide them in the right direction.

The wolf was howling, his voice shrill and wild and spineshivery. He was answered by two others, so distant that their cries could hardly be heard. She crawled into the wagon and fumbled her way to her bedroll.

She took her Hawken, which made enough noise to wake the dead, and carried it out into the clearing away from the fire. She took her time loading it, ramming down the charge, priming the pan, for she was beginning to be afraid that her shot might not be answered by another from the mountain.

The stars were so bright that she could see their pale glimmer reflected in the creek. She aimed skyward and pulled the trigger. The booming roar of the gun echoed again and again and again, as it bounced about among the heights rimming the valley.

When her ears stopped ringing, she realized the wolf had gone, scared off by the noise. She could hear nothing for a long time. Then there came a sleepy twitter from a bird in a nearby bush, and she sighed.

Pa would have shot to return her signal, if he'd heard it, so they were out of earshot. Or worse...but she shook off that thought. Losing Mama and the baby had been enough bad luck, surely, for one family to endure.

She drifted off to sleep, sitting by the fire, to wake with her neck stiff and sore and her back ready to break in two. The sun was lighting the top of the mountain up which her people had gone. A dog fox was barking, his tone sharp in the chilly morning, and a hawk—maybe an eagle—was quartering the sky.

The fire had died to ash-covered coals, but she soon had it blazing again.

She ate from the pot of cold beans without fixing anything else. There were enough beans there to last her, alone, for days. She wasn't about to waste more food, in case it took her menfolk a long time to find their way back.

Maryla led the oxen to water and put them in a fresh patch of grass. She tidied up the wagon, which was in a mess from months of constant travel, as well as her mother's illness. She checked the clothes, which she had spread on the bushes to dry, and turned those that were still wet. The dry ones she folded into the big trunk in the wagon.

She did, in fact, everything she could think to do, and when it was all done and done again, it was not yet noon. Nobody had come, and nobody had hailed from a distance. The dim prickle of fear she had been fighting down all night threatened to overflow into actual terror.

She was big and brave and had handled a lot of hard things, but she refused to think about what might happen if...no, she would not think about that. But it wasn't easy not to.

She ate more beans, put the remainder into a bowl, and scrubbed out the pot with sand and creek water. Then she sat on a sun-warmed rock beside the stream and stared up at the mountainside, as if willing would bring her family back.

It didn't. The oxen ate the grass within reach of their tethers and needed to be moved again. That gave her something to do for a bit. When she was done, she went back to her rock and sat again, staring upward, as the sun slipped, with painful slowness, down the western sky.

She cooked nothing that night. When she had nibbled a few more beans, she crawled into the wagon, tied the flaps tightly, and cried, cuddling the old rifle to her chest as if it were a companion. She was ashamed of herself, and she knew her grandmother would have scolded her, but she had never in her life been entirely alone. It was strange and frightening, and she wondered if she could bear it.

The first day was a Tuesday. Pa had been keeping track with his home-made calendar, all the way from Missouri, and she was sure of that. She thought about hitching up the oxen and going on alone, if Pa and the boys never got back to camp. Yet she knew it had taken everything they all could do to wangle the wagon, the team, and themselves up and down the cliffs and across the rivers behind them, once they took to the trail again after losing Mama. No one could do it alone.

By the third day, she knew that if she was to keep up with what day it was and what month—and even what year—she'd better start marking off the time on Pa's calendar. Yet she could see his long-fingered hands doing that, and she couldn't bring herself to touch it.

Instead, she made a long slick pole, trimmed from the deadfall in the creek, and notched it for every day. If nobody came, she would know the day she died, and that would somehow be a comfort.

The next day Rags came limping out of the trees, barely able to move. She looked up and saw him, and her heart seemed to stutter for an instant. He had returned alone, with dried blood caking his coat; it meant there was nobody left alive to come back with him.

She ran to him and dropped to her knees, putting her arms carefully about his neck, to avoid hurting the scabbed wounds. Under her hands, he was very thin, and she could feel him quiver with effort as he licked her face and tried to tell her something with whines and short barks.

He didn't have to, though. She knew as soon as she saw him. They were alone, and she was just glad to have one member of her family left.

That night, curled against her in the shelter of the wagon, the old dog died. One minute he was there, faintly warm and quivering with the effort of his breathing. The next he was gone, the skinny body in her arms an empty shell. Somehow she had known he was too feeble and wounded to live.

The next morning, with tears streaming down her face, she dug a shallow grave beside the creek and laid him in it. Then she dragged a flat rock, using one of the oxen for muscle power, to cover him over so no scavenger would disturb him.

She seemed even more alone, after that, for she had hoped he would live, in spite of knowing better.

As the days passed, she kept watching the oxen, trying to keep from thinking about the thing she must do when the time came. The patient beasts had hauled the wagon over the long miles; she had petted them and fed them, watered them and ridden on their broad backs.

She felt as if they were all that was left of her family, since Rags died, but she also knew that when the snows came, they too would die. She had no hay to feed them through the winter. They would starve, if she kept them here.

At last she loosed the largest animals, letting them roam about the valley, but they always came back to the wagon, day after day, until the snow began to fall. Then she drove them down the mountainside, hoping they would come to some gentler altitude where they could find dried grass to keep them alive.

After that she was too busy to worry about them. She shot the smallest ox, Tansy, and butchered him, skinning the beast and scraping the hide. She cut the meat into manageable pieces, after hacking apart the joints, and secured them high in the aspens and willows along the creek, so wild animals couldn't leap high enough to get them.

The hide she secured across the canvas wagon cover, scraped side up. It would help keep out the wind, she hoped, when the weather turned really cold.

It took days to finish dressing out the meat. She endured them, bloody and exhausted, but when she was done she had enough meat to keep her alive, she hoped, for a winter. It would keep, frozen in the worsening weather, high in the snowy trees. She thought of Jesse Gunter and his moose, and hoped no wolverine would find her store.

She would not have thought she could bear to eat her old friend, yet now she knew she could do anything, whatever it might be. If she lived through this winter and was able to find her way out of the mountains when spring came, she would go her own way without caring what anyone thought about it.

Her grandmother used to say that God sent trials to make you strong enough to live on your own terms. She hadn't understood what the old lady meant, at the time, but now she was beginning to. If she earned her life, here in the high and lonely reaches, then she would also earn her freedom.

* * * * * * *

FROM *DIE TAGEBUCH* OF KATRINA HOLZER

We are moving through country so dead, so dry, so forlorn, that only the desert of the Sahara might match it in desolation. Sagebrush covers the gray soil, which is a blessing, as it alone keeps our oxen toiling along, pulling their burdens. Now we follow a new river, the Snake.

Behind us lie Bear River and more loss of life. We have traversed league after league of this dusty way. Now we move between low-lying ranks of lion-colored mountains, their backs smoothed by the harsh wind and grit. It seems they crouch with heads lowered, paws extended into the brushy flats, watching us creep past their feet like a line of ants.

Herr Doktor Schildkraut would ridicule me for such imagery, but he has not walked more than a thousand miles behind oxen. He has not suffered drought and deprivation. He, in short, probably knows less than he thinks about the geology of the planet and its effect upon the suffering souls who must live upon or cross it.

Indeed, those who instructed in the Akademie are all less wise than they believed, I have learned on this terrible trek. Reality is unlike their concepts of it, I have found.

Life is more precious, death less appalling, and labor of the most demanding sort is not simply the lot of oafs and peasants. Anyone can labor and benefit from it. The woman my sons will find, if God wills it so, will be another person from that one they left lapped in luxury in their homeland. I trust she will be a far stronger and better one.

Thanks be for the Snake River, which loops back and forth beside a sheer cliff on one side and gentle slopes on the other, for much of its way. Difficult as it may be to cross, and we have crossed it at a point where three islands interrupt the dangerous stream and make it easier to secure wagons and animals, it allows us to continue our journey without dying of thirst.

At several points along our way, we have found ourselves looking, awe-stricken, at waterfalls pouring down the slick stone of the Snake River cliff. Along the waterside there is a fringe of weed and scanty growths of trees of several kinds. In this arid place, the green rests our eyes and eases our sore hearts.

So plentiful are the dried droppings of bovines nearby that we do not trouble to haul in firewood. Much of this fuel is left by the trains traveling before us, for which we must be grateful. To one hardened to the trail, eating food cooked over burning dung is no hardship.

Those whom I knew in Vienna, the ladies and their husbands who are so particular as to food and drink and dress, would be shocked to see me now, sunburned and toughened with travel. I have become far stronger than I ever dreamed of being.

Some task awaits me in this new country, I feel, and though I often dream of the Stoners, I also dream of bright young faces turned to me for instruction. I would that I had Albert Stoner's store of books—but perhaps he will arrive there, late but safe, and together we may teach the disciplines that even pioneers need to know.

CHAPTER TWENTY

It had been a terrible journey, plagued as Albert was by guilt. He had known Elizabeth was frail from the beginning. Yet his own longing to follow the westward migration had overridden his good judgment. Now that his wife was in her grave (and who knew how long she would remain there, what with the work of scavengers?), his soul felt cankered with grief.

The loss of their infant had been painful, for she was a bright and lovable baby. But the loss of his Lizzie had struck him a blow from which he felt he could never recover. It affected his behavior toward his children; he understood that, though he seemed unable to control it.

When he snapped at his sons or Maryla, he felt even more guilty, though he was sure he had to keep them going in the paths their mother wanted for them. His daughter, in particular, was a special thorn in his conscience.

He had allowed her to do a man's work in the fields, in direct opposition to the wishes of her mother. If she had hated the work and done it only passably, as Elizabeth had, it would have been all right, he felt now. But Maryla had loved the hard labor, the outdoor life, and she had hated those indoor chores proper for a girl. He had indulged her for his own convenience.

Now he was harder on her than on any of his sons. She must become the woman his wife had longed for her to be, if he had to break her spirit. As he climbed the slope, leaving her behind with the wagon to do the woman's work that was right and needful, he felt a strange mixture of pride and regret.

He did not, however, turn back. He had made his decision, and he would stand by it, no matter how stricken she might look.

His sons, on the contrary, were looking extraordinarily cheerful. An afternoon in the forest hunting, away from the labors of travel, suited them, he knew. He felt the same way.

At this time of year there should be plenty of game fairly close in the forest. Fresh venison or marmot or grouse would taste good to appetites weary of skillet bread and beans and coffee.

An eagle wheeled overhead, its raucous cry echoing among the surrounding heights. Albert felt his heart ease, just a bit, as he followed his sons, single-file, up a game track that should, in time, lead them to good hunting. The pungent scent of fir in warm sunlight filled his lungs, and for the first time in a great while he felt soothed and comforted.

Phil, moving silently ahead, stopped in his tracks. Albert realized that he had spotted a marmot sitting on a stump. He shot it neatly in the head, the blunderbuss resounding like thunder. The echoes sounded like a small war as they boomed round and round and finally died away in the distance. When Albert came up, the boy was already gutting the animal.

"Good shot," he said, bending over the kill. "But I didn't realize how far the sound was going to carry, up here so high. Those cliffs across the valley must bounce the sound back. I hope there isn't any hostile around to hear it."

The thought of running into Blackfeet, Shoshone, or some other bunch of red-tails who might be looking for trouble sobered him. Maybe this expedition wasn't such a good idea...but they were halfway up the slope now. To go back meant he had to face his daughter again, and his mixture of guilts made that a sorry prospect.

Again he moved after Jon, with Phil scouting ahead, playing Indian, most likely, and thinking about his capture by the Cheyenne back in the Plains. Albert, on the other hand, was thinking about the stories Jesse Gunter had told him.

He kept his eyes peeled, his ears alert. Something felt cold in the middle of his back, as if hidden eyes watched, but when he turned, nobody was in sight.

They climbed now more steeply, and when he turned again he could see over the treetops, across a long vista leading to another mountain. The valley below was hidden behind a tree-covered ridge.

The path he followed edged onto an outcrop, where an old rockslide had formed a platform thrust from the side of the height. Albert paused there, surveying the thick-furred forest below.

He could see game trails from here, thin threads of paler color winding among the trees over rocky bits, disappearing again in the intricacies of the forest. Nothing moved there, but he had the feeling that he was just missing what he should be seeing.

The arrow came from above, not below, and it whicked into the side of his chest with wicked impact. There was no pain, just appalled surprise. He found himself lying flat, his left hand straining to reach the painted shaft while he tried to call out to Jon. A croak was all he could manage.

Miraculously, Jon heard. He turned and saw, his face paling under its tan. Then he was beside Albert, kneeling, trying to stanch the flow of blood around the arrow.

"Tell...brothers...to hide," Albert managed to gasp. "Break...off shaft."

Jon turned and whistled. Mark and Phil, much higher along the trail now, turned and looked. Jon gestured toward the thick growth downslope before turning again to attend to his father.

An arrow skewered Jon through the neck, and he fell across Albert, his blood warm on his father's chest. "God!" Albert cried, his wound almost forgotten in the pain of this new loss. "God, punish me, not my sons!"

Even as he cried out, he saw Mark fall and go tumbling away down the slope, to disappear from his view. "Phil, run!" he croaked.

When he opened his eyes again he looked into a grim face, half black, half white, with a diagonal red stripe running across the aquiline nose from jaw to temple. There was no knowing what lay behind that terrible mask, but he could not mistake the knife in the dark-skinned hand or the descent of the blade toward his own throat.

"Forgive me!" his heart cried out to his children, to his wife, and to God, before he died. Then there were peace and darkness.

* * * * * * *

In the space of a few moments, Phil's life changed forever. When he looked back at Jon, he could see his father lying on the rocky ground. His brother's gesture told him to run, and he did, following his lifelong training for obedience.

The blunderbuss weighed him down, and, with no target to shoot at, he dropped it. When Mark was hit and fell, he veered off the downward slope and went into a tangle of brush that fringed a clump of boulders.

They were done for, he knew. The old mountain man had told him about the Blackfoot, angry at everyone and ready to fight for no particular reason. This must be a wandering band from that tribe, attacking without warning. He curled into a knot among the bushes and forced himself not to cry, though it was very hard.

He could hear men talking, laughing. When the bushes parted and a painted face peered down at him, he made no attempt to resist. His gun was up there, where he dropped it. His knife was too small to do much good against the big warrior who plucked him out of his hiding place like a berry from a vine and stood him on the dusty slope.

Phil felt quite ready to die without a struggle, until he saw the three scalps dangling from a thong at the man's waist. Papa's familiar gray-streaked red, Jon's curly black, Mark's dark brown...these were the men who had killed and scalped his people!

Without warning, Phil jumped onto the startled man and clung like a burr, arms and legs wrapped about his almost naked body, while he bit as deeply as he could into the oily skin. He set his teeth firmly, while his victim beat at his back, pulled at him with both hands, even got his companions to try separating this young wolverine from his bleeding chest.

Someone struck Phil hard on the back of the head, and he felt the world tilt and darken. That was better. Now he'd be with Papa and Jon and Mark and Mama.

Pain woke him, a pounding in his head that was almost unbearable. When a foot pushed at his side, joggling him demandingly, he rolled over, felt a wave of agony wash over him, but managed to stand. His eyes seemed blurry; the shape of the warrior he had attacked wavered at the edges.

The streaked face glowered down at him above a blood-streaked chest. The other four warriors gathered around, staring with enigmatic eyes at their captive. They were all big men, painted with spots and streaks, stripes and dashes of red and black and ochre.

Phil felt certain they were looking for trouble, as Gunter had told him. He felt a sudden pang of longing for that solid and dependable friend, met and parted with so soon. Jesse Gunter would know what to do, he felt sure.

The man said something in a harsh voice, the guttural syllables meaning nothing to the boy. Phil didn't respond; he stood stubbornly in his tracks, gaze fixed on the black and white face, his mouth set grimly.

They could skin him alive, but if he could help it, he wouldn't give 'em the satisfaction of a scream or a groan. The warrior spoke for some time, gesturing toward Phil, away across the mountains, then back to the boy.

The marks of Phil's determined teeth made a double row of dark red arcs on the coppery skin, but the man didn't seem to care about that. When he finished his speech, he turned away and started up the mountain.

The smallest of his companions looped thongs about Phil's wrists and fastened them behind him. Then he lifted the boy as if he were a gutted deer and slung him over his wiry-muscled shoulder.

Carried so, Phil crossed the low pass toward which the game trail meandered, and once on the other side he realized that horses waited for his captors.

Tethered in a clump of aspens, cropping what grass they could reach, six horses came into view. The Indians hurried to reach them; once there, they dumped Phil unceremoniously onto the ground and sat down themselves in a circle. They passed the scalps around, each examining them admiringly before passing them on to the next warrior.

Phil, his teeth full of grit from his rough landing, managed to struggle up and sit against a tree, watching the men closely. He had no idea what they intended to do with him. It would have been easy to knock him in the head and add his scalp to their collection, but as they hadn't, he felt they might intend to keep him as a slave. The old timers on the wagon train had spoken of such things being done.

After a time the polka-dotted fellow dug from his pouch some twists of jerky, which he passed around to his companions. Nobody offered Phil any, though his stomach was growling audibly by then.

The afternoon was wearing on, and already the valley on this side of the mountain was filling with shadow. He thought longingly of the beans and skillet bread Maryla would have ready, back in their lost camp that already seemed a thousand miles away and years in the past. Then he had a chilling thought.

What would become of his sister, all alone back there, with winter coming on fast? There was no way she could take the wagon on alone, for they'd proved more than once that it was all they could do, with their united efforts, to get it over the streams and canyons they had already passed. Would she try to walk out?

Or, worse yet, had the Blackfeet already caught her? But no. There was only one coppery scalp on their string. Unless...but he refused to think of her being a captive. It was worse, Jesse Gunter had said more than once, for a woman to be captured than it was for a man.

Phil found tears forming in his eyes. That wouldn't do at all. He jerked his thoughts away from sad things and began planning his revenge upon these men who had slaughtered his father and his brothers. That would keep him from crying, it was certain.

Staring at the cross-legged group beside the horses, the boy brought to mind everything he had learned from Gunter concerning torture. He'd string up that biggest fellow, for instance, hand and foot to aspens on the left and right. Then he'd build a fire—not too big—under his crotch.

While his enemy baked slowly, Phil would peel off his hide, cut out his tongue, trim off his eyelids—filled with such satisfying visions, the boy drifted off to sleep. His stomach might be empty and his future doubtful, but he was exhausted, and the young can sleep any time, any place.

When he woke, Phil was stiff and sore and felt as if he'd been tied in a knot and left out in bad weather. When he tried to wiggle, he realized he had been loosed and re-tied, in the night. Now his hands were bound in front, and his ankles were connected with a sort of hobble that would certainly keep him from running, even if he had someplace to run to.

He squinted up into the sky, which was streaked with pale cloud, already catching the sun. Around him he could hear the chittering of birds and occasional words from the warriors. He rolled onto his side and stared at the shadowy group beneath the aspens.

He realized, after his eyes got used to the light, that they were playing a game, of all things. They had spread a small hide on the ground, and onto it they were tossing pebbles, two or three at a time. When those fell wrong, the one who tossed them would grunt irritably and pass them on to the next.

It was sort of like a game of taws, he thought, though instead of shooting the marbles between finger and thumb they pitched them with an odd motion of the wrist. He couldn't imagine what they might be doing.

At this point, they should either be going on with their expedition, he thought, or they should head home with their captive. Only when they kept looking over their shoulders at him did he understand they were gambling for possession of him.

He sat up and tried to brush the twigs and fir needles out of his hair and clothing. Itchy things crawled under his shirt and down his trousers, as well, and he managed to stand and shake himself hard. A rain of debris fell about his feet, and his stomach gave a doleful growl, as if to protest being neglected for so long.

The polka-dotted man rose and hurried toward him, as if to prevent an escape, but Phil backed against the tree nearest and glared at him. A stream of words from his new owner meant nothing to the boy, and he said nothing in return.

Let 'em stew. If they killed him, he'd be with his folks. If they didn't, he'd get his revenge, if it took him the rest of his life.

Before he could figure out what was going on, the warrior hauled him up, carried him to the horses, and dumped him onto a gray pony. Using tough thongs, the man bound his feet together beneath the horse's barrel.

Without a knife to cut himself free, Phil knew there was no

chance to get loose. He sighed as the man sprang onto another animal and led his mount away from the others, deeper into the maze of peaks and valleys now warming in the early sunlight.

The boy's skinny butt was rubbed raw before his captor halted for the night. They had traveled all day, only stopping to water themselves and the horses at occasional streams tumbling down from the heights, even so late in the season. The warrior pitched him a strip of jerky just before stopping to camp, and Phil had the doleful feeling that would be all he got for the day.

He thought longingly of Maryla, back there at the distant wagon, lost among the mountains. She'd had a pot of beans ready to boil when they left camp, and they'd go mighty well right now.

He refused to think of Pa and the boys. They were gone, but Maryla was all right. He was as certain of that as he was anything in his world. She'd find a way to pull him out of this, if any human being could.

CHAPTER TWENTY-ONE

Maryla lay in the wagon, rolled in quilts and blankets, but still she shivered. Wind gusted down from the adjacent peaks, rattling the wagon cover on its hoops, driving a harsh whisper of snow against the canvas. She feared this was only the first of an unending series of blizzards that would sweep the mountains all winter.

Without the familiar sounds of the oxen moving about the small valley, the silence was immense and almost more chilling than the wind. Such small interruptions as the sounds made by canvas and flapping ox-hide made it more intense, rather than breaking the stillness.

This was the first of many frozen nights she must somehow manage to survive. She had listened to Jesse Gunter's tales, sitting beside Philip, both of them cross-legged on the ground by the nightly fires, as the scout told of such winters, spent alone in his trapping camps.

She shivered again, harder. This was harsh country, unforgiving of mistakes. Pa and the boys had proved that.

Outside there were only snow and trees, rock and heights that towered over this little space between mountaintops. Sometimes she heard the wolf, its howl high and eerie in the moonlight, but in such a blast as this not even wolves would venture out of their dens.

Even the owl that had lived in the trees along the creek was gone, or sheltered in a hollow. How could she endure a winter of silence, broken only by the howling of wind? The girl pulled the quilts tightly over her head, keeping a warm pocket where her breath accumulated, while she thought hard about her fate.

To freeze to death, Gunter had said, was an easy death. Perhaps she would be lucky enough to die in that way, sleeping away the winter without any hope of waking with the spring. There was no one to know now, or to care. It would be painless, effortless...but something inside Maryla refused to consider that way out of her predicament.

Her mother had always chided her for being so like her grandmother. "Unconventional!" Elizabeth would say. "Strong-willed and careless of the finer feelings of others. You are just like her. Breeches! It must run in the blood!

"If I could tell you the things she did, just to get her own way—she wanted to manage her own life, as if that were the prerogative of any woman! But such matters are not for the ears of a maiden."

Maryla wondered for the hundredth time what her bright-eyed grandmother had possibly done that was so terrible. The memories she had of her were filled with interest.

The stories she could tell! The things she knew! And the tasks she would tackle, even in her sixties, that seemed beyond the strength of someone her age!

Grandmother was one who would not give up her life or her liberty on any account, and the girl only hoped she could find strength to equal that first Maryla's. Being ladylike wouldn't keep her alive in these circumstances, that was undeniable.

Her eyes closed, and she rested, lulled by the soft slippage of snow down the curve of the canvas above her. She must have fire—an interior fireplace that wouldn't burn the wagon itself—and then she slept.

The sound that woke her brought her instantly to her knees, pushing back the quilts, feeling for her big old flintlock. By touch, in the darkness, she checked the flint, primed the pan. Then she listened again, her heart thudding desperately.

A gruff snuffling came to her ears, the crunch of snow beneath feet, an inquiring grunt. A bear?

Surely the bears would have gone into their dens by now, she thought. Yet it was very early still. Perhaps this one was only now going to his rest.

The smell of the ox-hide or of the meat tied in the treetops beyond the wagon must have brought him here. Or maybe it was the scent of the bread she had baked over the fire and stored in the wagon.

Rage flared inside her. She had no rations to share with any bear! If she lived through the winter, she would need every scrap she had and whatever she could scrounge.

A thought popped into her head, as she listened for more noise outside. A bear was a lot of meat!

At that moment, claws scraped against the icy canvas and grated over the frozen ox-hide. Maryla leaped out through the rear flap of the wagon cover and skidded around the corner of the vehicle. Even though she was clad in three sets of shirts and pants, the wind sliced through her clothing and her flesh, seeming to reach her very bones.

She blinked hard, trying to see through whipping veils of snow. Something entirely too huge and dark loomed, at point-blank range, against the paleness of snow and the billowing wagon cover. Black on gray, the bulk was within arm's reach.

She hardly took the time to aim, so close was the animal. Her finger tightened, the gun roared its deep boom, and the bear stood on its hind legs, pawing at its neck, roaring with fury.

She backed hurriedly around the corner of the wagon and clambered inside again, fumbling for her powder horn. Reloading in the darkness was not easy, but she forced herself to slow down, breathe deeply, as Gunter advised anyone to do in tight corners, and ram home powder, patch, and ball in the correct order. A misfire could mean her death.

Outside she could hear the groaning breaths of the wounded beast as it moved along the side of the wagon, scraping its shoulder against the canvas as it made its way around to the back. As it came in line with the flap, she poked the gun barrel through a slit. It touched something solid that flinched at the contact; again she pulled the trigger without aiming.

The big beast fell into the snow, threshed for a moment, and went still. Maryla knelt inside, listening hard, but no other sound than the wind and the snow—and her racing heart—came to her ears.

She reloaded the rifle, except for priming the pan, and laid it inside the roll of quilts. Half frozen from her foray into the icy night, Maryla returned to her bed and lay shivering for a very long time, the rifle a cold length beside her.

Then she began to grow warm again, her young blood pulsing through her veins steadily, dependably. She thought of her grandmother again. She would have shot the bear, too, given the same circumstances, Maryla thought. Then she dropped deeply asleep, while snow drifted in pale riffles onto the furry heap outside the wagon.

Maryla woke suddenly. She stared up at the pale canvas above her, and her first thought was that she must line it with extra quilts and blankets. That thin layer wouldn't save her from the bitter weather to come, it was clear. Then she recalled the bear.

She had slept...how stupid! If he had come to in the night, he could have reached into the wagon and killed her with one swipe of his huge paw. Thank God! He must really be dead.

She felt sticky, her eyes gummy. She'd have to melt a bucket of snow, she suspected, for surely the creek had frozen overnight. She combed her tangled hair, stuck her arms into her father's heavy woolen coat, and put on her own stout boots. Then Maryla untied the wagon flap again and looked out into the pale vastness of morning.

Everything was white. Bushes, trees, and rocks were smoothed into a seamless snowfield. The bear was completely covered over, though his bulk lumped the even flow of whiteness at the back of the wagon. No disturbance of that layer was visible, and Maryla sighed again. If he had stirred, the snow would have slid.

He was well and truly dead; she wondered where that last shot had struck the animal. Then she thought of that great furry pelt, the vast amount of meat, the useful claws and teeth of the creature.

She had watched the Indians as the train camped near their villages. She had listened to Swift Water, as she explained to other women in the train how her people managed to live on the plains and in the mountains.

Maryla Stoner might not be the scholar her father and older brothers were, but she knew her memory for things that interested her was almost infallible. All those skills she had heard described and watched being demonstrated were still inside her mind. She would dig them out and use them or die trying.

She would skin that bear, scrape its hide with her mother's big kitchen blade, and scrub it down with snow, salt, and perhaps sand, if she could dig down to any along the creek. There would be more ashes than she needed, once she got a fireplace built as well.

She jumped awkwardly into the snow. Her foot turned on a hidden limb of the bear, and she went down atop the buried carcass, but it was cold beneath her and no longer troubled her mind. She was already planning her next moves.

Fire came first. A big one out here, so she wouldn't freeze while cutting up her prey, then a secure place to build one inside the wagon. That was going to be tricky, with the vehicle full of flammable stuff, but she'd manage it. Her grandmother would have, she knew.

Maryla tramped through ankle-deep snow to the edge of the creek, where a clump of aspen bent beneath heavy layers like old women huddled in white shawls. Once she pushed through the outer branches, she found the deadfall she had used earlier as firewood. She hauled out a length of trunk that was fairly dry, protected by the igloo of snow above it.

She trudged back and forth, dragging batches of sticks and chunks of fallen trunk, until she had a pile of wood near enough to the bear to keep her from freezing while she worked on the carcass, yet far enough from the wagon to keep from catching the canvas afire.

Kindling the pile was not easy. She had plenty of paper—Albert had discarded things far more valuable, but he faithfully kept his books in their great chest. Yet somehow Maryla could not bring herself to use pages from the precious volumes as tinder for her flint and steel. It would be, in a strange way, like burning her father.

There was plenty of dry material in the wagon, however. Bits of ragged clothing, worn out on the trail, proved to be excellent tinder, once reduced to a tiny pile of threads. When a tendril of smoke curled up, pale blue against the whiteness around her, she sank back and began feeding twigs into the growing blaze.

At last she had a brisk flame that she pushed beneath one side of her fire-pile; soon it was sending out waves of heat, while billows of pale smoke rose into the sky. When it was going well, she turned to her victim and surveyed the gargantuan task that lay before her.

Pa had not taken the skinning knife with him, and she blessed him for that. Taking the hide off that monster would be terribly hard with a kitchen knife.

Sighing, she grubbed into the snow and found one of the stiff legs. She heaved the animal over, using a pole for a lever, and when he lay on his back, his arms awkwardly upright and his head twisted to one side, she began slitting the belly skin.

She feared the cold had frozen him through, but evidently the layer of snow had insulated the body somewhat. The skin sliced cleanly, as she repeated the motions she had used on smaller game. Slit the belly, slice along arms and legs, peel back the hide, turn the animal over and work it loose, using the knife to sever the many filaments that held the skin to the body of the beast.

She took off her heavy coat and, before long, two layers of clothing, for between the fire and the demanding work she had begun to sweat. Gunter had warned everyone about sweating in very cold weather; she intended to dry herself well when she finished and change into dry clothing, too.

The snow dwindled to occasional flurries, and a pale spot in the sky told where the sun hid behind the clouds. The fire burned low, and she replenished it.

The hide was now free, spread on the snow and covered with warm ashes from the edges of her bonfire. That would keep it from freezing, she hoped, until she could scrape it clean.

She had to gut the bear and cut up this wealth of meat before it froze into iron chunks that would be impossible to handle. Before dark, she managed to do that, roasting bits to eat along the way in order to keep up her energy.

Tying the bundles of meat into Mama's old bed sheets, she placed it well forward in the wagon beside the big trunk where the bedding had been stored. Fresh meat left in treetops would not be safe from wolves, now that the snow had come, no matter how high she might secure it. The ox meat was frozen solid, and that shouldn't attract visitors, she hoped.

The bones were big, but she dragged them on a blanket as far as she could, hoping no scavenger would come too close to her shelter. By the light of her fire, she scraped all the flesh from the bear's skin. Fingers numbing, she rubbed in snow and ash and snow again until the thing felt fairly supple. Then she salted it, rolled it and stored it inside the wagon. It might save her life this winter.

Howls from the slopes above her told Maryla the wolves were gathering, drawn by the blood-scent. She scuffed fresh snow over the stain near the wagon, unable, for the moment, to do more.

It had been a hard day's work in anybody's terms, and Maryla was exhausted. The still-hot bear meat she munched as she lay in her blankets warmed her, but the food didn't keep her from falling into a bottomless sleep. If wolves came, she was too tired to care.

CHAPTER TWENTY-TWO

By the fourth day, Phil wasn't certain of anything any longer. He ached from heels to head, and he couldn't have found his way straight up, for they had circled peaks and meandered down glens with swift streams at their bottoms.

They had climbed higher than the clouds more than once, and they had now come down into a green valley where game browsed within eyeshot, and small herds of buffalo watched them pass through red-rimmed eyes. At the far end of the valley, which was just within range of his vision, Phil could see a smudge of smoke, and his nose, now cleared of camp smokes, caught the tang of burning wood.

It was too far to see what sort of people or houses might wait there, but it was clear Polka-dot was heading in that direction.

Phil leaned forward, taking the weight off his tail bone. He felt as if he'd been skinned raw and beaten with sticks, and he suspected even worse was to come. So far, he'd made no trouble for his captor, but once he was untied, he planned to raise a quarter section of hell for anybody within reach.

If they killed him, so much the better. If not, then he'd find a chance to run, sooner or later, and he'd find his sister, if they both lived long enough. But he knew how to keep his thoughts to himself, did Phil Stoner.

His Mama had been too sharp-eyed and quick-witted for comfort, and he'd trained in a hard school to hide any mischief he intended to commit. If he could fool Mama, he could fool a bunch of Indians, he was sure.

But when Polka-dot cut the thong binding his feet under the horse's belly, and someone unseen gave a tug at his arm, he rolled off his mount in a heap and slept like the dead until someone else kicked him awake in the early morning light. That someone was a very old woman who looked tough as a boot string. She jerked him upright, surveyed him from head to toe, and cut off the thong binding his wrists.

He knew by looking at her she was another one cut from Mama's pattern. He didn't try a thing as she half dragged him toward a tipi and pushed him down beside the fire burning beside the door flap.

On a tripod over the coals twirled a chunk of venison that smelled better than any food the boy had ever smelled before. His mouth began to water as the woman cut away a strip of meat and flung it at him.

It was hot, and he had to juggle it from hand to hand before he could bear to hold it, but by that time it had cooled enough to eat. It was stringy and unseasoned, but he could feel strength coming back into him as he chewed and swallowed.

Although she didn't look generous, the woman kept feeding him as long as he would eat. Then she nodded and jerked him upright by one arm. Pointing toward the creek that ran along a gully beyond the camp, she handed him a big clay pot and gave him a push.

Chores! He'd had them back in Missouri. He'd had them along the trail. Now it looked as if he'd have them as a captive. But he knew if he gave satisfaction until he felt up to escaping, he'd continue to eat well. Despite her witch-like wrinkles and her grim, toothless mouth, that old woman obviously intended her slaves to be fat and willing.

Phil hobbled off toward the creek, still feeling the effects of his long ride without a saddle or blanket between himself and the knobby backbone of the horse. But it wasn't too far, and the water was clear and green, running swiftly over colorful pebbles and boulders. He crept down a track to an eddy that offered easy access and filled the jar.

His new owner kept him busy, carrying wood for her insatiable fire, skinning out animals other people brought to her, tending the ancient horse that seemed to belong to her. As time went on, Phil found her to be some kind of healer or doctor.

Bitter Water Woman took him with her into the woods and taught him how to choose the right plants for stopping the flow of blood, for soothing headache or upset stomachs, and for many other sicknesses. He was learning enough of her language by then to understand something of her explanations, as she tutored him.

About the time he decided he was learning too much useful stuff to run away from her, she traded him off to Spotted Horse for a better horse and a steel knife. That was the chance Phil had waited for.

Spotted Horse was a harsh man, to his own children and far more so to Phil. When the boy moved too slowly bringing tools or water or a gourd of coals for kindling the fire, the warrior's hard fist was ready for a buffet.

The first time, Phil hadn't expected that, and the blow knocked him out cold. After that he was ready to jump like a rabbit to avoid a repetition.

But he'd learned patience in his time with Bitter Water Woman. He didn't allow his fury to show in his eyes, for he kept his head down and his hands clenched at his sides. When Spotted Horse settled himself beside his tipi and harangued his sickly wife, Phil waited without comment or overt action. When he was given a task, he did it without hesitation or comment, biding his time.

He was been so quiet and cooperative they soon left off watching him closely. He waited, teeth gritted, for his chance, and when Spotted Horse sent him into the forest after wood, he was ready.

He'd stolen a flint knife, a piece of deer hide, and some pemmican, hiding them under a boulder on the slope above the village. He lit out, after retrieving his supplies, on a cloudy fall morning and didn't stop running until he crossed the ridge above the valley. There he found a shallow stream running down the other side, and he took to its stony bed to hide his tracks.

It took Spotted Horse three days to find him. The beating was a bad one, but it only fueled Phil's resolve to get away again. After his fourth escape attempt, Spotted Horse seemed ready to knock him in the head.

Phil, by then, wouldn't have objected too much, but old Owl Feather, who traded with anyone who came along for anything, worthy or unworthy, swapped a spavined horse for the rebellious boy.

Phil now understood most of what his captors said. He decided Owl couldn't possibly be worse than Spotted Horse, and he went along with the old man peacefully enough, though inside he was still watching for his chance.

Leaving the village behind, they crossed the stream beyond and headed up a long canyon. At least, he thought, the scenery was different, and he was away from the stink of the camp and the constant ruckus of the dogs.

He was securely bound onto his horse, a roan with a spine like a razor. This time, however, there was a thin blanket under his butt, which helped a bit.

The roan's lead rope was tied to the big sorrel Owl rode, and Phil had no control over his direction. This meant the mean-spirited animal often deliberately sidled under low-hanging branches or sharp stubs of dead trees, trying to rake him off his back. No amount of guiding with his knees allowed Phil to influence the animal's choice of a route.

They traveled for many days, most of them rainy or snowy. By now Phil had toughened to endure the weather without much in the way of clothing or shelter, but he felt as if he might have turned permanently blue, there in the chilly heights. When they stopped at last below a great cliff, where a lodge had been tucked into a thicket of young firs, he was more than glad to rest.

A tall fellow came to meet Owl, followed by two toddlers and six dogs. Phil sighed as he was freed from the roan and allowed to sit beside the fire with the mangiest of the dogs.

He was being traded again. By now he knew the symptoms, although the talk was in sign language. When Owl rode away alone, the new owner's family packed up their tipi, loaded their horses, and headed north and west, taking Phil toward some fate he couldn't even begin to guess at.

Once again he thought desperately of his sister. How could Maryla find him now?

CHAPTER TWENTY-THREE

Maryla drifted up from the depths, groggy and disoriented. Her feet were cold—she pulled them up and curled onto her side. But something else had disturbed her rest.

The wind had died away. She could hear, as if they were under her wagon, the crunch of sharp teeth into bone. Wolves were after the bear's remnants. She was glad she had left the guts with the bones; otherwise the animals might be drawn to the wagon by the scent of the meat inside.

She remembered all the things the Cree woman had used innards for, but alone as she was, Maryla figured she didn't really need a lot of tendon and stripped gut bags. That was material needed for keeping a whole family going. Besides, the stuff stunk enough, just removing it and dragging it away.

She wished for a moment she had managed to stay awake and keep her fire burning. That would have frightened away predators that might come too near.

Besides, wolves and cougars and wolverines didn't hibernate. She was beginning to understand the smell of her presence and her food supply was probably going to attract other visitors than the bear.

The thought of waking to find a cougar ripping away the flap covering the opening in the back of the wagon made her shudder. A fire would be a potent weapon against such intruders.

When pale light fingered the edges of her frail barrier, she woke again and pulled on her boots beneath the heavy layers of blankets. Today would be even harder than the one before. She ticked off items she must take care of before darkness fell, and at this time of year night came early.

First she bundled herself again in Papa's coat and tied up her head in Mama's wool shawl. Teeth chattering, she clambered down into the tracked snow and pushed together the remnants of her fire.

She had to remember to keep coals alive, she realized. Making fire anew every day would take a lot of time she couldn't spare until she had herself prepared to face the winter.

Once she had raveled more cloth, struck flint to steel a hundred times, caught the resulting spark at last and nurtured it to hardihood, she felt as if she had wasted the morning. When the flames began to crackle, licking upward at the pile of dampish pine and fir boughs, she put the big kettle, filled with snow, at one side, its iron base nestled into the coals, and turned to look at the creek.

When they had come to a halt here, what seemed like weeks ago now, but which was actually only days, she had noticed with pleasure the big slabs of stone lying flat along the water's edge. It would make getting water easy, for she need not get her feet wet when she took the bucket down to the stream.

Now she knew if she could move several of the smaller pieces, breaking big ones into manageable sizes, it could form a fireproof hearth on which to make her interior fire. The great skillet Mama had used for cooking over campfires would hold the burning chunks of wood she would chop small enough to fit inside.

When it heated through it would radiate a lot of heat from the thick iron. Covered with its heavy lid, it would also hold a smolder of red coals overnight without endangering her wagon.

It was a solid plan, she thought, one her father and even her grandmother would have approved if they had been here to advise her. Maybe they were, she thought, and the notion was not at all fearful. Maybe they and Mama and the boys were all hovering around, waiting to go to Heaven until they saw her through this terrible winter.

Once out of the circle of warmth from the fire, Maryla found her teeth chattering again. Still, she stumbled through the crusted snow to the creek. It was not frozen entirely over, though there was a thick frill of ice at either edge.

She scraped away the snow, using boots and numbed fingers, and bared the stepped layers of rock. Some were thick, some thin; many were cracked across the width of the layers.

She found a stout sapling among the aspens bending over the stream, broke it off, which was fairly easy in the frozen air, and pried at the top layer of rock, putting all her weight and strength to the task. In the biting chill, she felt her back might break before the rock did.

There came a crickle of sound, then a crack. A plate of stone buckled upward, and she pushed it over to slant against the rise of the creek bank. The thing was too heavy to carry, so she returned to the wagon for one of the ragged old blankets Mama had kept for sleeping on the ground.

With the help of her lever, she worked the stone onto the cloth and tugged it along, heels digging through snow into frozen ground beneath, until she reached the wagon. Getting it up into the bed of the vehicle was going to be a job, but she had to eat first, she knew. Already the combination of cold and effort was depleting her strength.

She didn't disturb her store of frozen ox-meat. Instead she took one of the smaller chunks of bear she had reserved for immediate use and spitted it on the spike Mama kept for that purpose. She braced its butt by digging it into the cold ground and leaned it over a rock so the meat was above the coals that now glowed and shimmered with heat. Another rock set against the grounded end of the spike counterbalanced the meat, allowing her to continue her efforts at the wagon.

The sky was silver-pale now, and the sun was almost visible through the glaze of cloud. She thought she might be very lucky the blizzard had been short-lived, for if it had kept on at full blast she would have frozen before she had a chance to prepare her wagon to become a winter home. It wouldn't do to take anything for granted—she had to get that damn rock into the wagon now.

Maryla was tall and strong, and that was a good thing for her. She heaved the slab to lean against the tailgate of the wagon, which left the top some inches below the level of its bed. Then she went to her knees and set her fingers beneath the edge of the stone.

She put her back and knees into sliding the thing upward, inch by inch, while her hands cramped and numbed and her spine felt as if it would crack under the strain. "Bastard must weigh a ton," she said aloud, taking grim pleasure in the forbidden word. Mama would be shocked.

But the rock-plate moved. Once she had it going, the ice left on it helped to ease the motion. When she pushed herself upward, taking the strain on her legs, the slab flopped noisily into the wagon, which creaked and groaned at the weight.

She smelled her meat beginning to roast, and though her hands and her skeleton felt as if they had been subjected to some of those Indian tortures Jesse Gunter used to tell about, she grinned. The stone plate covered almost all of the wood in the very back of the wagon. For a space of roughly three feet by three, it would protect her floor from her fire.

Before digging out the skillet, Maryla sat on a blanket beside her fire and sliced off roast bear. Her belly felt lank, and she ate, grease running down her chin, until she could hold no more.

Immediately she felt desperately sleepy, but the girl knew she couldn't risk taking a nap. She had to get things ready now, for in a day, or an hour, or even a couple of minutes the relatively fine weather could turn bad again.

She washed her hands and face in snow, for the first time understanding why Mama was so particular about cleanliness. Then she turned to the wagon again, rummaging until she found the great skillet, whose handle was a good three feet long and whose two-foot diameter could hold a lot more fire than she could risk inside an enclosed space with a canvas cover.

Small flat rocks from the stream leveled the slab, and others would hold the skillet in place, even when wind shook the wagon like a dog shaking a rattlesnake. That had happened already, bouncing her about inside as if she were a seed in a gourd.

Then, very carefully, she cut a hole on the southeast side of the canvas cover, hoping the prevailing cold winds would continue to come out of the northwest. She had to vent the smoke, and already she was thinking of a way to carry it out efficiently.

She rested beside her fire again, ate more steaming bear meat, and gazed warily at the sky. It was past noon now, and she had not yet insulated her shelter. Her bones felt as if they had been run through Mama's grain-grinding mill, and her hands were chapped, fingers cracking.

Gloves—there were some woolen ones, knitted by her mother, packed in the clothing trunk, she thought. She had to have them, if she could find them, for her hands were really all she had to help her stay alive.

Sighing, she took Papa's axe and moved wearily toward the nearest clump of pine and aspen. There was a fallen pine just right for chopping into small bits for kindling. She cut several young aspens, as well, for green wood burned longer than dry, and she knew there would be days at a time when she couldn't get outside to find more fuel.

Those rounds she cut into short lengths, just right to fit inside the skillet. They would hold the dried fuel to a slower burn, she hoped. Load after load of wood went under the wagon for future use.

Whenever she could manage to go outside, once the weather really set in, she would get fresh fuel every day. Then when the blizzards turned vicious, she could use her store of gathered wood, which would remain relatively dry under the shelter of the wagon.

The sky was turning dark as the invisible sun went down behind the mountaintop beside the valley. She scooped a batch of red coals from the outdoor fire into her father's short-handled shovel and tipped them into the bed of wood chips she had ready in her skillet.

Smoke began to billow into the long cave formed by the wagon-cover. She added green alder chunks and put the lid over the smolder of fire, almost covering it, but leaving enough space at one edge to keep from smothering it. If she got cold in the night she would add more wood, but for now she wanted to reinforce her canvas roof.

The big trunk of quilts and blankets still stood across the wagon, just behind the driver's seat. She had been using those the family had used as they traveled, but now she opened the container and smelled the musty scent of old wool and the faint remnant of lavender sachet Mama had always kept there.

Tears came to her eyes as she tugged the heavy folds free of the chest and laid them out, draping them over the book trunk and the windrow of farming tools her father had piled so hopefully along one side of the vehicle. There was plenty of rope and strong cord coiled there, too, and that was going to be very useful.

Using her mother's shears, she cut the extra lengths off the heavy coverings and secured them to the wagon hoops with loops of cord, making an inner wall three quilts deep. That should keep heat in and the bitter chill out, she hoped.

She laid thick layers of folded blankets on the floor, keeping a safe margin around her fireplace, but otherwise insulating the floor to keep the cold from creeping up through the hardwood planks. It was possible to freeze to death from below, she suspected, if you didn't take precautions.

The coals were popping under the skillet lid, and smoke eddied upward in a long curl, to be drawn away fairly efficiently through the hole she had cut in the canvas. It also let in a draft.

Tomorrow, she resolved, she would find a way to makeshift a stove pipe. She might use a breeches leg, reinforced with hoops of willow twig to make a tube.

She checked the outdoor fire, covered its bed of coals with ash, and took the remnants of roast bear inside with her. Again she ate voraciously, her body demanding the heavy fat of the meat after her exertions. Then she wiped her hands and face on Mama's best dish towel and lay back in her nest of quilts and blankets.

She must have slept immediately, for the sound of padding paws, snarls, and harsh sniffing woke her. Wolves, just outside, were exploring the bloodied snow where she had dressed out the bear.

Maryla rolled onto her side and reached with Mama's pot hook to push the skillet lid to one side. That revealed a warm red glow, into which she pushed several small sticks of wood. By its light, she checked the load of her flintlock. Yet she hated to use powder and shot on wolves. Fire would send them running, she knew.

She rose to her knees and took one of the long dry sticks she had stacked along one side of the wagon for the purpose. Kindling one end in the fire-skillet, she pushed aside the back flap and leaned out into the night.

Startled red and green-gold eyes shone in the blaze of the torch. Six gray-furred shapes backed away from the wagon, and one stepped through the ashes covering the day's fire. With a shrill yip, the wolf danced sideways, nipping at its burnt back paw.

Maryla waved the torch as if it were a wand like those her grandmother told about in the magical tales she used to tell to entertain her grandchildren. She climbed over the tailgate and set one foot on the chunk of wood she had used as a doorstep.

"Eeeeeyohhhhh!" she shrilled, drawing circles and zigzags of red fire against the night.

The pack whirled in the snow and melted into the darkness. No sound marked their flight; though she waited for a bit, her toes, even in the thick wool socks, beginning to freeze, she could detect no further threat of predators.

Maryla stuck the end of her stick into the snow, well away from the wagon. Though the flame was short-lived, the end still glowed red as she retreated into the wagon and tied the flaps fast.

Replacing the lid of her skillet, she pushed her feet up as close as possible to the hot iron until they were warm. Then she curled into her bedding and fell into exhausted slumber. Even the renewed wail of the wind didn't disturb her rest.

It wasn't until Maryla woke the next morning, still hearing the vicious hiss of wind past the wagon, that she felt the full impact of her present situation. Down on the prairie across which they had traveled it was still autumn, and up here winter had only just begun. She had months of solitude ahead of her. She shivered at the thought.

Always there had been family around her, and neighbors not many miles distant. She was used to talk, to jokes and laughter, quarrels and sulks and making-up.

"I don't know how to be alone," she said aloud, just to hear a human voice. Hers sounded very thin and weak and muted, hardly human at all.

As if in reply, the wind buffeted the canvas, making even the interior quilts quiver with its force. The little warmth of the skillet fire whisked out through the smoke-hole, and she sat up to put more wood into her makeshift fireplace. Smoke billowed up and curled around her head, making her cough, but she persisted until the blaze was clear and bright.

Only then did she dare a peep through the rear cover of her shelter. Pulling the canvas aside, she realized that though the wind was blowing hard, it carried no snow.

It meant she could do some more work to secure her food and fuel supplies for the winter. Strangely, she hesitated, wanting to curl into her pile of quilts and blankets, pull the bearskin over her, and give up the fight.

"It's easy to freeze," she said, echoing Jesse Gunter's words. "A man just lies down and quits, and he goes to sleep and never wakes up agin. I've seen it a many a time. Makes me wish I could be a quitter, sometimes." His rumbling voice was clear in her mind, as she repeated the words.

"I'm no quitter," she said to the absent guide. "Stoners never quit. My Pa and my Grandma would shove me back out of heaven, if I was to let go that way."

She heaved the heavy layers of covers to one side and fumbled for her boots, which stayed close beside the fire to keep the leather from stiffening. Another pair of wool socks went over those she had been wearing, and she jammed her feet into the boots, though it made a tight fit.

She reached into the pile of clothing she had bunched against the quilt-wall and dug out a woolen sweater of her father's, drawing it over the clothing she already wore. That, with the heavy coat, should keep her from losing too much heat to the wind.

She chewed some more bear meat, knowing she would also have to pick fir tips and pine needles to boil for tea. Gunter's Cree wife had said people grew sick and weak, over the winter, if all they ate was meat.

There were a thousand things she must do, if she was to live through the cold weather; it was with difficulty that Maryla forced herself out of her shelter to begin the day's stint.

As she tugged more heavy segments of log to the wagon, stacking it under and around until the vehicle sat on a solid mass of wood, she felt the silence in her bones. Snow seemed to muffle even the whistle of wind in fir boughs; she found herself straining her ears, trying to find some comforting sound to tell her she was still in the world of the living.

"If I keep on this way, I'll go crazy," she told herself. "I've got to find some way to keep myself straight. Talking to myself is going to get mighty old real fast. What can I do to keep my head on right-way-up?"

She finished securing her bear meat, part inside the wagon, part tied high in the nearest tree. As she worked, she thought hard, although it seemed as if her brain might be freezing like the creek that had already ceased to gurgle beneath the ice.

"Frozen stiff, that's the creek and me," she said. "But I've got to find a way to thaw me out and stay alive."

Then she remembered the nights around the big fire, when Mrs. Holzer read aloud from one of Pa's books to anyone interested in listening. She hadn't been too interested at first, Maryla admitted, but there was something about the rich tone of the widow's voice, the roll of the words she read that had gripped more people than Maryla into a fascination with poetry and philosophy.

Those very books were inside the wagon, safe in Pa's trunk. She could read for herself, right there safe in the wagon. She wasn't a very good reader, it was true, but she knew how to sound out the words she didn't know. Goodness, Pa had used words she'd never seen written down anyplace, and she'd surely know them if she saw them in a book.

"But if I'm going to read the good stuff, I really ought to do it better," she grunted, as she chopped a length of fir into suitable sizes for her fire. "I better start with those damn readers I hated so, when Pa made me learn 'em."

Then she thought of ciphering. She'd always hated arithmetic, though Pa and the boys seemed to think it was some kind of game. All the books were there in the trunk, because Pa had intended to teach school at last, when they came to Oregon. Everything was there, waiting for her.

"If doing something I really hate will keep me mad enough to stay alive, then I'll do it," she said. She hauled herself into the wagon and tied the flap fast, for the wind was rising again, after subsiding a bit during the day.

"I've got enough light, with the fire. There's Mama's candles, too—I'll never use 'em, if I don't get the good of them this winter. I sure and certain can't carry them out, if I live till spring."

She set Mama's broth pan on one side of the fire to simmer her fir-tip tea. Then she removed her extra layers of clothing in order to move around more easily and began to dig into the quilt box. Mama had wrapped her candles in cloth and laid them between layers of old sheets, and there they were, a bit melted by the heat of summer travel but still usable.

Then she dug down to the top of the book trunk, for she had

stacked items she thought she might need on any handy surface. Pa was a mighty orderly man, she thought, as she looked again at the neatly arranged books.

School books were on the left, stacked solidly from top to bottom, with primers and such on top. If she just mined downward, top to bottom, she'd know most as much as Pa by the time she finished, she thought.

In the middle were thick philosophy books, atlases, the dictionary. She took that out, knowing she would certainly need it before the winter was over. On the right were the books for pure delight, as Pa had called them. Shakespeare, Malory, More, Spenser and Marlowe, and Pa's beloved Greeks.

Katrina Holzer had read from several of those, and Maryla shivered as she thought of reading them for herself. Was this what her father and brothers had found between the musty leather covers of books? This thrill of excitement?

Among the thick volumes lay a thinner, lighter one, and she took it up. THE JOURNAL OF LETITIA MARYLA CORBY was written on the cover in faded script.

Grandma? Her own words, from the time when she was young? What a treasure!

Then Maryla laid the book back in the trunk. This must be saved for a treat. Every time she finished one of the hated schoolbooks, she would read a page or two from this precious volume; the reward might keep her struggling through the black-letter print as she studied things she should have conquered years before.

"I'll just take a peep tonight," she promised herself, as she turned to her strange supper. She sipped the tea before it cooled, scalding her tongue, and she ate her bear meat before it was quite well done, in her haste to open her grandmother's journal.

Lighting a candle, she dripped wax onto a pewter plate to hold it steady. Then, hands trembling with excitement, Maryla opened the cover and began to read.

* * * * * * *

THE JOURNAL OF LETITIA MARYLA CORBY
13 APRIL 1805

It is with Eagerness that I begin this account of my Experiences in Life. As my Godmother said when she presented this little Book to me for my Birthday, "May your Days be many and useful."

Yet as it is a small Volume, though containing many Pages, I must be Cautious not to Waste, for there is no Money with which to Purchase Another. Therefore, I shall Write very Small, and perhaps this may Last until I am Old and Wise and able to offer sound Advice to the Young.

12 OCTOBER 1805

I did not Think, when I received this Book, that I would find so little time to Write in it. Though Much has occurred that is of Interest, Time has been lacking in which to Inscribe it herein. Spring passed in the Country with Grandmother, who died in May, the Summer in Scotland as Governess to a Gentleman's young Daughter...but now it is Fall again, and I must look to finding other Work.

Mr. Sutherland, who employed me, has taken his Family Abroad, and I cannot leave my Father in his present Condition.

Father's health is no Better. Indeed, he grows more Pale and Weak by the Day, and I Fear that he will soon join my Mother beyond the Grave. My Brother Jonathan will not admit that my Position will be dire when that Occurs, for he intends for me to become his Clerk and Servant, subject always to his Will, without Pay and without Respect from Him or his Clients.

That I will not agree to do, though I have not yet Spoken to him of my Thoughts in the Matter. Plans must take Shape before the Worst comes to Pass. I am thinking with all my Wit of a Course that I may follow when my dear Father is no more. Let the Law maintain what it will, I am not the Chattel of any Man, far less my tyrannous Brother.

* * * * * * *

Maryla forced herself to stop there. She shivered with curiosity. What had that earlier Maryla decided to do, when her father died? She almost opened the book again, but, with strength she had not known she possessed, she set it again in the trunk. With that fascinating puzzle to follow, after her day's study, she could keep her mental balance, she thought.

Her grandmother's strength and common sense, though Elizabeth had thought little of them and had considered her mother-in-law in some degree a reprobate, had always impressed Maryla. Surely she herself had those qualities, at least in part. Enough to discipline herself in order to survive, she hoped.

She was weary, for the work she must do, in such bitter cold, was exhausting. After the candle was snuffed and put away, she must sleep. The books she would save for the very worst weather, when it was death to venture out of the shelter of the wagon.

But the thought of that journal, waiting in the trunk amid the scents of old leather and paper, formed a warm kernel in her mind, around which she might build her life. Her grandmother might well save her, though she knew her mother would have been astonished and, perhaps, appalled at the thought.

CHAPTER TWENTY-FOUR

It was three days before the next storm penned her inside the wagon. Then it settled in as if to bury the world in snow, and Maryla found herself welcoming the opportunity to begin her work.

The first step to take, of course, was a review of a Primer, which she finished before the candle had burned down an inch. She had, of course, read that book when she was tiny, and now she found it laughably easy.

Would it be cheating to take out the diary again? No. She had said that every time she finished a book she would read more from the journal, and she had finished this book. It would not be that easy from this point onward, but the first time, she was going to stretch a point.

* * * * * * *

3 FEBRUARY 1806

Although the Tides of War now ravage Europe and Napoleon Bonaparte bids fair to Rule the World, my own small Tragedy looms Larger in my Heart. Father died last Night, his final Breath devoted to my Mother's dear Name.

The small Hoard of Silver that I have saved against this Time is safely in my Pocket, tied about my Waist with strong Cord. Above that—my Brother would Quake to know it—I wear Kneebreeches and Hose, with a Waistcoat over a plain Shirt of Linen. My Boots I purchased at a shop purveying Clothing for Children, and they do not Seem so Small when Blackened and Polished.

My last Glance into the small Mirror that has reflected my Countenance for Eighteen Years showed me a Plainish sort of young Man, tall and slender, not yet Bearded but serious of Mien. His dark Wig is straight and his Portmanteau is in his Hand.

The Sum derived from the Sale of my small Possessions has secured Passage upon a Schooner sailing for Holland. I hope that the Fortunes of War will not Divert it from its Goal.

From there I shall take Ship for the New World, hoping that it will not be so Cold and Difficult for a lone Female as the Old has become. This Roundabout Route may well Deter Jonathan, should he endeavor to Trace my Movements.

* * * * * * *

So that was why Mama objected so to my wearing trousers! Maryla thought. She knew Grandma had disguised herself as a man and escaped from her brother in that way, and here were her own words describing that adventure. How exciting!

Maryla almost succumbed to temptation and read farther, but she managed to control her curiosity. Below the Primer was a first book of mathematical propositions, and she knew she would need great incentive to dig through its long ranks of simple sums. They were easy ones, she knew, but she dreaded working her way down the pages.

"Tomorrow I shall begin it, if the storm doesn't let up," she said, speaking to her grandmother, whom she felt to be very close beside her. "And when I finish it, however long it may take me, I will visit you again."

She laid the book in the trunk and closed the lid. Then she returned to her bed-pile and lay gazing at the faint flicker of firelight on the quilt-ceiling until she dozed off, still thinking of that first Maryla, who'd had her own difficult and dangerous journey ahead of her.

Maryla worked her way patiently through the arithmetic book, scribbling sums on the stone hearth with charred twigs, and scrubbing them out with handfuls of snow. It took several days, because she was determined to understand what she did, not simply to skim through the book as she had when she was a child.

Nothing else promised to keep her mind active and her loneliness under control. Constant work was the cure for almost anything, she had learned early in life.

Outside the wind shrieked more loudly than the wolf ever had. Snow battered her shelter, but the lining of quilts and the panful of fire, around which she curled herself as closely as possible, kept her from freezing.

The candle's light was cheerful, picking out bits of color on the rapidly darkening quilts. Mama's Sunday dress from ten years past, Papa's shirt that he tore while cutting wood—even the sooty quilt scraps held memories, she found. That, too, kept her mind focused and active.

But she was anxious to read from her grandmother's diary, once she had completed the last sums in the book, and knew that she now understood everything she had worked so hard to conquer. She would never become a mathematician, she felt sure, but she now knew far more than most, though it had taken the better part of two weeks to go through the book.

Again she drew the thin journal from the trunk and opened it. Even in candlelight, the ink seemed faded and the script was sometimes hard to make out, but she was determined to decipher it. Her heart thudded with excitement as she began to read.

* * * * * * *

18 MARCH 1806

I Write this in a cramped Space under Hatches, by the flickering Light of a gimbal-mounted Lamp. About me, many People retch and Moan. The stench of this Place is horrible, but the Storm that rages Overhead precludes any Expedition onto the Deck.

The Lamp swings madly, making me almost Ill as it Cavorts. The Quality of my Penmanship also suffers, but I am, praise God, not suffering as do most of Those about me. The Children, in Particular, are in sorry Case.

Barring any Catastrophe, we should make landfall within the next five Days. Though the Storm has borne us off Course, the Mate assures me that the Captain is most Skilled and will bring us Safe to Shore at our proper Destination.

Mr. Stoner is a Pleasant young Officer, and he seems to find the Person I pretend to be Companionable. We have Shared many a quiet Moment beside the Rail, looking up into the Vault of the Sky and Speculating as to the Nature of the Stars or down into the fathomless Deep, wondering what Marvels might be found There, beyond those a Sailor sees almost Daily.

I have not Often met such an unexceptionable young Man, those whom I encountered in my former Life seeming, all too frequently, Arrogant in their Assumption that one who Works for her Bread may be Considered fair Game. Mr. Stoner has won my Respect, in that he is Equally civil to young Women going out as Servants and to Mothers of Families.

Those he helps as he can, without Thought of Recompense. He has won my Friendship, though he little Understands who and what

I may Be. I feel some little Regret at the Thought of deceiving such a good Fellow, and also of saying Goodbye to him at the End of our Voyage together.

There, however, my Life may Begin. I have not yet Decided whether to enter this unknown Land as a Male or a Female. Knowing the Attitudes of Men toward unattached and undowered Girls, it is perhaps Best if I continue as I am, for a Time. So Lucretius Martin will Continue to Exist for some While to come.

It is a Frightening Thought, that of entering a wild and untamed Land where Red Indians roam the Countryside, burning and Pillaging where they Will. What other Dangers may Await me there, of which I have not yet Heard?

And yet I would not return to London if I could. To wear away my Youth to Old Age slaving, unpaid, in my Brother's meager Office, copying Writs for Lawyers and other such Deadly Dull Materials, is not a Thing toward which Anyone might Look with Favor. If I die the first Moment of Landing on this alien Shore, I will not Regret my rash Decision or my Departure from Old England, where not a Soul holds Affection for me in Heart or Mind.

* * * * * * *

Maryla caught her breath. Her grandfather had been a sailor, that she had known. But what a wildly romantic notion it was to think that when he met his future wife, he believed her to be a male like himself.

She grinned. More and more, she understood her mother's shock and dismay at this unconventional mother-in-law who took her life into her own hands and made her way in the world, unassisted by anyone. This explained much about her energetic grandmother that the girl had never even thought to wonder about.

Although she was sorely tempted to read further, Maryla closed the volume and replaced it in the trunk. It was late, and she must keep to a regular schedule, or her life would come apart and leave her floundering, without any pattern or guidance.

She put a green chunk into her skillet fire and slipped the cover more nearly to enclose the glowing heap of coals. She pinched out the candle, also, setting the pewter dish on one of the trunks, out of the way. She had found that a regular schedule, rigidly adhered to, helped her to pass the days and the nights with more composure.

Lately she had begun to toss and turn in the night, letting blasts of chilly air beneath her covers. Her nightmares were frightening, although as yet she had not brought one into wakefulness with her.

She had begun to feel that if she could remember them, she might find a way to lessen their impact on her spirit.

As she fell asleep, she found herself seeing, in the darkness behind her eyelids, the face of her youngest brother. "Phil," she said aloud. "Phil, where are you?"

Her own voice woke her, and she huddled the covers more closely about her and shivered. If Phil were safely dead, why should his face float inside her sleeping mind?

Wondering, she slept at last.

The weather broke for a few days, after that night. Though the snow was now hip-deep, Maryla wrapped her legs in strips of blanket over her three pairs of trousers and the tops of her boots, and forced herself out into the biting cold. Her store of wood in the wagon needed replenishing badly, and she spent some time scraping snow off the fallen aspens beside the creek and chopping them into manageable chunks.

She had depleted the stacks beneath the wagon, too, and she dragged her weary feet back and forth, forming a deep-cut path to her supply. When the wagon again sat solidly on woodpiles, she dragged herself into shelter again. There she found her skillet fire died down to coals, requiring her to feed it with chips of dry wood until it was burning again.

She had learned to set one of her Mama's small skillets in the coals inside the larger one, shaving into it bits of bear meat and adding snow until she achieved a rich stew. Beans and Mama's dried thyme added body and flavor, and once it had cooked and cooled, it warmed her through and through.

She slept the rest of that day and night, waking only to add fuel to her fire. When she woke fully at last, there were streaks of light around the covering at the rear of the wagon, but wind shrilled through the firs at either side and pattered more snow against her frail roof.

She had come to look forward to her days of study. For the first time in her active life, she understood her father's fascination with learning. As she moved to the next level in her reading she found the stories becoming more demanding, but at the same time they were more interesting, as well.

The classic myths that her father used to tell in the evening, in winter, were there on the pages, with drawings to illustrate the doings of gods and goddesses and rash mortals who dealt with them. Now that she had reviewed her basic reading, Maryla rushed through the next reading book quickly, and on the second day she closed it firmly and reached for her grandmother's journal.

* * * * * * *

20 FEBRUARY 1806

I am Ashore, in a small City, newly Built to the Eye of one from Europe, but yet Bustling with Enterprise. Mr. Stoner kindly Advised me to search out Lodgings with Mistress Carroway in Lark Street, which I have done. The Payment for a Month's Lodging took much of my Small Store of Money, but the kindly Mate also agreed to Introduce me to an Acquaintance, a Lawyer who has Need of a Copyist.

While I Objected to such Labor, Unpaid and Unappreciated in my Brother's Office, here I am more than Pleased to have the Opportunity to undertake it. Any Work that is Honorable and which brings Enough Coin to Support me is more than Welcome.

Bless Father, who taught us a neat Hand and our Greek and Latin, as well. He was only a Curate, poor all his Life, but he gave me all he Possessed of Learning and of Determination. This will Stand me in good Stead as I forge a new Existence here in this fresh Country.

God be With Me in this New Endeavor.

* * * * * * *

That was entirely too short and only whetted Maryla's appetite. She decided she had earned the right to read just one more entry before closing the book.

* * * * * * *

30 MARCH 1806

I have neglected my Journal, though often I Thought to indite herein some of the strange and Interesting Matters encountered here. Boston is, despite its small Size, a major City in this new Country. Mr. Marshall, in whose Offices I work as Copyist, is heavily Involved in Politics, and his Clients are Prominent in local Affairs.

I find a new Interest in these Matters as I copy. Today an Interruption caught my Ear, and I looked up to see my Old Friend Albert Stoner standing beside my Employer. Both Gestured for me to leave my Work and Attend them, and I did so with very good Will indeed.

To find a Friend again in this Strange Environment is a Grateful

Sensation. I had Thought Him long Departed and his Ship well on its Way eastward across the Ocean. It seems there was some Need for Refitting, and the Vessel will remain in Harbor for some Months, which is most Pleasant to Contemplate.

* * * * * * *

That was better, Maryla thought. Now she knew her grandmother was settled into respectable work, with an old friend at hand. She could resume her studies without wondering what happened after that all too brief entry of February 20th.

Down the girl went through the layers of books, working her way deeper into the classics, mathematics, even beginning to struggle with algebra and geometry, although she had to admit defeat with both. She needed someone to explain matters to her, and only the wind answered her questions.

She wished desperately that she had paid attention when Papa taught her, along with her brothers, beside the fire at night. It would have been so easy to listen, instead of teasing Rags or daydreaming. Why had she been so stupid?

Then she realized that if she already knew what lay in these books, she would have nothing to keep her sane during this endless winter. It had worked out for the best. Perhaps other matters would also resolve themselves, if she lived to walk out in the spring.

She kept to her resolution, as well, waiting until she completed each book before returning to that fascinating journal.

* * * * * * *

1 APRIL 1806

I find much Pleasure in the Company of Mr. Stoner. Mr. Marshall, finding that the Press of Business has lessened, allowed me the Afternoon free today, and Together Albert and I roamed the Streets of Boston, a Matter that I had Hesitated to Risk, even in my present Guise. This is, after all, a Country Strange to me as Yet, and I am Unwilling to Venture into Places that might Pose a Problem.

Although it seems Unlikely, I find that my Friend seems to Regard me with unusual Attention and Affection. Can he Suspect my true Nature? Surely not! And yet I find Myself wishing, from Time to Time, that he might see through this Masculine Disguise to find the Self that lurks Beneath. Is that Foolish? He will be Away again soon, I do not Doubt, with his Ship.

And yet when I mention this, he shakes his Head gravely. Could it be that he is Considering a Change in his Profession? From Occasional Comments he has made, that might be True. I find myself strangely Delighted at the Prospect of having a Companion of his Congenial Nature resident in this City of Strangers.

(Yellowed envelope, containing letter in faded script, inserted in Journal of L. M. Corby)

12 April 1806

My dear Lucretius Martin—

I wonder what may be your true Name, for surely it is not Lucretius, though the Martin might be correct. During our long Voyage together, it slowly came to my Mind that although you seemed a polite and comely young Man, there were certain Matters that indicated Otherwise to my knowing Eye.

Such a delicate Hand, such a small Foot are not usually found in Males, however Young they may seem. As we Spoke together about Matters that Few find Fascinating, I knew that Yours were a Voice comfortable to my Ear and a Mind that I valued. As we grew to Know one Another, and I found that you were not what you Seemed but far More, it came to me that This was the Woman I would Wed, if I find Favor in her Eyes.

Whatever your Name, whatever your Reason for this Disguise, I know that it cannot be Discreditable. I will keep your Secret, if you wish it. But I ask that you consider my Suit carefully, for you will not find One who Admires you more or feels for you a deeper Affection than

Your Friend,

Albert E. Stoner

CHAPTER TWENTY-FIVE

The days passed, and time would have seemed endless without the distraction of the books and her grandmother's journal. Maryla had settled into a routine that held her together. She never allowed herself to think of her mother, of the baby who died, or of her missing menfolk, but went steadily along her path without looking back. Lured by the wonders she was discovering, she went through the trunk and the journal, learning about her grandmother far more than she had ever suspected there was to know. Each time she took up the thin book, she almost held her breath, waiting to find out something new.

* * * * * * *

13 APRIL 1806

I am Placing Albert's Letter inside my Journal for Safekeeping. All my Hopes have come to Flower, and he Knows me as I am. With such a Spouse at my Side, I need never Fear to find my Brother a Threat again. Even He, Arrogant as he Seems, cannot Dispute the Bonds of Marriage.

As well, there are Plans in the making that promise Well for the Future that the two of us may Share.

JUNE 15, 1806

Never did I Expect, when I first began to Write in this Book, that I would enter into it the Account of my Wedding. It is Difficult for me, after such a Time of Vicissitude, to comprehend my Great Good Fortune in meeting Mr. Stoner, and it is with joy that I set down these Words:

Today I became Mrs. Albert Edward Stoner.

Mr. Marshall, on learning the Truth of my Situation, became a

Friend at once, for he has, I have learned, a most sincere Affection for my Spouse. When he realized that I had Copied for him for Weeks without in any wise Revealing my true Gender, he was charmed.

At once he put me into the Charge of his dear Wife, who exclaimed over my Story and began at once to make Plans for the Wedding, which though very Private was most Proper and well Conducted. Not once did she Blame me for fleeing from my Brother, although the Law considered him my Master until I was Wed. Now, God be thanked, that is no longer the Threat it was Before.

Although lacking a proper Gown for the Event, I wore that which Mrs. Marshall had Worn as a Bride. It seems Strange that so plump and Matronly a Lady should ever have fitted into the Garment, but she seemed Well Pleased that it became me so Well.

Albert has resigned as Mate of the *Sullivan*, and has decided that the fine Land of this Continent offers much Opportunity for Farming. (Mrs. Marshall assures me that all Proper Sailors long to become Farmers, once they Retire from the Sea.) Being a Londoner all my Life, I cannot say, but I am willing, whatever he Proposes, to follow his Lead.

Although he is not Wealthy, he has saved his Pay for Years, and with that Sum we will be able to take up Land in Pennsylvania, where the Indian incursions have become Infrequent and Inconsiderable. I do Hope that Father, from his place in Heaven, can see the great good that has come to his Daughter, whose Future was a constant Worry to him as he lay Dying.

God be with us both, as we go Forth to become Farmers in this new-born America.

* * * * * * *

Maryla sighed. Although she had never entertained the notion of marriage with any enthusiasm, she remembered her grandfather. A suitor such as he would be acceptable even to her, she thought, for he had obviously been a man willing to make her grandmother a partner instead of a sort of servant.

With some difficulty she struggled through another book, this one written in Latin. Her father had insisted upon teaching her the rudiments of the language, and luckily he had annotated his books with notes and translations.

She managed to get through half of Caesar's *Gallic Wars*, although it was very heavy weather for her. She was sure that as long as she lived, she would remember that *Gallia in tre partes divisa est*.

The story wasn't much different from her own country's movement into foreign parts, where native peoples resisted their coming, but half of it was enough. She felt as if her brain had been stirred with Mama's big iron spoon. Enough was enough. She opened the journal again, to soothe her wearied mind.

* * * * * * *

11 OCTOBER 1806

Finding one Moment to Spare for Writing here, I must make Note that Mr. Stoner and I have now reached the Location of our Land, which we Purchased through an Agent from the Property of one now Deceased. Although the former Owner perished at the Hands of Savages two Years agone, we are Assured that such Incursions have now become almost Unknown here.

The House is not one that a Londoner would Recognize as Such. A mere Pile of Logs laid crosswise and chinked with Mud, it has no Window, a Floor of packed Earth, and only one Door. This, I am told, is to Foil the Attacks of Savages who might Otherwise gain Entrance through such Openings.

At once, Mr. Stoner used his new Saw and made three Cuts— two Windows, front and Rear, and a Door opening into the back Garden, where a few Vegetables, gone Wild but still Persisting, have Survived. This is as much to provide Escape, at need, as to give much needed Ventilation.

There is Much to do here. The Land must be Cleared to a Further Extent. The House must be put into Repair against the coming of Winter, which I am told is Bitter here.

My Height and Strength, which my Brother Deplored, have become Valuable Assets instead of Flaws to be regretted. I find I have Skills never Suspected, for I am able to Chop with the Axe, Till with Hoe and Spade, and to build with the Hammer and Saw almost as well as my dear Husband.

Together we shall Flourish in this New Country and, in time, we will have a Child to assist us in our Endeavors. This is a rather Frightening Consideration, for here there is no Midwife within Call, not even a Neighbor near enough to come to my Aid, should that be Necessary.

In May, I believe, I shall face my Confinement, and though I do not Suggest it to Mr. Stoner, that Thought fills me with some Dismay. Not for the First Time, I long for my dear Mother, now so long in her Grave. But those are Unbecoming Sentiments, and I am now a Woman Grown, able, surely, to face the Perils of Life on my own.

* * * * * * *

The next few days were fairly clear, with occasional gusts of wind but no new snow. This made it necessary for Maryla to renew her fuel supply and to cut down a fresh batch of meat from her aspen-tree storage. Bear meat had begun to pall, and even the addition of Mama's herbs to her stews and roasts did little to tempt her palate.

She floundered through the deeply piled snow, and the exercise made her feel better. The constant smoke was flushed out of her lungs, and the activity made her hungry again. By the time she had her tiny realm in order, her lining of quilts taken down and shaken hard to remove the buildup of soot, she was happy to return to her old habits.

Yet she did not feel entirely secure. She dreamed of Phil, almost every night. After arguing with herself that this must be merely her wish to think some one of her people was still alive, she admitted, at last, that perhaps it was a true vision.

Her dreams were interspersed with sudden glimpses of Indians, mere patches of faces or activities, although Phil was always the center and focus of her nightly visitations. It was frustrating, for there was nothing she could do.

It was impossible to leave her haven until the snows melted with spring. Even then she would have no idea in which direction to look for him. And if he were a captive, what could she do to rescue him? The question haunted her.

To avoid sleeping for very long at a time, she dug more fiercely into her books, adding fine translations of Vergil and Catullus, of Aristophanes (one of his was a naughty play about women bringing their husbands to reason by forbidding them their marital privileges) and Aeschylus.

When she reached the thick copy of Shakespeare's plays she felt jubilant. As she read the rolling syllables aloud, she could almost hear the voice of Katrina Holzer accompanying her own efforts. She rationed Shakespeare, in the same way she did her grandmother's journal, using it to help her continue with the more difficult volumes.

* * * * * * *

21 MAY 1807

Although my Health seems Extraordinarily fine, Mr. Stoner has Insisted that I remain in Bed for a Week after the Birth of our Daughter Hannah. This leaves my Hands unoccupied, except for the Care of the Infant, and I find it Good to Note in this Journal the Fact that I am now a Mother.

Although my Concern continued until the final Day, the Birth was Easy and Quick. Mr. Stoner Attended me with the Care and Affection of a Woman, and when he put into my Arms this tiny Child, red-faced and Indignant to find Herself in the World, I knew I had chosen Well the dear Companion of my Life.

Hannah is a quiet Babe, who suckles Vigorously and Sleeps Deeply. Her small face has already Lost the Spots that covered it at Birth, and she looks, to her fond Mother, a perfect English Rose. May she have a Long and Useful Life.

* * * * * * *

That was entirely too short, and Maryla dipped more deeply into the little book.

16 AUGUST 1808

Today was born a son, Albert Edward Stoner II. Mr. Stoner is quietly Proud, for since the tragic Loss, through Fever, of our dear Daughter, he has Longed for another Child, and this small Son seems to fill him with Gladness. I have not Written here of that Loss, for it seemed Impossible for me to Mention, even had I Possessed the Time in which to Write of it.

This Confinement was less Isolated than the first, for we now possess Neighbours, only some five Miles Distant from our Home. Mistress Clapham is the Mother of Four, and she is well Versed in Midwifery, a matter which was of great Importance, as this Delivery did not proceed with the Ease and Expedition of my First.

Mr. Stoner has said that he Fears my Life might have been Forfeit if he had been Alone at the Birth of our Son. I, too, believe that to be True. It is only with Difficulty that I may Write, even Now, and so Weary am I with my Efforts that I will Close until more Strength is Regained. The loss of Blood has weakened me.

Only Today have I felt like sitting up and Writing in my little Book again. For some Time, it seemed that I must join my dear Father and Mother in the world Beyond, but after a long Period of Weakness I have regained some Strength. Mrs. Clapham has been a wonderful Friend and Nurse, and my Husband agrees that without her Aid I might well have Died.

It is a strange Sensation, moving so near to Death that one sees his Shadowy Face. There was no Fear—not for Myself, though I bitterly dreaded leaving my dear Albert and my Child. Of course I was unable to Suckle the Infant for a very long While, but Mrs. Clapham provided a Goat, whose wholesome Milk nourished our Son through his early Days.

Now he is a fat and healthy Boy, so loud and Active that I can only Dandle him for Moments at a time. Small Hannah would be Walking by now...And talking, very likely. But I must not Allow myself to Dwell on what is Past. Our Son is a great Comfort, healing, to some extent, his Parents' Hearts after that Tragedy.

We are most Fortunate, Albert and I, to remain Together. Our Family gives Thanks each Day for this great Blessing. It is unfortunate that Time prevents me from Writing as I should in this my Book.

Only my Confinement has allowed me to Add these Notes of Grief and Joy to its Pages. But in Future I have vowed to do Better, for some Day one of our Progeny may desire to Learn of our Lives in this new Country.

* * * * * * *

It was as if, Maryla thought, her grandmother had some premonition that one day her granddaughter would be in this terrible predicament, clinging to sanity only by means of the slender lifeline that was her journal. The feel of the limp binding in her hands seemed to link her to that long-dead lady. The stout spirit who had written the faded words still breathed courage into her.

Days turned into weeks and weeks into months. Without her faithfully notched stick counting off the ending of each day, Maryla would have lost any sense of the passing of time. It seemed as if she had lived in this sooty, canvas covered cavern all her life; the memories of Missouri, of her family, of the long trail they had traveled together were more like dream than reality.

Only her continuing visions of Phil, almost every night, reminded her that her brother might still be alive. It was, in a way, comforting to know that once she escaped this snow-imprisoned place she would have something real and specific to do. Without such a mission, she would have felt almost fearful of the end of her captivity.

The number of books she had not read dwindled. By March she was almost to the bottom of the trunk, and stacks of volumes crowded her small patch of floor. She began returning them to the trunk, mathematics at the bottom, readers next, classics and Shakespeare on top, for if the winter drew on too long she would surely be forced to reread some of her store.

The Journal dwindled very slowly, for she rationed herself even more strictly as the unread pages became fewer. As life became more complex for that first Maryla, however, her time for writing in her journal had become skimpy, the entries so short that her granddaughter found herself wishing she had done more.

* * * * * * *

30 NOVEMBER 1809

Again I am Abed after Childbirth. It seems that only at such Times do I find the Opportunity to write in my small Book. Yet our Lives are very Busy and Happy, despite the Hardships we face each Day and the occasional Danger from Indian Attack.

Small Lucretia is much like her Sister, as I remember her. I pray that the same Fate will not be Hers, for to lose two Children in such Manner would be terrible, indeed.

Albert is Pleased with his new Daughter, and our Son is ecstatic at having a Playmate. I find that my Heart, wounded by my earlier Loss, is Cautious about taking in this Morsel completely.

Yet I find myself, each Day, succumbing more completely to her Smile and her Ways. Indeed, it seems Impossible not to love an Infant, and I know myself Lost already.

3 DECEMBER 1809

The Winter now upon us is Harsh, and we find Ourselves confined to our Cabin, unable to do more than Attend the Livestock. Our Fire roars by Day and by Night, for with such young Children it would be Unwise to expose them to this unusual Cold. Even so, the Water in our Pail is skimmed with Ice each Morning, and I must Thaw the Haunch that hangs in the Storage Shed before it may be

Cooked.

     This allows Time to Write, of course, yet I would that this Winter would end far sooner than it is possible for it to Do.

CHAPTER TWENTY-SIX

FROM *DIE TAGEBUCH* OF KATRINA HOLZER
1850, December

I have neglected, until now, my duty to chronicle our last weeks of the journey westward. Illness overtook me before we turned away from the valley of the Snake, into the interior of the Oregon Country itself, following a small river into the tumbled mountains lying between us and the greater river that provides passage by water to the green valley we seek.

There were obstacles almost every inch of the way. When I became delirious the burden of my care fell upon my small companion, Klaus, while his mother and brothers wrestled their wagon and livestock up and down steep grades and over more arid mountains. The herbal teas and tinctures provided by Marta eased me through the worst of my fever, which was, thanks be to God, not cholera.

I barely recall the perilous trip by raft down the tremendous width of the Great River, although Marta tells me that we missed disaster by the narrowest of margins when our raft almost crashed into an island of stone. I was semi-conscious at the time, only returning to my normal state of alertness after being nursed for some days at the home of the kindly Scot, Dr. John McLoughlin.

As soon as I was strong again, we set off up the wide river that ran into the Columbia. In only a day and a half of travel along a well beaten track, we arrived at the Falls, where a considerable community has been established.

Marta and her sons have claimed a small acreage upriver, suitable for providing sustenance for the family. So many folk have now taken up residence here that Dr. McLoughlin suggested Marta might set up as a nurse, sickness being very common among the travel-worn emigrants who arrive here.

She is learning much about local plants and cures from a woman of the Klickitat tribe. Already patients are making their way to our door (actually a canvas flap that closes our rude cabin).

I have founded a school, although I must admit feeling somewhat guilty about doing that. Herr Stoner desired so strongly to teach here at the end of his journey that I consider myself something of an interloper. However, he is absent, and I am here, and there are many small children, too young to work in forest and field, to keep occupied.

I learned in Vienna, while tutoring, that the younger the child the easier it finds learning. My present school consists of six youngsters, the oldest seven, the youngest three. The smaller ones work hard to compete with their older companions, and we have worked our way through the alphabet and our numbers, and are now beginning to build words with the one and calculations with the other.

FROM *DIE TAGEBUCH* OF KATRINA HOLZER
1851, January

Winter here is less rigorous than I had feared. Indeed, it is less snow-ridden and icy than winters in my homeland. Grass is still green in spots along the riverside, and the plenitude of fuel means we keep fires roaring day and night. Marta insists that chill causes illness, and the health of her charges seems to bear out her contention.

We have seen nothing, heard nothing of our friends the Stoners. Jesse Gunter left us here upon arrival, taking his wife northward to visit her Cree kindred who live in the Bitterroot Mountains. He returned yesterday, although he insisted it was not his habit to travel in winter.

I suspect that the crowded camp of his parents-in-law may have driven him to distraction, for he has set up camp at some distance from the town and visits us only on occasion. It is plain that his free life in the wild has made him uncomfortable in a large community. I suspect he may never live willingly in any village, even among the Cree.

When last he came, I asked him to speculate as to the fate of our former companions. His weathered face wrinkled as he squinted into our fire and spat deliberately to make the flames dance.

"I'm afraid they didn't make it, Miz. Holzer," he said. "I've asked everybody I met who might know, and there's no word of a late wagon comin' on alone. Nobody has seen or heard of any of 'em, and in this country, at this time of year, that's not good. Not good at all."

I had known that, of course, yet I have dreamed about Maryla and young Philip more than once. I have a feeling deep inside me that those two, if no others, may survive. Herr Doktor Langenmach, who specializes in philosophy and theology, would deride me, I know, for giving way to intuitions.

Yet I have come to the belief, since undertaking this journey, that human understanding is limited. Human intuition is not.

I shall continue to hope that we shall see some of the lost family once again. They did not have cholera—that is the basis upon which I build my faith.

* * * * * * *

Maryla felt the winter to be unending, as her imprisonment in the wagon grew longer. Blizzard followed blizzard, covering the valley so deeply that the top of the canvas would have been enveloped, if the warmth inside had not kept the snow melted into icy sculptures under the edge of the wagon bed.

Swords of ice dripped from the canvas, skewering each protruding hoop to the snow beneath. Even with her fire kept at its highest safe level, her pail of snow beside the tailgate flap, intended to melt overnight, often re-froze and had to be set directly onto the coals in the skillet.

She had worked through the thick Atlas, all the textbooks, all of the readers, and almost all of the classics. There was only a skimpy pinch of pages left in her grandmother's journal, and the Shakespeare was worn away to the sonnets, which were not very interesting to her. Poetry had been the delight of Mama and Jon and Mark. She and Pa had preferred the plays.

She had begun to reread the classic myths already, saving her precious journal for times when she felt she must run out into the driving snow, screaming, and join her people in death. Only her grandmother's solid good sense, expressed in the cramped penmanship that crowded the small pages, kept her balanced enough to survive.

She was healthy enough, though she missed the exercise she had always known, and she kept losing weight. Her food supply would have kept an entire family alive, at need. She had Mama's herbs and dried stuff, as well as tea made from fir-tips to keep her from getting scurvy, but the energy needed to keep warm was burning up her body faster than she could eat. Yet it was her heart that starved for companionship, while her mind cried out for even more nourishment.

She counted the notches on her stick and realized it was late

May. Surely the snow would begin to thaw before long! Thinking about that, she opened the journal and read.

9 MARCH

It has been very Long since I have had the Time to take up my Journal. Our Lives, though very Hard, have been even more Busy, and each Night sees us fall onto our Couches too Weary to do aught except Sleep. But there is a joyful Occasion at Hand, which must be Writ here, though my Space is now almost Filled.

Our young Albert has found a Wife. Tomorrow my Son will be Wed to Elizabeth, Daughter of our Neighbors beyond the River. She is a lovely young Person, sweet and Biddable, though I find her altogether too much the Conservative in her Person and Actions. However, so long as she Pleases Albert, that is no Concern of mine.

There has been a single Incident that caused Friction between us, when she found this Journal lying in my Chest, and read the first Pages. Shocked at my Subterfuge when I escaped from England, she took it upon Herself to admonish Me for such Conduct.

It is Best to Pinch such Buds when first they reveal Themselves, and I set her back upon her Heels very Firmly, but, I believe, without Rancour. Now it seems that we have a good Understanding, which will be Useful as she and our Son intend to dwell in our House until we can build a Cabin for their Use.

11 JANUARY

The Months since our Son's Wedding have flown, and now he is a Father. Albert and I find much Joy in young Jon, and his Aunt Lucretia Spoils him, I fear. Elizabeth has not regained her Vigor as yet, and as the Weather is too Chill for any Outside Work, we have had a Holiday in which to Play with our Grandson.

As I find my Pages dwindling, I wonder what Matters may fill the very Last. There has been no savage Incursion in some While now, and it is to be hoped that our Lives may continue to be Tranquil. But I shall save Space for such Occurrences as may fall to Us in Time to come.

* * * * * * *

Now there were only three pages left, and Maryla read very slowly, already feeling sad that she was coming to the end of her belated relationship with her grandmother. But there was too little to save—either thaw would arrive, setting her free, or she would go mad or die, here in her canvas and wooden prison.

3 MAY 1830

Little did I Suspect, when last I Wrote here, that these final Pages would Recount the Removal of the Stoner Family into the wild Country to the West. The Land, once so Rich and Sustaining, has little Vitality Left, and Albert Longs to find the rich Soil of which Travelers tell us. West of the Mississippi, they say, can be Found large Tracts of unspoiled Land, ready for Logging and the Plow, to be Claimed by First Comers.

Our Son and Elizabeth will, of course, Accompany our Journey, for They, too, understand that we must Depart. Perhaps there my Son may find Opportunity to Teach, as he has always longed to do. Their small Son, Jonathan, is very Young for such Travel, but with God's Help we shall all come, in time, to whatever Place He has destined for our Use.

My Sorrow is that of leaving our Daughter behind. But Lucretia is now Married to a Parson and must remain, of Necessity, with her Spouse. There will always be a Spot in my Heart where she Dwells.

The last Page I Reserve for a short Account of our Arrival at Journey's End.

* * * * * * *

Maryla sighed. The last page was the back of the one she had just read, and the back cover of the book was impossible to write on, being made of fabric that was now faded and beginning to split. As she turned that page, she knew what she would find there, for she had lived all her life, almost, at the end of that old journey.

Yet once more she could hear Letitia Maryla's voice in her mind as she read the fine script.

* * * * * * *

20 JUNE 1830

We have arrived at our Destination, though not that for which we originally Set Out. My Husband has been ill with Fever, and as we have Camped upon a gentle Slope, with wooded Mountains above us and about us Soil that promises Much, we have Determined, young Albert and I, to remain here. The Plenitude of Trees promises building Materials for our House, and it is still early enough in the Season to Plant Crops and to begin a Garden.

The View from our Camp is wonderful, stretching away West across a long Valley, in an Array of Mountains that lead, I am Told, to that Desert of which Travelers tell. I am as well Content to remain Here, my Family about me, my Grandson growing in good Health, and another Grandchild expected in the Spring.

Albert has regained his Strength and is setting about the Labors of the Farm with much Enthusiasm. It is true—a Sailor is, at Heart, a Farmer, if he has the Opportunity to fulfill his Heart's Desire.

So I come to the End of this small Book. Long ago, when I began to Write here, I did not know what Fate might await me. Now I am Content with what God has set in my Path. May He remain with my Folk until they come, in their Turns, into his loving Presence.

LMS

* * * * * * *

Maryla closed the Journal and set it in the trunk. It was hard to believe she had an aunt she had never known and of whom her parents had never spoken. Was Lucretia still alive, back there in the east? Were there cousins there who had never heard of the Stoners who came to Missouri and now were reduced to a single survivor?

The thought of kinfolk, no matter how distant and unknown, seemed a comfort; she closed the trunk and rolled aside her bearskin bedding. Perhaps the day had cleared and she might go out and renew her store of wood.

Before she reached the flap, a sound brought her to a halt as she crawled past the fire. A dripping sound...A DRIPPING SOUND!

She lunged toward the flap, pushed aside the quilt that kept out some of the draft around its edges, and untied the strings. The glare of sun on snow almost blinded her as she stared, heart pounding, into a rapidly clearing afternoon, in which fresh snow was already beginning to melt from the surrounding firs and the wagon cover.

Was this the thaw for which she had waited so long? If not this one, then another, before too long, would unlock the frozen country and let her go free. She must begin to prepare, right now, for her trek westward.

Three days later, a light snowstorm re-frosted the trees and laid a thin covering atop the old snow, now iced over like a wedding cake. But it was plain this was only a mountain storm, not a blizzard raging down from the north.

Maryla, after so long in sub-zero temperatures, felt almost too warm as she moved about the campsite, laying out the clothing in which she intended to travel. Everything in the wagon was tainted and stained with smoke and the stink of the bucket she had used when it was too cold to go outside to relieve herself.

She felt her own lungs must be as sooty as the inside of a chimney, and she had no wish to take that scent with her. She had to clean herself thoroughly, no matter how grubby she would get as she traveled.

She scrubbed her father's thick woolen coat with snow until it seemed clean. The heavy trousers he had worn in winter, the thick woolen shirt, were shaken and pummeled in turn, then left to freeze overnight. In the morning, most of the dirt shook out of them, leaving them acceptably fresh.

In the brilliant sunlight, she stripped off her heavy underwear and threw it onto the fire she had rebuilt near the tailgate of the wagon. Her father's extra set would do her, and she was now disgusted with the musty stink of her body and her confines.

She dived into a snowdrift and scrubbed her own skin as unmercifully as she had the clothing. Streaks of soot and grime disappeared as she worked.

She was grateful, if a bit puzzled, that her monthly Curse had disappeared during the stress of the winter months and her drastic loss of weight. She wished she might ask Mama—or perhaps Mrs. Hirschorn—what might have caused that oddity.

She was now a rack of bones, she thought, looking down at her body. Her ribs stood out and her breasts had all but shrunk to nothing. Her knees were a bit knobby, and her muscles, always so dependable, had dwindled. She must condition herself, as the weather began to clear, in order to make the difficult journey through the mountains, when the time came.

Dressed in clean clothing from the skin out, Maryla felt renewed, stronger than she had all winter. The energy her body had done its best to conserve began to grow again, as she cooked great roasts of her stored meat and devoured as much as she could hold. Meat made muscle, her father always said, and she would need all she could muster, once she began her trek.

Her wind had suffered along with her muscles. She pulled on Jon's best boots, which were newer than her own and just enough too big to allow room for three pairs of Mama's hand-knitted socks. If he had worn them into the mountains, she thought ruefully, instead of the moccasins Jesse Gunter had taught him to make, she would be stuck with her own worn pair, which wouldn't last very long in rough country.

There was no real need for a heavy coat, she found, once she began her first climb up the slope, though she knew one must go with her. You never knew what weather would come upon you in the mountains.

The high, dry air and the warmth of the sun seemed to negate the deep snow through which she struggled. That first day she climbed to the top of the lower slope, stopping at a layer of scree that had slipped down from the cliff whose face had sheltered her small valley from the worst of the winds of winter.

There the path curved around the rough patch onto a wooded slope. She intended to go all the way up. It was unlikely, after so long and so much storm and snow, that any trace would be left of her kin, but she would look anyway.

For weeks she explored the heights around her campsite, finding no sign of what had happened to the menfolk. Eating ravenously each time she returned, she built herself to her former condition and beyond.

She found that she had grown, even during the winter, and now would have stood, she thought, little less than her father's considerable height. Her shoulders were wide like his, and her legs long. That was useful to her now as never before.

The day came at last when she must say goodbye to the wagon, the remnants of the meat in the treetops, and the trunk of books. That was a bitter loss, for she must leave behind every token of her family's existence except for her grandmother's thin journal, which she carried in the pack she had made of blanket and wrapped in her now supple bearskin.

That pack was judiciously loaded with meat dried over her fires, while waiting for the snow to melt. She carried inside it socks, mittens, the skinning knife, an extra sharp blade that she concealed in the side of her boot, a small pot, a carefully selected variety of herbs, old linen for bandages, in case she might need them.

One of her mother's fine handkerchiefs went on top of the load. That still held, despite the smoke, a faint scent of lavender.

Maryla felt as if she carried with her a bit of her mother, as she set out up the longer, gentler slope that seemed to lead between the heights to the west, where she must go. At the top of the first climb, she looked back.

The brook's snow-augmented flood glinted in the morning sun. The evergreens seemed very dark against the winter-killed grass, and the wagon, now a grimy gray, seemed like a toy set between those providential clumps of young firs.

The long winter seemed like a dream. Her family might have been people known long ago, now lost in time. Only Phil still haunted her thoughts, and she had decided she must live with his nightly presence.

Otherwise, she was alone as she had never been. Yet now she understood loneliness and it was no longer a burden. Her mind, formerly filled with daily matters, now contained enough riches to keep her content, if she had to remain alone forever.

That was not her intention, however, as she plodded up the slopes, over the rough shoulders of mountains and down the steep sides of shadowed glens. Maryla would go out, and she would find, if he still lived, her young brother and people of her own kind. Perhaps even some of those she had known on the trail, Gunter or Mama Hirschorn or Katrina Holzer.

She turned her back and went over a small rise that blotted out the valley. She was, at last, on her way.

CHAPTER TWENTY-SEVEN

It was the longest winter Phil could remember in all his life. He'd slept in a lodge crowded with three adults, four children, and innumerable dogs. Lying beside the door flap, where the chill around the deer hide covering seeped in and froze him, he seemed always to be chilled, even when wrapped in every scrap of fur he could scrounge.

This latest family was—maybe not the best, as he couldn't imagine using that word to describe any of his list of owners—the least bothersome of them all. He lay now scrunched into a ball, his back turned to the creeping fingers of cold, and counted back.

That first polka-dotted fellow had traded him to the old woman, who traded him to Owl. He'd swapped him to Spotted Horse for a broken rifle; Horse, in turn, traded him to the family of Redbird Eater for a couple of worn buffalo robes.

Redbird had been the laziest man Phil ever saw. He lay around his lodge, letting his wives and children do everything. When he got hold of Phil to boss around, he took great pleasure in sending him out into the worst weather to do the nastiest chores.

After Phil began peeing into the water jars and putting sharp pebbles into Redbird's bedding, the warrior suddenly traded him off to his present master, Crooked Arrow. He didn't ask any extra trade goods as payment for the considerable array of bruises and contusions he sent along with Phil to his new master.

Except for allowing as many flea-ridden dogs to sleep in the lodge as could crowd in among his family, Arrow wasn't a bad fellow. But that didn't mean Phil wasn't planning to run as soon as the snow melted.

If he could slip away carefully enough, he knew now he could probably elude capture. He'd learned a thing or two during his life with the different bands and tribes.

He felt sure if he'd known as much back on the Plains, when that Cheyenne caught him, he might have managed to steal back the horses and get away scot-free. Or not, of course.

A moccasined foot kicked him on the knee. It was Badger Woman, Arrow's older wife. It was almost dawn, time for his unending chores to begin again. Phil wondered how he could ever have thought his work on the farm was endless and boring. This was more deadly dull and exhausting than anything he could have imagined.

He stumbled outside and kindled the fire that served the three lodges grouped haphazardly about the ashes left from the day before. If it didn't snow again, the old ones would sit in the lee of the windward shelter and warm their bones while the children ran and leaped and rolled in the deep accumulation.

The women crept about, talking quietly among themselves, while the men remained in the lodges, trading lies around the indoor fires. At this time of year, there was nothing but dog-work to do, and Phil was the one chosen to do it. Being a slave, he had decided a long time ago, was not what he intended to take up for life.

When the snow began to melt at last, Phil began hiding bits and pieces in the edge of the forest every time he went to bring in firewood. A deer hide, hairless but intact, went into a shallow hole beneath the drooping branches of a fir tree. A parflèche bag of rancid pemmican joined it, and Arrow's dogs were berated for stealing it from its place in the lodge.

That pleased the boy a lot.

Those dogs scratched and whined and shared their itches with him until they almost drove him mad. They were as unlike Rags as dogs could possibly be, except for the fleas. Rags had his share, but these animals made him seem clean as a carrot.

Phil managed to pilfer an old bow, strings, and some arrows from one of the old men, who no longer saw as clearly as he used to. Phil felt a bit bad about that, but he decided he would struggle with his conscience later, when he was out of this mess.

He didn't know how to use the weapon, but he figured he'd learn mighty quick, once he was on his own. If a six-year-old Shoshone could kill rabbits and grouse and woodchucks with the bow, surely he could manage to stay alive.

Pa always said a man could do anything he set his mind to, and he'd pretty well proved it, most of his life. Phil intended to live up to what Pa would expect of him.

When a relative of the family came over the ridge with his own kin, heading for spring hunting grounds, Arrow and his family seemed to forget everything except catching up on the news of the winter. That night Phil and the dogs were pushed out of the now impossibly crowded lodge to make room for some of the newcomers.

Before the last fire had burned down, the boy crept away from the camp, waded along the brook, and eased over a thick mat of fallen fir needles to his hiding place. Once he had his supplies, he moved like a shadow over the springy carpet, leaving behind, as far as he could tell, no trace of his passing.

When he came to a clearing where a fire had downed a tangle of trees, now overgrown with brush and fireweed, he jumped onto the nearest charred tree trunk and sprang from foothold to foothold, crossing the area with unexpected ease and speed. Except for some scratches from brambles, he arrived at the other side intact and feeling fairly confident any pursuit might well hang up there.

It might be, he thought, that he wouldn't be missed for a long time. And if Arrow did find him gone, it was more than possible he'd decide this reluctant slave wasn't worth the trouble of recapturing. It wasn't as if he was a woman!

A ravine with a swift stream, icy with snow water, crossed his path. He scrambled down into the cleft and followed its course, trying to keep from slipping on wet stones that lined the banks and the bottom. He left no tracks there either.

Four nights later, Phil had to admit being on his own wasn't as easy as he had thought. It was amazing how much the silent wives of Crooked Arrow did; he hadn't realized that his own labors were just footnotes to theirs, small tasks too unimportant to waste their time doing.

His worn deer hide cloak and breechclout were tattered now, and his moccasins (cast-offs of one of the older sons) were only a sort of cuff about his ankle. The only thing that had improved was his skill with the bow. He was no sure-shot, but he could now hit a woodchuck, if he got lucky, or a rabbit, if he didn't.

Raw meat was getting very old. He had no flint and steel to kindle a fire; though he had watched Bitter Water Woman make fire with a drill once, he found it impossible for his awkward hands to manage the trick. So early in spring, everything was wet, even the undersides of logs, and if he had kindled a spark it would have been damped out instantly.

But the bloody meat kept him from getting weak, and he found himself, more quickly than he had expected, looking over a ridge onto a wide stretch of plain, gray-green with sagebrush. At the western edge of the sky were low tan mountains that looked dry, even with their heads still capped with snow.

That seemed too forbidding a place for one small boy to tackle alone. In these mountains there were streams, now burbling with runoff, where he could find more and more small animals foraging for fresh greenery. He decided to remain in the shelter of this range, following it northward until he located that great Snake River that Jesse Gunter had told about.

He had counted off the days, using all his fingers and half his toes, when he discovered, sheltered beneath a rocky overhang, a pile of discarded flint where some painstaking warrior had chipped out fresh arrowheads. Now he was at a lower elevation than earlier, and old grass, still fairly dry, hid beneath fallen rocks and the fallen trunks of pines and junipers.

He gathered a pile, let it dry for some time in the sun, and began experimenting with two big chips of flint. Before dark, he had a spark. Before the moon rose, he had a good blaze going in that sheltered spot, hoping the smoke would not betray him to any enemy who might be traveling along the range.

* * * * * * *

The family's winter camp had become confining to Elk Who Broke Through the Ice. His own lodge was not as crowded as some, of course, but it had been very cold for months, and his two wives, his daughter and her man, and two small ones made it cramped and noisy. His twin sons would have crowded it even more, if they had lived, but he would have suffered that gladly to see their bright faces at his fire.

That was the bitterness that drove him out of the sheltered camp and into the chilly spring of the north. He had entrusted his twin sons to those white Christ-people at Waiilatpu, and they had cursed them with spotted sickness so that they died.

If he had been there, he would have helped his friend Tilaukit and the others kill those who had destroyed, through their strange magic, so many of the Cayuse people.

The words of the white missionaries had bewitched even his own mind. That was the only way he could explain his decision to entrust to them his sons, who had been just old enough to wonder about everything and to run about learning to snare rabbits and to shoot small birds with their little bows.

He had felt there was much the pair could learn from the missionaries, who possessed wonderful tools and weapons. Even now, he was tormented by the teachings the pale-skinned ones had put into his head like a swarm of vicious gnats. Their words drove out good sense, making it seem that nothing he knew could be true.

Yet he had always known the spirits of the animals and the rocks and the trees. He had listened with his heart when he hunted, knowing that he and the animals existed together in harmony, even when he must hunt and kill game, or an enemy or predator must hunt and kill him.

Every action would, in the end, work together for the good of all. It was the way of nature, and none of his people had ever doubted that. Only a mad person could doubt it.

Yet the newcomers had taught that one's heart was a liar, and that only in their book could any truth be found. They claimed that happiness lay in the time after death, but he had seen, even while enspelled by their strangeness, that they were not happy people.

Why, if happiness could come at all, should it not be found in this life as well? The question tormented him, as did their alien ideas about obedience to the wills of others. Always, his people had followed only the dictates of their own hearts. These contradictions would drive a man mad, when he had too much time to think.

Three winters had passed since his sons died and the mission was destroyed. Broke Through the Ice had taken part in the successful war that followed, and he had scorned any part of the indemnity paid by the whites. Nothing the white men possessed could repay him and his family for the loss of the twins.

He had taken his horses and his family and they had gone away from their old homeland near the great river. In a distant valley among the Bitterroots, they made their camp in summer, going farther south in winter. They had spent the past cold season in a good spot, warmed by plentiful wood and fed well with the stored seeds and roots and pemmican and dried fish the women had prepared.

Yet he was still troubled in his mind; winter was a terrible time for him, lacking any activity that stopped the whining of the gnats in his head. People who distrusted the very land that sustained them and the voices of their own hearts must be mad, and it seemed they could drive others mad, as well, even long after they were dead.

It was too early to hunt, he knew, but he left behind his family and went afoot into the mountains. He did not want even a horse to interrupt his bleak mood, and when he met two Nez Perce and a Bannock who were also fleeing a winter of confinement he was well content. All shared that late-winter mood, and none talked unnecessarily.

They moved through the burgeoning spring together, almost wordless most of the time, living on small game and grouse as they moved to the south and east. As the air warmed, Broke Through the Ice began to feel as if he were thawing with the season.

Small tendrils of ease crept up through him, and he began to hunt seriously, rather than in the lackadaisical manner he had used before.

Snow now lay only on the shaded sides of trees, and he could see claw marks where newly waked bears had come out of their dens and measured their height against the great fir trees. Deer would be cropping the newly budded branches along streams.

Spring always brought better spirits, and when he set out on this morning, he felt that today would bring him success in his hunt. What he found, however, was no game track but the marks of feet in a patch of dust on the side of a hill.

They were very small feet, bare of moccasins. Something about those tracks caught his fancy; he noted the direction in which they pointed and went back to find his companions.

A child meant adults. Perhaps there was an early band of enemies raiding into this country after horses. They must find who this was and what purpose his people might have, here in the land of the People.

* * * * * * *

FROM *DIE TAGEBUCH* OF KATRINA HOLZER
1851, April

We are amazed at the mildness of this past winter. Although spring is not yet here, shrubs are setting green buds, and herbs and grass are pushing up through the winter-killed growth. In another two months or so, they tell me it will be time to turn the soil and begin planting crops.

Preparing for that event is time-consuming. Having left behind such weighty equipment as plows, our farmers are anxious to meet with traders coming up by ship from the south to the fort on the river.

I, too, am anxious. Who better than a trader to know another trader (or two)? When our train parted, one segment going to California and the other coming here, Jesse Gunter helped me to ask all those taking that route to pass the word that I was going to Oregon. Perhaps my prayers will be answered, and my sons have somehow learned of my presence here.

Meanwhile, we are sending representatives to the English port on the Columbia to purchase seed, small tools, and other necessities. Andreas Hirschorn has gone with Herr Hollings and Jesse Gunter to see to this.

Luckily, both Marta and I have small hoards of gold and silver with which to make such purchases. Those unfortunates who lost wagons in rivers or down mountainsides, along with all the cash concealed within them, must make do with laboring for others in exchange for what food and supplies can be spared.

I showed Andreas the miniatures of my sons, painted when they were very young but, I hope, still like them. He has promised to look very closely at everyone he meets, and I know that he will.

He intends, I believe, to go with Gunter up the Columbia to trade with small outposts there, ventures set up by French and British entrepreneurs. This new country is becoming veritably crowded with white people, it seems.

One advantage we have found is an increase in customers for Marta's herbal concoctions. Over the winter, she traded with several women from native tribes for dried plants, which they recommended for an array of ailments.

In particular, dried lobelia was most effective in treating bronchial and lung problems, of which there were many during this damp Oregon winter. The rain and chill of this climate are conducive to such matters, and having a locally grown medicine is convenient.

We await the return of our traders with much impatience, although it will be weeks or even longer, we know, before we can reasonably expect them. Without realizing it, I have come to rely upon Andreas. His strong back and quick wit often solve problems that arise. His mother, of course, conceals her worry, but we both understand that travel through this country is never altogether easy or without hidden dangers.

CHAPTER TWENTY-EIGHT

After crossing the ridge above her winter's camp, Maryla found herself moving down into dryer and less thickly wooded country than she had just left. Atop the highest pass, she could see decreasing billows of mountain spreading westward. Beyond those, she remembered that Gunter had spoken of wide flats, covered with dust and sagebrush, which must be crossed before finding the Snake River.

She had a water bag her father had bought from a trader at Fort Kearney, but filling it too full made it so heavy that it overbalanced her on steep slopes and slowed her down too much on the level. She would never cross a desert, with such limited supplies of food and drink, without luck so incredible that she doubted the possibility.

She had planned to head as nearly west as possible in order to try to locate the salty lake toward which the Mormon trains had headed. She knew little of the Mormons, but they were her own race. Surely they would help her join another train, when they began traveling again, that would take her to Oregon.

She closed her eyes and tried to visualize Jesse Gunter's maps drawn in the dust, and to recall his directions, muttered around the fire at night. She wanted to go north anyway. As long as she could remain in these mountains, where streams were frequent and game was stirring with spring, she felt that was the best she could do.

Somewhere north of this place she would find the river. Following it would certainly be easier than trying to travel afoot through the flats.

This alternative route might, she realized, take her completely out of the tracks followed by emigrants, traders, or even trappers. Yet the idea of trudging, alone and without any supplies she couldn't carry, through that forbidding country made her shudder.

Gunter's words came back to her: "You find the Ghost Mountains, the ones the Frenchies call the Tetons, and that old Snake'll be wiggling right along by their toes. It's rough country to cross, but

Swift Water'n me have made it, times a'plenty."

She studied the stars by night, remembering the heavy volume among her father's books that described the constellations' progress through the sky and the methods used by sailors to keep their bearings on the featureless ocean. Thinking of her grandmother's voyage from England, she had found those things fascinating.

She had memorized quite a lot of the information about navigation, though the mathematics defeated her. Even without such understanding, she hoped to find that those methods worked equally well amid the huge billows of the mountains.

"I shall take a bearing on the pole star," she said aloud to her lost father. "If I come safely to a place where other people have settled, it will be your doing, Pa. I'd never make it without your books and your teachings.

"You never let anything lick you in your life. I don't intend to, either."

The direction she chose was hard, for high country rose in her path, through which she had to seek out a way without trying to climb over impossible steeps. Streams wandered down from the snows, which were beginning to melt, even at higher altitudes. She learned to follow them, although too often she found herself faced with unclimbable cliffs or ice-coated blocks of stone that forbade any attempt at passing.

She persisted, resting frequently enough to hunt and eat well, although often she had to hide while traveling bands of Indians passed on their way to spring hunting grounds. Avoiding trouble was best, as Gunter said, and she always found a way at last through the heights.

The runnels would curve abruptly at the last possible moment, revealing further stretches of mountain and forest that she must conquer in turn. It got colder, of course, as she moved northward. One morning she topped a ridge and saw before her a shining wedge of mountaintop rising over the intervening slopes, which were already becoming dryer and more forbidding.

After days of travel through forested mountains high enough to reveal that snow-clad peak, she found it was only one of a row of pale giants rising beyond a valley and a river. So unusual were the shapes and the setting that she knew she had come to those mountains Gunter and his wife told about.

"If you pass along the east side of the Ghost Mountains," Gunter had said, "you'll go up into the Yellowstone country. Colter's Hell they used to call it when I was a younker. That's mighty strange up there, with steam coming up out of the ground and creeks smoking like kettles of soup.

"If you go around through the steep pass to the south and then head northwest you'll come to the Bitterroots in the end. There's timber and water, though it gets dry if you head west. A hard trip for anybody and deadly to some. But if a man stays in the shadder of the heights there's enough water and game to see him through.

"I went that way the first time I headed for the far north, and that was the year I met Swift Water and her folks, huntin' along the river." He spat and coughed. "Later I reckoned it was better to climb alongside the Snake into the Yellowstone and cross the Divide to the north.

"You allus know when you've gone over, because the cricks and rivers run west instead of east. Unfailin' sign."

Gunter knew best. Maryla set her steps to follow the river, which had to be the Snake. It would run up into the heights and disappear, and she would have to follow another stream entirely when she came down.

That might mean she wouldn't have to cross the desert alone. There ought to be someone down there along the Snake—Gunter said there was a Rendezvous, when he was trapping, at Jackson Hole. He said some trappers still made their winter camps there. There might, so early in the year, still be someone in camp.

And then she recalled the scroungy, filthy-bearded trappers the train had encountered along the trail. Gunter had bragged that Swift Water civilized him, which was plain from his behavior. Those others had been holy terrors, and some had been firmly asked to leave camp by the fathers of girls they clearly intended to pursue.

No, better to go on alone than to get into a serious situation—she'd had her warning from Leo Freeman! So she trudged along the riverbank, ready at any moment to duck into the shelter of the trees and bushes lining its course. It wasn't men who sent her to cover, however.

Spring was progressing, and bears were waking from their long sleep, coming out to nibble on green shoots. They looked thin and grumpy, and she had no desire to come face to face with one. Lying beneath coverts of willow and alder or aspen, she could hear them talking to themselves in grunts and whimpers as they stripped off mouthfuls of luscious buds.

Four times she had to hide, as she followed the river beside the silver-gray mountains. Only once did she hide from human beings. Elk and moose and deer were moving about, but she didn't want to risk a shot that might attract any family moving along the valley. She'd had her fill of meat over the winter, anyway.

Instead, she contented herself with woodchucks that fell to her skillfully flung rocks, birds of various kinds, and rabbits she caught in the snares she set each evening before finding a secure resting place.

It took days to reach the end of the Tetons, and yet more days to climb among the further mountains flanking them, as she moved higher and higher and the forest became thicker and more snowy. When she came to the first of the steaming springs, she marveled. She hadn't quite believed Jesse Gunter, but here was the proof of his wild tales.

As she gazed down, thinking herself hidden in a copse of alder, heavy hands fastened onto her arms from behind. The stink of bear grease filled her nostrils, and a harsh voice yelled something beside her ear.

Damn! She'd been fairly caught, just like Gunter had warned. A minute of inattention could mean a long time of regret. But she didn't struggle now. Let her captor think she was a typical white woman.

Two more hunters came up through the brush along the steaming creek and stopped to admire their companion's captive. One began gesturing, and Maryla knew he was dickering for her. Her captor kept shaking her, as if to show how strong and healthy she might be, pushing up the price.

He succeeded, evidently, for after tying her wrists firmly with thongs, he handed her over to the shorter of the men. This one seemed to be middle-aged, his belly beginning to sag, his eyes surrounded by wrinkles. He tugged on the thong secured to her bound wrists and led her away along a river bank that offered fairly easy travel.

Maryla said nothing, even though he was taking her back the way she had come. Having to cross the same country twice was going to slow her down a lot, but at the moment she could think of nothing to do about the situation.

For three days they moved through the burgeoning spring, Maryla carrying a load of meat from the elk her owner had killed on the second morning. He seemed to be a pretty good hunter, and so far he hadn't offered to molest her, but she reserved judgment.

Men, her mother had told her, were not to be trusted in matters of this sort. She had to keep an eye on him, whatever happened. He might be in for a surprise.

It had been Mama Hirschorn who explained to her the results of rape. Mama had avoided the subject of babies and how they came to be, and at the last she'd been too sick to worry about anything.

After Leo's attack, Maryla had gone to Andreas's mother, as he suggested, and the older woman explained, without embarrassment and with much clarity, just what would have happened. She had also emphasized the possible result.

To escape from Indians, you certainly didn't need to be pregnant, Maryla decided. It was hard enough to climb and run and hide and slither through bushes without having your body unbalanced by a baby. No, if this old fellow made advances, then she'd show him what she could do. Until then she'd just watch and wait.

The sun was almost down on the third day when they came over a ridge and saw below them a small camp, tucked into the bend of a creek and surrounded by firs, aspens, and brush. If you didn't know it was there, she thought, you'd never give the place a second glance, for the mottled hides forming the lodges blended with the remnants of dried grass and the rocky soil on which they stood.

Her captor gave a sharp call, so much like that of a jay she would have been completely deceived by it. In a moment a figure came out of the nearest lodge and peered upward. Now they were moving down the slope, and Maryla saw that this was a woman, very old and wrinkled, yet she walked easily and her grip was strong when she took part of the burden of meat.

As the three moved toward the lodge, the old woman was obviously questioning the man. Maryla decided quickly that he was her son, for her tone was exactly like that with which Mama addressed Phil when she wanted him to do something he didn't much like.

Once inside the lodge, the old woman gestured for Maryla to fill water pots from the stream while she talked further with her son. It was amazing how much you could understand, just from gestures and expressions, the girl realized. It was a shame they didn't speak Latin—she'd studied enough during the winter to make a stab at speaking it.

When she returned, the woman was gone. Only the man remained in the shelter, poking listlessly at the small fire burning in its center. Maryla poured the contents of one gourd pot into the iron kettle hanging from a tripod over the coals.

Already, elk meat was beginning to roast on its own rawhide thong, and in the kettle was a mix of meat and unidentifiable plants. It smelled fairly good, which was a relief. She was as hungry as those bears she'd avoided, back in the valley beside the Tetons.

The man was opening her pack, which she had carried all the way without interference. The knife he took out and set aside for himself, never suspecting she had one inside her boot.

She had abandoned so much along her difficult route it was the only thing there that caught his fancy, although he had already taken her flintlock. Evidently he didn't care for the molded lead in the pouch or the powder in the horn. He dropped them casually behind him.

Maryla pretended to be indifferent as he pawed through her things. Only when he took out her grandmother's journal did she look up sharply. He riffled the pages, sniffed at the cover, and looked puzzled. When he tossed it toward the fire, she was there to catch it and tuck it inside her shirt.

"You leave that alone!" she said, using the exact tone his mother had used.

He rose, his face wrinkling with anger. She backed away as he rounded the fire pit and reached for her. Both her hands came up, fisted together in a knot, and caught him beneath the chin. His teeth clacked together audibly, and he staggered backward.

He was bigger than she, heavier, and she knew he had to know a lot of tricks she never dreamed of. Without waiting to think of something clever, she kicked him in the stomach. His breath whistled out as he went down; before he could recover, she caught up a stick of firewood and cracked him over the ear. His eyes rolled back, and she hoped she had a few minutes grace before he came to again.

Recovering her knife, her Hawken, and her pack, she sliced a long slit in the side of the lodge facing away from the others. Rifle in hand, pack retied, she crept through silently and headed for the creek, whose thick fringe of trees and bushes would give her cover.

Once there, she removed her boots and waded upstream. The creek drained from the slope they had descended, and its course would take her up it again, she felt certain.

Though it was dark, there was a rind of moon above the fir trees. She kept in the shadow, feeling forward with each foot before risking a step. It would be easy to freeze at this height, so early in the year.

The moon crept down the west, and she found herself at a point where the water poured out of a hole in a rocky cliff. It was time to climb in earnest, she knew, putting on her boots again.

The terrain was steep, crumbly with rotten stone. She had to creep, testing handholds and footholds as she went, or risk tumbling down into the rocky creek and breaking bones.

By dawn she was over the top of the ridge and well on her way. She decided not to try retracing their steps, for she dreaded running into other hunters. She bore westward now, as much as the terrain would allow.

For two days she moved as fast as possible toward her goal,

which she hoped would be the mountains flanking the salt lake. When she came out of the highest country and camped, she found spring well advanced at the lower levels.

Birds were already fluttering about, trilling spring songs and carrying nesting materials. The air was so much warmer that she discarded her heavy coat, depending upon her bearskin to serve in case of more cold weather.

Now travel was a bit easier, for the mountains were smaller, their slopes gentler. As she came over a pass, very late one evening, Maryla stopped and dropped into a crouch. Beyond the next hill rose a column of smoke, and she wondered instantly if any lookout had spotted her as she was silhouetted against the skyline.

Crawling along a thicket of elderberry bushes, she went to earth, chewing on buds, a trick she had learned from the bears, and nibbling a bit of leftover woodchuck. She didn't intend to stir until dark.

Once night fell, she felt more secure about moving. She hid her pack and moved toward the spot from which the column of smoke had risen. It was better, she had decided during her enforced inactivity, to know who was there than to imagine all sorts of terrible things that might not be true.

Maryla went up a long slope, moving like a lizard on hands and knees, and flattened herself to the rocky soil when she reached the top. A glow of warm light showed that the fire still burned, and she crept forward until its spark was completely visible.

She could see no people sitting or standing around the blaze. Indeed, there was only a single small lump within the circle of firelight. Surely this was no ambush—she had seen no other human being anywhere, though there had been traces of traps and trails marking the activities of those who had trapped here in other years.

She crept forward, silent as a shadow, until she knelt over the huddled shape. She raised her head and listened, but only the whisper of wind across stone and through branches came to her ears.

That gruff, sniffling snore...she had heard it all her life. This was Phil!

She jerked back the hairless deer hide and stared down into startled gray eyes. She'd found him! By God, in all this tangle of wilderness, she'd located her brother. Her dreams had been right—he was alive, wriggling between her hands, trying to loose himself from her grip.

* * * * * * *

Phil had been dreaming about Spotted Horse, and when the hands caught him, he struggled to get free. He hadn't run and hidden and crept and slid so far, just be get caught again and sent back to hauling water and cutting lodge poles for his captors.

Above him loomed a bone-thin face, red-streaked by the dying firelight. A straggle of hair hung over the eyes staring into his, and even as he fought he thought there was something odd about the color. Then he went limp.

"Red!" he gasped. "Red hair! You're white...."

"Phil, you ninny!" That voice was as familiar as anything in his world. "It's me, Maryla. Quit fighting!"

He goggled up at his sister, feeling a sense of unreality. How had she come here? He'd been carried up and down mountains, back and forth across creeks and rivers, until he didn't know, himself, where he was. How on earth had she found him?

He flung his arms around her and hugged her close. She smelled different. She'd cut off her hair. But there was still one person in his world who belonged to him, and they were together now.

CHAPTER TWENTY-NINE

It was good to get out of the settlement, Jesse decided. Riding through the fresh-fir-and-spruce-scented morning, he knew he probably wouldn't ever get tangled up with any big batch of people again. The Cree village was noisy and crowded and stunk, but the white-eye town was worse.

He was glad he hadn't had to stay at the English fort and do the trading. They'd left Jeff Hollings there with the gold and the trade goods. He'd make a good deal for the Oregon City bunch and buy a wagon to haul the stuff back in.

The Hirschorn boy had taken it into his head to go with Jesse upriver, and he was glad of the company, though he wouldn't have welcomed more than a single companion. Americans didn't have any feel for the land, the trees, and the critters.

While they were particular about building privies, they weren't so particular about washing their own hides. Between the Cree stinks and the Oregon City stinks there wasn't a hair's worth of choice. Though different, they were equally unpleasant.

Jesse looked ahead eagerly. It would take days to reach The Dalles, where he hoped to do some trading with the local tribes who came there in spring. There he'd rejoin Swift Water's Cree bunch as well.

The trail skirted the Columbia when it was possible and followed creeks and draws to find ways over great stone barriers when it had to. It was rough and steep, and even on horseback it wasn't fast.

By the time he got to his destination, he hoped Swift Water and their son would be waiting. About this time of year her people usually came for their usual spring trading, and he was hankering to see his own family again.

He turned to Andreas, who was riding awkwardly beside him, still trying to get comfortable on the big sorrel Mrs. Holzer had bought for the trip. "It's been a while since I seen our boy," Jesse said, spitting at an unwary clump of weed.

"You have a son?" asked Andreas, his eyes widening. It was obvious nobody had ever suspected Jesse Gunter of having a family, other than his Cree wife.

"Damn sure do," he replied. He grinned as he set his heels to his horse, taking advantage of a grassy meadow. "He's mebbe eighteen now. His Ma'd know. He's been training with his uncle, up to now, learnin' to be a full-blowed Cree.

"Now it's time for him to come with us and learn how to deal with white men. That's goin' to be the biggest problem he'll face for the rest of his life."

Andreas looked thoughtful. "You don't believe that learning our ways, being civilized, will improve the lot of the natives?" he asked, his tone interested. "Frau Holzer thinks it will broaden their horizons and improve their lives."

Jesse grunted. "Miz Holzer's a bright lady, mighty helpful and honest, but she don't know nothin' about Injuns or Americans, either one. Americans are goin' to take every inch of land, every pelt, every tree, as soon as enough of us accumulate here to do the job.

"We're goin' to leave the Injuns with bare rock and wore-out loincloths and not much else. I may not live to see the job entirely done, but it'll come. You'll prob'ly see it, young as you are."

"But I have watched the Indians, along the trail and since we arrived in Oregon. They do not seem like people who will allow this to be done without trying to halt it." Andreas sounded worried.

"You're right." Jesse spat again, viciously, at a clump of Oregon grape. "They'll fight. I've seen just about every tribe you can name in battle, and believe me, it's goin' to be bloody. They go tail over teakettle, when they decide to, which is why you hear so many scary stories about Indian massacrees.

"They don't go by our rules. Hell, we don't go by our rules, 'less it suits our purposes. The tribes have sense enough not to start a battle they don't believe they can win, usually because they outnumber the enemy at least two to one.

"I've heard some white soldiers fuss about that, call 'em cowards. Hell, it's just plain good sense, which our kind don't seem to be all broke out with.

"They've also got a real handicap. They don't lie among theirselves. When they start bein' lied to and skinned to the bone by bad traders and bad politicians and bad soldiers, they're goin' to rise up, and this country will be bought with blood. Makes my hair rise, just to think about it.

"An' that's why I want my boy to know white men. Know not

ever to trust anythin' they say and not much they do. That way he'll be prepared.

"It may be the time'll come when he'll have to head for the north, with his mother's folks. Get entirely out of reach. Down here there don't seem to be much hope. Leastways, not to me."

Andreas, young and idealistic and honest as he was, seemed shocked; he also looked pale and worried. "My family...," he began. "What will happen to them? To all of us?"

"Hell, boy, we'll win. We know how to make gunpowder, which the redskins don't. We have more folks than you or I can count, back there in the east, just hankerin' to head west. An' there's no end to 'em in Europe.

"Most tribes limit their numbers to fit the place that supports 'em. The women pick the dried seeds off the wild carrot and drink 'em in water. When they want a baby, they stop takin' it. When it's not convenient, they drink some every mornin'. That's how they keep their numbers under control.

"We never limit anythin', we just breed like rabbits and move along to take over what we want. It's our nature, and there's no way those poor folks can understand it. They'll fight, and they'll lose, and it makes me sick inside to think about their independent ways gettin' lost in the shuffle." He smiled at Andreas's puzzled look.

"It's a great life, as I learned for myself, free and not under any-body's thumb. I guess, when it comes down to it, that's what sticks in the craws of our kind. Most folks like us can't abide anybody that doesn't have a boss or a governor or a king tellin' him what to do every day of his life.

"You watch—first thing folks will do around that new settle-ment back there will be to put in a gover'ment and laws and rules, just like the English have done at the fort. Then it'll be just like any-place else, and I'll never go back."

He stared ahead, for the easy space was coming to an end as a spur of rock thrust from the great cliffs to the south into the tum-bling waters of the river. "We'll go up this way. There's a crick that runs down from way up there." He pointed to the almost vertical shadow that marked the route around the obstacle.

They camped for the night above the creek, finding a flat patch among the towering firs. "Anchor yourself agin one of these trees," Jesse advised the boy. "If you turn over in the night and roll off downhill, you won't stop till you either bust wide open on a rock or hit the water down there."

He had long ago perfected his method of sleeping in such a spot, and soon the two of them were rolled in their blankets, each with his back against the trunk of an immense tree. Ordinarily Jesse slept like the dead, but this night his sleep was broken by dreams.

He woke several times to listen to the dark forest above and below them. He could never recall just what he had dreamed.

Unsettled and still weary, he rose before dawn and roused his companion from the heavy sleep of youth. Andreas yawned and grunted, but being reared by a strict mother, he said nothing as they built a fire and boiled coffee. Moving over this rough terrain in the dark would be foolish, but as soon as the sky turned pale and it was possible to see to travel, they were on their way.

Above them, unseen but always there, was the white cone of the mountain south of the river. Beyond the broad stretch of water, as the day grew brighter, he could see other snow-covered cones, their shapes as regular as if they had been turned from a mold.

The Cree had tales about those mountains, considering them holy places. Jesse always had a strange feeling when under the scrutiny of the White Ones; he was glad when they moved again into the low country along the river.

Among the maples and young firs, pushing through prickly thickets of Oregon grape or wading streams fed by veil-like waterfalls, he felt more comfortable. There he felt as if the Eye of God, with which he had been threatened as a child, was no longer fixed upon him.

They crossed rivers along the way, some deep and swift, some shallow. He often followed one upstream to find a better place to ford it, but always they headed east again at last.

When The Dalles came in sight, huddled among abrupt ridges that sheltered the settlement from the high prairie to the south, he gave a sigh of relief. His dreams had not eased as they traveled, and he feared what he might find there.

However, he was greeted with calls of recognition by the traders and the raftsmen who had taken up residence there, in order to assist emigrants in their perilous descent of the river. Beyond the small clump of huts, just visible on the other side of the tributary, he could see a camp that must be that of his Cree kindred.

He dismounted, assisted by a dozen pairs of hands. "What news from downriver?" asked a burly fellow, whose beard looked ample enough to keep him warm in winter without the help of the furs of other creatures. "I hear you had an easy one."

Jesse grinned, accepting a jug the man offered. After a long swig, which warmed his inside a bit, he said, "Easy enough. You have much snow over here?"

"No more than usual, but the Cree tell me there was more than enough upriver. They lost a bunch of old folks over the winter."

"Then I'd better go see to my family. You save me a bit of that stuff for later, will you?" He turned and headed for the Cree camp, which was half hidden in the willows beyond the mouth of the river.

The Deschutes was wide, where it entered the Columbia, and he both resented and understood the significance of the placement of the Indian camp. The river formed a barrier.

It was clear that uneasiness was growing among the whites as to their safety when they were too close to one of the tribes. He knew his words to Andreas were true. The massacre of the Whitmans by the Cayuse a few years before had obviously made everyone edgy. Sadly, white men made no distinction between one breed of Indian and another, although Jesse could have told them lists of distinctions until he grew a long gray beard.

He moved to the riverbank and waved an arm, giving a whoop to catch the attention of the watchers among the cottonwoods. Then he went upstream to the shaky dock, where a boat was kept for such crossings as had to be made. It took a long slant from upstream to allow time to cross. Otherwise, any boatman would have been swept into the Columbia. The crossing took a while, and when his keel grated on the rocky shore Swift Water was waiting.

Beside her was a tall young man, his eyes, curiously pale for an Indian, betraying his excitement. Sliding Otter was Jesse's pride and joy; when he stepped out of the boat he found himself engulfed in a totally uncharacteristic bear hug.

"Well, by damn, I'm home agin!" Jesse said, putting his free arm around his wife. "Otter, you been growin' agin! I left you last fall and you was only up to my eyebrows. Now it looks like you've gone and outgrowed your old Pa!"

The boy grinned. "I can look down on the top of your head," he said, with much satisfaction. "I am taller than anyone in our clan. Perhaps I will be the tallest Cree ever born."

"Just makes it harder to keep your head down, younker," Jesse grunted. "You be careful, you hear? There's white men comin' out here that'll shoot you just for the color of your skin. You keep your temper and your tongue, and that may help you some."

As he settled into the Cree encampment, he watched his son with interest. The boy had spent most of his life with his mother's brother, while Jesse and Swift Water trapped and traded. Jesse was pleased with the result. If they'd dragged the boy around with them, from winter camps to Rendezvous, he'd have learned bad things from the white men.

Drinking and wenching and obscenities and cruelties of all

kinds were the main features of the Rendezvous he'd attended. At the time he'd thought it was great fun, but now, decades later, he wondered why. Looking back, it seemed like a tiresome waste of time. He might've been with the Cree, with his son instead of drinking himself stupid and wasting entirely too much gold to think about comfortably.

But that was neither here nor there. Jesse Gunter didn't waste his time regretting the past. Now he intended to make sure his family's future was as secure as he could make it.

Andreas hailed from the other bank of the river. Sighing, Jesse started for the dock, where the boat waited. But Otter touched his shoulder. "I will go after him. You are old and need rest."

Shocked speechless, Jesse stared after the tall figure striding toward the dock. "Old am I?" he yelled after his son. "I'll show you old!" And then he had a sobering thought.

"I am old," he said to Swift Water. "We're both gettin' on, if truth be known. That young sprout'll be handing us grandchildren before we kin say scat."

Sighing, he turned, his arm about his wife's shoulders, and headed for her tipi. "At least, we'll be able to take off on our own now, without worryin' about trappin' or keepin' on the good side of your folks or mine. That suit you?"

She turned her head and smiled. His heart lifted, for she did not often smile. Things were going to work out for them in their old age, after all.

CHAPTER THIRTY

It was time to run. That column of smoke that led Maryla to her brother would attract other gazes than her own. She feared it from the first and hadn't waited to compare stories or even to ask about her father and Jon and Mark.

As soon as Phil was awake, she smothered this fire, caught up his skimpy supplies, and pushed him from the cranny in which she'd found him.

"But Maryla, I've got clean away from 'em. It's been days and days since I left," he protested.

"It's been less than that for me. I expect that either the hunter who bought me is going to be chasing after me or else somebody else entirely will come over that hill before long. Whichever it is, we're going to be gone.

"Unless, that is, you want to stay here and say hello and go back to whatever you were doing all winter." She looked at him sternly, though she longed to hug him again.

He looked properly quelled. "All right. I'll carry my stuff...I'm not a baby."

That was a good sign. She had never tried to boss Phil—she had too much bossing of her own to want to hand it along to anybody. But now it was different. Now she was solely responsible for their safety. If they were to reach some haven of security, it was up to her to make certain Phil jumped when she said to jump.

Before they were more than well started, she heard a shrill whistle that might have been a night bird but was more probably someone hunting one or the other of them. They climbed the cliff behind the niche, struggling from handhold to foothold as they went up it.

When she flopped over the top and found herself on a ledge that seemed to angle around the shoulder of the mountain, that was the route she decided to take. "You follow me right close, and keep your eyes peeled," she said to Phil.

She set off along the ledge. So quietly did Philip follow that she looked back often to make sure he was still there.

"You've learned to be a pretty good Indian, yourself," she said when at last they paused in the shelter of a stream-bed to drink and rest.

"I ought to've. I been workin' for every kind of Injun you can name, since Pa and the boys were...killed." He choked but recovered his control. "They've traded me for everything you can name, too, from worn-out bearskins to no-good horses. I've been makin' trouble, ever since the old woman. She was mean, but she taught me a lot. Like, for instance, we can eat the roots of those cattails growin' along the edges of the creeks."

Maryla looked at her brother in astonishment. Somehow, she had never expected him to take any interest in such things. And then she remembered—food was always an important element to Phil. If you could eat it, he was automatically interested.

"You dig 'em out of the mud and do 'em just like potatoes; she used to bury 'em in ashes under the fire. They're not bad—we ate a lot of 'em, when it was thawed enough to dig among the dry shoots."

That was useful information, and when they topped the mountain and crossed over onto a stream-scarred slope, she looked closely for the green shoots that marked growths of the rushes. As they moved downstream, they paused from time to time to dig tubers.

When they camped at last, far from the creek and well sheltered in a thicket of aspens, she risked building a fire. Her father's flint and steel had served her well through her wanderings, and luckily her captor had not taken them out of her pack.

They roasted a large batch of the tubers in the ashes and when she bit into one, after cooling it a bit, Maryla found it rather flavorless but very filling. Not knowing when they might risk another fire, she and Phil stored the other cooked ones in their packs and covered the fire with dust and ashes.

She moved well away from the area before stopping to rest. Smoke could be smelled as well as seen, and she had no intention of falling into the hands of any Indian again, whatever his kind.

At last, full of warm, bland but filling tubers, she lay in a hidden ravine, watching over her sleeping brother. They needed to share watches, but she knew Phil could never stay awake. She had to sleep as well, but it was a long while before she could relax and drift into dream.

Maryla woke with a jump. She had dreamed, indeed, and since finding Phil alive she felt a certain trust in those nightly visions.

Though no detail remained with her, she felt a sense of danger that made her neck hairs prickle.

Someone, she was instantly convinced, was on their trail, drawing near, even now when dawn was not yet even a promise in the east. "Phil!" she whispered. "Phil, wake up. We've got to move. Now!"

She was on her knees, rolling their sleeping hides. Phil yawned widely as he helped secure their bundles and followed her up the side of the ravine.

There was a game trail that made the climb easier and quieter than it might have been if they'd had to struggle up that bank through the thick spring growth. Though it was very dark, Maryla felt her way upward with both hands, having secured her pack and the rifle to her back.

As she fumbled her way onto the top of the embankment, she heard a whistle behind them, down in the draw from which they had just come. Whoever followed them was evidently close on their heels now.

Phil butted her in the rear, trying to hurry her along. She knew he had an even greater dread of capture than she, and she rolled into the brush and scuttled deeply into the edge of a stretch of forest.

Behind her a faint rustle told her Phil was keeping up and she didn't stop until she found a huge root-ball, where some giant fir had been uprooted by a storm. They tumbled into the hole together and held their breaths, listening to the night-sounds.

Almost beyond hearing, there was the ghost of another whistle. She felt Phil shiver against her, and she put an arm around him for a moment before unhitching her rifle and digging out her powder horn and bag of rifle balls and patches.

Something crashed through the brush at their backs, and hard hands seized her before she could resist. She heard a grunt of pain, and suddenly her hands were free. She reached back and grabbed a handful of face, twisting and squeezing it as hard as she could.

The hands loosed their grip, and she turned to her enemy, finding Phil fastened to his leg with his teeth sunk into the fellow's calf. She kicked the other leg out from under the warrior and as he fell she grabbed the Hawken and thumped his head hard with its butt. He went out, but the impact had lost the prime in the pan.

They'd made a lot of noise; she could hear others coming through the bushes now. She glanced at Phil and saw the pale glimmer of his face in the starlight.

"I thought Indians didn't fight at night," she muttered.

Phil almost giggled. "We found us a batch that don't know the rules," he said. "You hit 'em high, Maryla. I'll hit 'em low."

When the first dark shape appeared against the sky above the root ball, she sprang out of the hole. Grabbing a handful of dirt, she flung it into the featureless face. Then she battered the unfortunate fellow with furious fists, while Phil raised gasps of pain with whatever he was doing below.

Something came out of the shadows, striking her a stunning blow, and Maryla felt herself sinking to her knees. "Phil!" she gasped. Then she went out entirely.

She heard gruff voices before she was entirely conscious again. They seemed to be arguing, and there were several of them. Too bad. If there had been only the two, she and Phil might have killed them and escaped.

She felt something warm against her side and Phil's shoulder nudged into hers. "They're arguin' about what to do with us," he whispered. "That first one wants to scalp us here and now. His leg is goin' to be sore for a long time to come." There was infinite satisfaction in that whisper.

Maryla knew too well how likely that was, but she said nothing. They couldn't have done anything different that she could think of. Sometimes things just worked out wrong, as she had learned over the past months.

Phil nudged her again. "That big fellow, he's a Cayuse from up along the Big River. He says there are white men up there who'll pay in things like colored cloth and good knives for us. He just told the toad-faced one that he was going to waste a chance to get such things if he killed us."

Maryla thought about that for a while as the argument went back and forth, punctuated by grunts and exclamations. She had learned by listening to people talk, as the wagon train moved slowly over the country, some of the reasons why men might want women that had nothing to do with raising a family.

She hadn't any desire to find out anything more about that. It might be best if their captors did knock them in the head right now and let them out of this tangle of disasters that had overtaken them. Yet, in the end, that was not what happened.

Maryla had been watching morning climb the sky while the men talked. At last there was a final grunt and the warriors rose. The big fellow Phil said was a Cayuse gave something to the lamed one, and her old enemy nodded. Then the Cayuse jerked her to her feet, checking the thongs around her wrists. He pulled Phil up beside her.

He fastened a long line around her neck, looping it around Phil's as well, and kept the free end in one powerful hand. He pointed and jerked, and the two of them went stumbling after him as he headed into the spring morning.

Maryla hadn't wanted to cross the desert alone. It was infinitely worse to cross it at the heels of someone who held a rope around her neck. Yet he seemed to know what he was doing, and they crossed fairly short stretches of sagebrush flat between small and hidden sources of water, some of which didn't reach the surface of the ground but had to be dug after.

Two days was the longest they went without water at the end of the day. Their water skin, which the warrior filled along with his own before leaving each waterhole, held enough to keep her and Phil from drying out entirely.

Phil began talking with the Indian, much to the fellow's surprise, on their third day together. As they traveled, Maryla began to understand a word here and there, although Phil had to translate most of what the Cayuse said. They were both using Shoshone, her brother claimed, that he'd learned when he lived with Spotted Horse.

The man's name was Elk Broke Through the Ice. He was middle-aged, and he claimed to have known the Whitmans at the mission, before the massacre. She could tell when he mentioned them, because his eyes became dark and angry, and twin lines bracketed his mouth.

He understood white men better than most others from tribes less familiar with their ways, and he claimed there was a place on the river where many white people lived. Other whites came there to travel down the river or over the mountains.

All this emerged as they trudged along at his heels or crouched around a stingy campfire at night. He was not a bad-tempered man, and he seemed to take more interest in them as they went. Though at first he had seemed extremely hostile, he became less so as they traveled.

It seemed to be an endless journey on foot, though Maryla knew they would have walked the distance behind the wagons anyway, even if no tragedy had occurred. The gritty soil, the unending supply of rocks, the occasional crumbled beds of lava stretched away before them, and she could hardly conceive of finding an end to that nightmarish journey.

They traveled up a winding stream at last, climbing into pine and fir-forested mountains, with higher, sharper peaks in the distance to the west. It was cold there, even in spring, and she and Phil hugged their bed-skins around their shoulders as they walked, feeling the icy wind tugging at their tattered clothing and their long and unkempt hair.

There was no opportunity to escape. There wasn't even a chance to wash, for the Cayuse wouldn't allow them to get too near the river. He seemed afraid they might escape again, and he kept a close watch on every move they made, much to Maryla's embarrassment.

They came at last to a ridge and looked down on a wide river flowing along the foot of a sand-colored cliff, with tawny stretches of cliff and hill beyond the rolling waters. Maryla knew they had reached the Columbia. If nothing else, there would be plenty of water, but she couldn't even guess whether or not that meant she might get a chance to wash.

The throng of people down there in the dingy town almost frightened her. It had been a long time since she was with other human beings. The dozen or so moving beside the river or among the flimsy frame buildings seemed to amount to far more than they really were.

Someone looked up and she heard a hail from below. Broke Through the Ice said nothing, but he drew himself upright and stalked down the trail with great dignity. As they descended, watching their footing on the crumbly path, the sun came out from beneath the overcast that had darkened the afternoon.

Maryla welcomed its warmth. Perhaps that was a good omen. She had come to believe in such things, though she knew Mama would have disapproved.

For the first time in a great while, she felt hopeful. Those were white people down there. They'd understand her words. They might even have some news of the wagon train and those with whom she had traveled for so long.

Whatever came, she was determined not to submit to anything just because somebody wanted her to, not to give up her freedom to do what she thought was right or to give in to stupid or nasty things because they might he "the Lord's Will."

She would not, in fact, behave in any way like a lady.

CHAPTER THIRTY-ONE

Jesse Gunter was getting ready to leave with his family, and Andreas felt sad. They had become friends, along the trail; he knew Jesse never intended to come back to the new settlement on the Willamette River, and he knew he would miss having the mountain man's wealth of experience to draw on, when there was need.

Jesse's son Otter had promised to visit Andreas, if he ever came in that direction, but Hirschorn knew how unlikely that would be. The lively young Cree would go with his parents until he met a likely young woman, and then he'd become a responsible member of his tribe.

Andreas had observed the process during his weeks in the Cree camp. That visit was very enlightening. Instead of the barbarous savages his mother and Frau Holzer had expected him to find, these were just people like any others. They had odd customs and lived in a more primitive manner than the pale-skinned people he knew back East, but he could find no basic differences in the way they treated their families and their fellow tribesmen.

Families were close, and they laughed a lot. Children played games it was hard to distinguish from those his own brothers played. Mothers hummed to babies, and young people squabbled and sometimes fought, but nobody really took it seriously. Only when they looked across the river's mouth toward the white men's settlement was there hostility in their black eyes.

He would not have felt comfortable threatening anyone among them. These people lived a hard life under harsh conditions. They were tough and smart and strong. It was a shame, Andreas felt, that the whites in the village across the little river seemed so willing to share their hostility.

Remembering what Gunter had told him on their trip upriver, Andreas realized the old trapper knew what he was talking about. These people at the trailhead, as well as his own family and those others in their train, intended to take for their own what belonged to the native people here.

These people at The Dalles knew it, though no one admitted it. Guilty consciences had to be at work to make such sour attitudes. He wondered if they even knew the Cree had not been involved in the Whitman disaster, but he felt that even if they had known it would have made no difference.

Though almost no one discussed it in those terms, all the talk about cutting timber and floating it down to the Columbia to be loaded onto ships, about plowing up the soil and planting crops, meant just one thing. This was land and these were trees that the native inhabitants would no longer be able to claim or to use.

"Civilization," Malcolm Netherbee called it. Frau Holzer also considered these things to be progress toward some wonderful goal. Yet Andreas knew he would never feel quite comfortable, sitting in his own house on his own legally acquired land, as long as he remembered the look in Gunter's eyes when he spoke of the inevitable loss of freedom to his own Cree people.

Movement in the town caught his eye, and he turned to gaze intently at the few figures visible, who were now facing toward the cliff rising above the town. At that moment the sun peered from beneath the cloud cover and lit a spark of copper among the tiny shapes now moving down the steep path.

A surge of excitement moved inside Andreas. He had seen that coppery sheen before. He turned and ran toward Swift Water's lodge, calling, "Jesse! Jesse! Somebody's coming. I think—I think either Mr. Stoner or his daughter may be with them."

Jesse's grizzled head poked out of the door flap. "By damn!" he said. "You sure?"

"Well, not entirely. But come with me and see. I never saw hair that color before on anybody but the Stoners." He felt his heart thudding faster than normal, and he wondered why.

He'd liked Maryla, it was true. They'd been friends for a while, and he'd grieved with the rest when her family had to drop out of the wagon train. That didn't explain why he felt this glow of warmth filling him as he followed Jesse to the shore and climbed into the boat they kept there, despite the alarmed protests of the townsmen.

He put his back into paddling the awkward craft, catching the current out into the Columbia and then whipping its prow into a little cove where they could anchor it. By the time they secured the craft and climbed the bank, there was a fight going on among those on the far side of town, where the travelers had stopped.

"I got 'er!" someone was shouting, while others yelled, "I'll pay more! I'll pay twice that!" A tall Indian stood listening, expressionless, to the bidding.

Andreas caught Jesse's eye, and the two of them ran toward the fracas. When he passed the last house, he came to a sudden halt, uncertain whether to go to the rescue or to dissolve into laughter. Behind him, Jesse began to chuckle; together they stood and observed the scene taking place behind the cluster of shanties.

The Cayuse stood erect, ignoring the behavior of the half-dozen white men who were gathered about a tangle of figures. One bearded fellow held onto a short braid of bright hair, while its owner battered his face with her fists. He grunted with pain at every blow and had the look of a man who has unwittingly grabbed a catamount and can't figure out how to let him go again.

His other hand was busy trying to pry a small boy loose from his legs. "Phil!" Andreas yelled, but obviously the boy had his teeth too full of leg to reply.

The onlookers, who were still bidding with the aloof Cayuse for the young woman, backed away to a safe distance, for from time to time a long leg or a short one darted out to kick someone on a knee-cap or in the groin. The voices began to die away, as it became obvious the pair might well succeed in pulling down their huge and brawny adversary.

Andreas started forward when one of the men stepped in to aid his comrade. Jesse caught his arm. "Let 'em take care of it. I'd guess they've took care of worse 'uns since we saw 'em last."

"But...." Andreas tried to protest, but Jesse shook his head. "If she's to think well of you, boy, in time to come, you better let her fight her own battles. At least, let her finish this 'un. If it turns agin 'em, we'll step in."

Heart thudding with anxiety, Andreas held himself in check as Phil ducked behind the big man's legs and Maryla pushed their victim backward to fall flat on his back, her braid twitching out of his grasp. Phil scrambled out from under the flailing legs and jumped onto the bearded face with both bare feet.

Maryla kicked her victim squarely in the stomach, stepped back, and said, "Now, Phil."

Her brother rolled off, and she kicked the man in the side of the head so hard his eyes rolled up. Andreas could see their blank whites even from where he stood.

"Anybody else think he's going to buy me like I was a heifer?" asked Maryla. Her voice was not one to inspire confidence in any of those present.

They began backing off, one by one, trying to pretend they hadn't really intended to buy a white woman as if she were a slave, though Andreas knew that was exactly what they'd intended to do.

Looking around at the dissipating crowd, Maryla saw the two men who watched. She looked hard, brushed short wisps of hair out of her eyes, and looked again. "Mr. Gunter? Andreas Hirschorn?" she gasped.

Phil came to his feet and looked too. Then he gave a whoop and leaped onto Jesse like that long-ago wolverine. "I knew you'd find us!" he was yelling. "I figured Maryla'd find me, and she did. 'Nen I figured you'd find us both, and sure-nough-to-goodness you've done it."

Gunter was stifling laughter as he lifted the boy off his chest and held him out to look him over. "Son, looks as if you've found us, instead. Another day an' I'd of been gone into the Bitterroots with my fam'ly, an' Andreas'd be headed back down the Columbia. You sure timed it fine."

Maryla dusted herself off, twitched her braid back behind her, and held out her hand. "I'm mighty glad to see you both. Mr. Gunter, would you think I asked too much if I begged a small loan?"

Gunter looked at her quizzically, and Andreas wondered what she might have in mind.

"Broke Through the Ice there brought us here. He intended to sell us, I know, but he paid the man who wanted to scalp us, and he brought us where we'd have some help. I'd like to pay him back, at least what he gave that other man."

Andreas nodded. That sounded fair to him. He liked a woman who had a sense of honor.

Jesse grunted and spoke a string of words that roused the attention of Broke Through the Ice. The tall fellow looked thoughtful.

They exchanged offers, Andreas was sure, just like two farmers dickering over an ox, until the Indian held out his hand and Jesse put into it two worn gold eagles. The Indian still looked a bit doubtful, but Jesse pointed to the men, now disappearing into various shacks, and began gesturing toward the coins.

He was telling the Indian what he could buy with his money, it was plain. Andreas sighed with relief as the Cayuse trudged off after his former customers to make his purchases.

Now, face to face with Maryla, he felt as if his throat had swelled shut. Words were trapped inside him, and he couldn't say a word. Instead, throwing caution to the winds, he reached out, grabbed her, and hugged her close. She wasn't one of those giggly girls. She was one who'd stand beside you in a fight and work beside you in the field. Worth ten of the other kind, he was certain.

He felt a moment of resistance. A hesitation. Then she hugged him back as hard as she could, leaving him gasping for breath.

Gunter said, "After a hug like that 'un, you two'd better be engaged at least. Maybe married. Out here, it's best to have somebody, and Maryla and Phil need a family. You got plenty of that, young Andreas. I think you to ought to hitch up together. Billin' and spoonin' is all very well for them what has the time for it, back East, but out here it's best to find somebody dependable and grab 'em. What do you think about that?" He was grinning widely.

"You two an' Phil make up a mighty nice little fam'ly, an' if you do your best you might come up with some more to keep him comp'ny. I take it, from the fact that these two are by their lonesome, that the rest of the bunch is...is gone for good." He glanced inquiringly at Phil.

"Yessir. Mama died. Then Pa and me and the boys went huntin', and the Blackfeet killed ever'body but me. We two are the last of the Stoners, I guess."

Andreas felt stunned by Gunter's suggestion; he hadn't thought to get married for a while yet. Maryla had been a friend—but then he thought that might be the best kind of wife to have, one who started out as a friend.

He'd seen others marry along the trail, once because a new-made widower had many children to care for and needed a woman to supervise them. One woman, widowed by cholera, took on a new husband simply to help her get her rig across the mountains and the deserts. They mostly seemed to do fine together. Of course. That was the best possible thing to do.

"What about it?" he asked Maryla, who wriggled free and looked him up and down.

"Well...." she drew it out long, and he felt his heart drop into his heels. "You promise never to expect me to act like a lady? Never, ever, no matter how long we're married or how many children we have?

"You promise to let me work with you in the woods and the fields and not expect me to always be doing housework? I'd better warn you, I'm no good at that sort of thing."

Andreas had suffered all his life from his mother's compulsive neatness; that posed no problem for him. "Himmel! Why have we all these boys in the family if not to teach them such things?" he asked her. "After knowing you, I cannot imagine being married to one who cannot fight her own battles and help me with the work."

Her grin, he thought, must match his own.

Maybe, in time, they'd have come to the same decision, but old Jesse had saved them a lot of preliminaries.

"We shall do it," he said. "As soon as we return home. Mama and Frau Holzer would never forgive us if we did not allow them a wedding."

Phil jumped from one foot to the other, and Gunter sighed with relief.

"Now I got you young'uns off my conscience, I guess Swift Water and Otter and me'll be on our way. You all head back to the settlement, and give 'em my best regards. If they ask when I'll come visitin'—tell 'em when I can, which is no lie. Trouble is, I'll never be able to."

"But how can I pay you back, if we don't see you again?" Maryla asked.

"I been carryin' them eagles for near about thirty years. They was the first coin I ever made trappin', and I kept 'em to make sure my trappin' would stay good. Now I'm finished with that, and I've no need for 'em any more. The Cree don't use money, and in the mountains there ain't no merchants.

"I hope old Broke Through the Ice gets his money's worth, though I doubt it. He'll take a roll of calico and two skinnin' knives back to his women and they'll all think he snookered the white folks something shameful."

Gunter chuckled, although he looked just a bit sad. "No, if you find somebody needs somethin', along the way, you just pass the favor along. That's the best way, anyhow," he said.

They waited, after all, until the next day to depart. Andreas watched Gunter's small family and their string of horses out of sight as they headed up the roll of land on their eastward journey. Then he turned his horse, followed by Maryla and Phil on their newly acquired mounts, and headed downstream again, toward that difficult journey that would take them back home to Mama and Frau Holzer and the boys.

He had not made their fortune trading, that was certain. But he knew his family and others from the train would value what he did bring back more highly than anything else he could have found.

"You know," Maryla said, "I'm going to be mighty glad to see your mother and Miz Holzer. They seem almost like family already."

Phil grunted, and Andreas smiled. In this new country, as Jesse said, it wasn't good to be alone.

* * * * * * *

Elk Broke Through the Ice did not allow himself to smile. He had learned, while at Waiilatpu, the value white men set on their round bits of gold. He had pretended ignorance with the white trapper, even though he knew Gunter suspected he knew more than he seemed to. It was always best to seem ignorant when dealing with these barbaric people.

He tucked one of the eagles into his medicine pouch. One never knew when he might have need of medicine that worked with whites. The other he held before him as he went into the trading shed, where he had been many times before.

There was a blanket, blue banded with scarlet, that his older wife had coveted since first seeing it. There were good steel hatchets and knives, cloth of many kinds. These were things his own people either had no way of making at all, or which took a great deal of time and labor for the women to create.

He had no use for yellow metal, and he laughed inwardly as the trader scuttled about, trying to offer him as little as possible for his golden coin. He knew what he wanted, and he said nothing, just stood with great dignity, shaking his head slightly each time the man tried to indicate that this pile of goods was all he would offer for the coin.

Only when Elk Broke Through the Ice had everything he wanted did he nod, the faintest quirk of his chin, and drop the coin into the dirty palm of the trader. Then he bundled it all into the blue and red blanket and rolled it into a pack.

He knew the Cree who camped beyond the smaller river. He would trade some of the things he had just purchased for a horse, for he had no desire to walk all the way to the spring camp, burdened with all of these things.

He rode for four days before he found himself in the summer range. Though it was still cold at these elevations, with snow lingering in shadowy places, he knew his people would have come here with the rest of the surviving Cayuse.

He rode down into the shallow valley where the lodges were clumped, and as he saw familiar shapes below and heard hails of greeting from family and friends he felt a great weight drop from his heart.

He had wanted badly to kill those two white people, the child and the woman, taking vengeance for his sons. Yet they had fought so valiantly that he paused to think about them, and his anger had cooled. These lives he spared seemed to balance, in some way, those two lives lost. Now he returned to his people laden with gifts for everyone, and the thought warmed his heart.

The gnats no longer shrilled in his mind. The spirits of earth and water, stone and plant and beast once more surrounded him with their comforting presences.

Elk Who Broke Through the Ice was at peace at last.

CHAPTER THIRTY-TWO

The village has begun to look more settled, less primitive now. Shops of varied kinds have been established, purveying goods brought from the port on the great river. Farmers have broken the soil and are planting a variety of crops, which should give us plentiful supplies of food for the next winter season.

Marta is more than happy. Her sons thrive, and the younger ones are learning rapidly at my small school. Andreas is a happy young man, and his Maryla seems equally so.

They toil together on the land claimed by the family. They hunt together in the forested mountains, and the game they bring is a welcome addition to our diet. Although by training and education I should be less than happy with the situation, I know now that it is strength, not weakness, ability, not manners, that are valuable in the real world in which we now live.

We have built the young couple a small hut to themselves nearer to the farm, ostensibly to shorten the walk. Actually we feel they deserve more privacy than our crowded house can afford to those newly married.

I was concerned about their adding too rapidly to our numbers, but Marta assures me she has instructed Maryla in the uses of the seeds of the wild carrot for controlling conception. The learned Doktors would sneer, but I have learned better, in my time here. Marta brought with her a plentiful supply, and as wild carrot flourishes naturally in this country, a fresh store will be harvested in the fall.

1851, July

Today came a letter, by the hand of Jeff Hollings, once more returned from the port with a fresh supply of necessities. When I saw the beautiful script Guenter and I taught to our sons, I felt almost faint for a moment.

Most dear Mother [it began],

We are joyful that you are spared to us and that you now are on the same side of this vast continent where we have made our home. So well established are our various enterprises that we are determined to come north in the fall, when our partner will be trained fully to continue our business.

At that time we hope to visit your new friends and to bring you home with us. When we three, all that remain of our family, stand together once more it will be a time of thanksgiving for us all. You will be happy to find how well we have prospered, using the moneys given us on our departure to build a thriving business here in San Francisco.

If you wish to write to us, you may send a letter to The Brothers Holzer, The Embarcadero, San Francisco, through Captain Jonas of the *Skybird*, when next he visits the Columbia. He will see it safely into our hands.

God be with you, beloved Mutter.

Karl Louis Holzer
Franz Gustav Holzer

My tears are, even now, washing out the ink and making their dear names dim before my eyes.

Now I can rejoice fully with Marta and her sons, with Maryla and young Phil. Although it seemed for a time that my life had turned to dust, now it is redeemed and shines brightly in the sunlight of this new and unstained land.

My beloved Guenter, wherever you may be in the fields of Heaven, you may rest content. Although there is no security in this world of mankind, I have come to a haven at last. When our sons join me here, I shall rest content wherever we decide to make our home.

POSTSCRIPT

My Own Oregon Trail

The Oregon Trail has more than historical meaning for me and my family. In the Sixties, for many reasons, my husband Joe and I decided to move away from Texas, and after subscribing for a year to the newspaper published in Corvallis, Oregon, we began making preparations for the move.

We had very little money. After looking around carefully for the best way in which to transport household furnishings, thousands of pounds of books, two adults, a teenager, and two young children across two-thirds of the continent, we purchased a forty-eight passenger school bus and stripped out all except the front row of seats.

While waiting for our home to be sold, we packed into that space my grandmother's upright piano (made in 1902), other furniture, boxes and boxes of books, dishes, cookware, clothing, etc. When we weighed bus and all on the public scales, the entire equipage totaled sixteen thousand pounds.

Behind the bus we towed our Chevrolet van, which was also loaded with luggage for the trip, plus odds and ends that would not fit into the bus. In July of 1968 we completed the sale of our home (we had a couple of thousand dollars left after paying off the mortgage and setting aside enough money for the trip) and set out.

School buses have governors on them: forty-five miles an hour was just about our best speed. The weight was such that we had no jack capable of lifting the bus, should we have a flat. But we were relatively young, filled with energy and excitement, and we knew we'd make it to our destination, whatever problems arose along the way.

The first day we stopped at a park in order to retrieve something from the van. As we pulled into the drive, from the other end another vehicle pulled in. In it were the father and two children of good friends who had been living in Florida for several years. We sat on a low stone wall and had a final visit with them—truly a final visit. The next year both those children died in a traffic accident.

We covered about seventy miles that first day, stopping in Tyler, Texas, to fill up with gas and find a motel for the night. As we sat in front of the gas station, one of the dual tires on the bus went flat. The station had a tire to fit, but we had to go downtown to find a tube for it.

In Tyler lived the parents of close friends who had just moved back from Hawaii. We tried to phone them, but their number was unlisted. As we sat in front of the tire store, Joe told me and the boys, "You watch that intersection. Our friends are going to come along and stop at the red light. When they do, run out and stop them."

They did. We did. That night we had a farewell visit with them as well, and it was several years before we saw them again.

It took us three days to get out of Texas, at the rate we had to travel and with the weight we had to move. We spent the third night in Dumas, Texas, after having our second flat just outside town. That one got fixed, too, without any problem.

The fourth night we spent in Pueblo, Colorado, amid a pounding rainstorm. The next morning we set out toward Monarch Pass. At that time carburetors were not fuel-injected. They were set to handle the air-gasoline mixture at whatever altitude they were to work. The mix was not sufficient to get sixteen thousand pounds up to almost fourteen thousand feet.

Even the van, detached from the bus, wouldn't make the climb. We had to be towed to the top (there are businesses halfway up the pass for just that purpose).

Going down was an adventure all its own. Luckily Joe had, in his youth, been a truck driver and knew to go down in the same gear required to go up a grade, so we didn't burn out our brakes or lose control.

We stopped at the bottom, thoroughly wrung out, to find that the man at the station there had just gassed up a car from Texas belonging to people we knew. He looked up the credit card slip, those being more leisurely and personally interested times.

Things were beginning to look a bit strange at that point, though as yet we didn't understand quite how strange they were to become.

We, being lowlanders, felt that had to be the worst climb we would meet along the way. After all, it was the Continental Divide, wasn't it?

Wrong! After Monarch came Blue Mesa. Even now it is a stiff pull, but twenty-odd years ago it was incredibly more difficult. The grades were much steeper going up, and the two-lane highway was a series of switch-backs, going down at a perilous angle. The three boys and I, using the bars in front of our seats, unconsciously pushed the bus up and tried to hold it back all the way down.

When we pulled into Cimarron, Colorado, not too late that afternoon, we were all exhausted. Or at least Joe and I were. We checked into the small motel there, ate supper, and Joe and I went in to take a nap.

While we slept, the three boys decided to explore the mountains, something we had not anticipated. When we woke there wasn't a boy in sight. Calling got no response.

The people at the motel, used to ignorant flatlanders who didn't know the dangers of the country and its creatures, sounded their klaxon, and at last the sons reappeared. We didn't know whether to kiss them or to kill them.

The next day we moved through Montrose and down into the desert of Utah, heading toward Green River. It was hot as Hades (no air conditioning inside, and the road was as hot as a griddle). We pulled out to stretch our legs, only to find that the right rear dual tire was melting like bubblegum.

"It's just going to have to rain," Joe said.

We were still a long way from anyplace, and at about forty miles an hour it takes forever to cover ground. It got hotter and hotter—and then it clouded over and began to rain. With occasional ice in it.

We drove into Green River to find people standing out in the downpour, staring upward in disbelief. In 1968, they told us, it had been five years since they'd had appreciable rain. There were good-sized children who had never in their lives seen rain.

We checked into a motel that gave a wonderful view of the buttes that loom over the town. After eating supper, we went to bed, but Joe couldn't seem to settle down. He had the feeling that something was going to happen. At about midnight, a drunk came fumbling at our door, to be met by my large and determined husband, automatic in hand. Needless to say he made no problem, and Joe slept like an infant for the rest of the night.

There were no tires to fit the bus in Green River, so we headed out toward Price and Salt Lake City. But it was Sunday, and nothing was open that had suitable tires. We limped through Salt Lake City, more and more concerned, and came at last to Tremonton, Utah, where there was a huge truck stop with every size tire imaginable.

There was also one of the most welcome and charming small motels I can remember. Deep old-fashioned beds, handmade doilies—it was wonderful. And, next morning, we went on our way northward, over the old highway that wound along the course of the Snake River, going through every small town, up and down the irregular terrain flanking the river.

It was a most interesting route, now destroyed by the straight, flat, highly efficient interstate highway. We collected large numbers of frustrated drivers behind us on the upgrades, but always we turned out to let them past, when there was a chance.

The green valley of the Snake seemed like the "green pastures" of the psalm, and for the first time I had a real understanding of much of the imagery in the Bible. We who live in well watered country have no way to comprehend in full the metaphors of a desert people, which come to life unmistakably when you pass through arid country.

There were signs along the way—humorous ones like IDAHO WATERMELONS painted onto water-rounded rocks that studded the countryside. Today's self-conscious highway bureaucrats would probably cringe at the thought, but such things made what could seem like a deadly journey into fun.

Late that afternoon we crossed the Snake into Oregon. Ontario provided a motel, from which we set off the next morning to cross the "easy" last leg of our journey.

This involved "pushing" the bus over seven passes. They've now been cut down considerably, but then they were steep, and the bus was heavily loaded, and we were just about tired out. By the time we came down the descent into Central Oregon, we were anxious to see the end of our journey.

The ponderosa pine forest came as a welcome relief. While Santiam Pass was a stiff climb, the lakes along the route, the huge fir trees, and the fresh scent of the air told us that we had made no mistake in setting our goal.

Already I was looking for a place to stop, to dig in roots and make a home again, but we were still some distance from Corvallis, and only small sawmill towns lay along our route. Near one there was a log cabin for rent that I still regret not checking out.

We came at last to our destination, almost ten days after setting out. It was registration time at the university there, and there was nothing for rent anywhere.

We searched out the countryside, finding at last an old house between Independence and Monmouth. It lay amid mint fields, a relic of what I call Swedish Victorian architecture.

It was a way station, cheaper than a motel, from which we could find a solid rental house. I liked its looks, but once we had camped there we found oddities. While lying in bed, I could see out through the front wall. The front closet smelled strongly of cat, a scent we could never eradicate.

It began to rain. Straight from a Texas summer, we found it so cold in the high-ceiled house that we either took steaming hot baths or went out in the van with the heater on in order to get warm. Our youngest son became ill, and that was when I realized there were "things" wrong with the house.

To give James medicine in the night, I crossed the large living room, which was connected with the kitchen by a wide arch. At the back corner of the kitchen was a doorway leading up a narrow stair to an upstairs room, which we did not need to use.

I have never been afraid of anything, but when I crossed that cold, dark space I could feel that door as if it were imprinted in ice on my side and face. The feeling was incredibly chilling, depressing, and might have been frightening to someone with good sense. I still get goose-pimples when I think about it.

When son Bill explored that upstairs room, he found a trapdoor, beneath which lay a mummified cat, secured within a space not much larger than a boot box. Once he was removed, we thought the smell might decrease. It didn't.

And what was the secret of that house? Though we moved out in a couple of weeks when we found a nice rent house in Silverton, Joe traveled through Independence and Monmouth on the automotive supply route he established in the next couple of years. While serving his route, he heard the story at last.

The people who had lived there had an odd reputation. They seem, according to rumor, to have had highly unusual leanings. When they moved away, they left their dogs locked into a shed, where neighbors heard them crying and found them. They left their cats locked in that front closet, to die of hunger and thirst, in desperation and agony.

People who would do that would do anything. I don't even want to guess what they did in that upstairs room.

In Silverton we came to rest, first renting for a year and then buying an old farmhouse outside town, where we lived for the next six years. It was there I wrote my first two novels. In Oregon we found friends, work we liked, and country we enjoyed exploring for seven years.

We came home again, of course, leaving behind a lot of friends, good memories, and a part of our lives. We go back frequently, for now I write books using my Oregon observations for backgrounds.

I have always wanted to write a novel about the Oregon Trail, particularly since taking, in our own peculiar way, our own way west in the tracks of the emigrants. I feel, in an odd way, that I, too, have been an emigrant like those of whom I write. I know the smell of the desert by day and by night, in sun and in rain.

I can understand the joy they must have felt when first seeing the green valley of the Snake and their relief when their journey was at last coming to an end. I have been there, and perhaps that has allowed me to give some hint of their feelings and reactions as I followed them along the Oregon Trail.

Ardath Mayhar

ABOUT THE AUTHOR

The author of seventy books, more than forty of them published commercially, **ARDATH MAYHAR** began her career in the early eighties with science fiction novels from Doubleday and TSR. Atheneum published several of her young adult and children's novels. Changing focus, she wrote westerns (as **Frank Cannon**) and mountain man novels (as **John Killdeer**), four prehistoric Indian books under her own name, and historical western *High Mountain Winter* under the byline **Frances Hurst**.

Recently she has been working with on-line publishers. *A Road of Stars* was her first original novel to appear in print-on-demand format. Many of her out-of-print titles are now available from e-publishers fictionwise.com and renebooks.com; many other novels are being published by the Borgo Press Imprint of Wildside Press and Amazon.com.

Now in her seventies, Mayhar was widowed in 1999, after forty-one years of marriage, and has four grown sons. She now works at home, writing short fiction and nonfiction, and doing book doctoring professionally. Her web pages can be found at:

w2.netdot.com/ardathm/ and
http://ofearna.us/ books/mayhar.html

www.ingramcontent.com/pod-product-compliance
Lightning Source LLC
Chambersburg PA
CBHW031400250626
47155CB00004B/1340